MARS REVOLUTION

THE CENTAURI ASSIGNMENT

A
NOVEL
BY
MICHAEL COLE

BASED ON A CONCEPT BY MARK ANTHONY DEL NEGRO

SEVEREDPRESS

MARS REVOLUTION

ISBN: 978-1-922861-63-4

CHAPTER 1

World Two.
Two miles from Espinosa Colony.

When Winston Tremayne first arrived on World Two, he believed he was helping mankind start fresh. At fifty-nine years of age, he was old enough to remember the last green days of Earth.

Earth. Even after thirty years, he struggled with the new designation, World One. It was said that change was necessary to pave the way for progression. First, it was rules—which only applied to the citizenry, despite the mantra 'all humans are created equal'. Next was political structure and term limits. Why bother with elections when the system had become too bloated and chaotic for the populace to keep track of things. With enough propaganda, tragedies, disasters, and divisiveness to pit the people against each other, nobody could identify the root cause of the world's problems. The few who did were powerless to do anything about it.

With progress came destabilization of regions, then global war, and ultimately something that was called peace.

Peace, the one part of humanity that did *not* change. There was peace, so long as everyone stayed in line and knew their place. Since the dawn of his birth, mankind had always ruled one another and called it peace. Peace at the end of a sword. A club, a sword, a whip, a gun, or a plasma gauntlet—only the technology changed. The nature remained the same.

Change—and by extension, progress—occasionally veered towards liberty, even if unintentionally. World One, a formerly lush planet, decorated with blue oceans and green pastures, had been transformed into industrial landscape. With the invention of fusion energy nearly leading to global disaster, and nuclear energy reserved solely for the government capital in Rome, an energy source was needed. Over a century of debate came to a crashing end. Methane had become the primary energy source.

With World One's supply rapidly draining, the Alliance turned to the stars for solutions. Thus, Mars became World Two.

Here, the cosmos had gifted them a planet within flight range. Its atmosphere was thin and clean, its surface dry and harmless, lacking disease or geological threat. Its volcanoes were dormant or extinct. There was no predatory wildlife or poisonous plants. World Two was just a rock in space, its landscape blanketed in freezing temperatures, its gravity a third of its blue-green neighbor's, its air unbreathable.

Then came the interference of man.

Those skies which were originally so clear, were now darkened. The ground was warm, and the core heavy. Experimental technology, originally implemented on World One's moon, had been perfected here on World Two. The atmospheric, temperature, and gravitational alterations brought success... and consequences. Those dormant volcanoes came back to life with a vengeance, accelerating the warming process, and filling the atmosphere with smoke and debris.

Nothing was more disastrous than the reawakening of Olympus Mons, the tallest planetary mountain in the solar system. It was three weeks after the gravitational alteration when geologists reported heavy seismic activity around the seemingly-extinct mountain. On July 17th 2046, the twenty-seven-kilometer-tall monster bled the planet's blood onto the surface. Being a shield volcano, its eruption was not explosive. Had it been, World Two would have been a dead planet, for it would release double the fumes as Yellowstone and Lake Toba combined.

In his studies, Tremayne repeatedly read the reports by the Geological First Officer, Simon Gracie.

"I felt the land shake under my boots and heard a deep roaring in the distance. At first, I truly believed the planet had come alive in the most literal sense. It was unlike anything I'd ever heard, even after forty years in my profession. I have studied super volcanoes, witnessed the 2139 eruption of Novarupta, and have sent doomed probes into the atmosphere of Venus. Nothing compared to this. A monster had awakened, and it was bleeding. Even from miles away, we could see its black-red rivers drooling from its mouth, hot clouds rising above it. The sky changed. No longer could we see the stars, whose presence comforted us during the bitter days and nights. No longer was this place bitter. The solar panels' job were made easier, for the planet was warming itself in a blanket of ash. Truly a fiend from Hell, the monster's blood torched everything unfortunate enough to come in contact with it—a fact five teams learned the hard way. It was then I realized we truly have changed the world, just not in the way we planned."

Dr. Gracie was correct. Olympus Mons was not the only monster awakened by humanity's meddling. As it turned out, Mars was indeed full of life. For millions of years, the ecosystem of Mars was hidden in the warmer subterranean regions. With the shift in the planetary mass and the seismic activity that followed, they were driven from the depths onto the world above. Some were herbivorous and benevolent, others were carnivorous and violent.

With the discovery of life came the biggest tragedy of the whole situation. Living among the subterranean creatures was a civilization of humanoid creatures. Not only did Mars contain life, but it was also home to *intelligent* life. Upon learning of these beings did Dr. Gracie learn of his greatest sin. The change in gravity, the eruption of volcanoes worldwide, and the countless earthquakes had reduced their global population in half. Men, women, children, all dead due to the abrupt shift in their environment.

Like the best of God's creatures, the Martians adapted, but were not without their grudges. They kept to themselves mostly, rebuilding their numbers in the deep caverns below. Creatures of the dark, they ruled the depths, leaving humans to rule the world above.

And rule humanity did.

One colony became five. Five became fifty. Fifty became a hundred. A hundred ballooned to a thousand, and the numbers kept growing. Distance developed culture, one that embraced individualism.

For years, things ran relatively smoothly. The colonists were all part of a drilling operation. Originally, it had started with a few hundred people. The objective was to extract methane from within the planet's crust, store it in giant containers, and ship it back to World One. Up until recently, there was little to no military presence. The Alliance did not originally see the point of wasting precious resources and personnel to babysit a few colonists.

As the population changed, so did the way of life. People learned to reap the benefits of their labor. Distance provided freedoms they were not used to for many years. People could read any material they had access to without being investigated. People were able to speak openly to each other and exchange ideas, including controversial ones without fear of arrest. Colonies could arrange their own school curriculums. People voted on their administrators. Even the Colony Governor, though appointed by the senate, tended to allow the people to vote on larger-scale matters.

Now, the population was in the millions. More personnel and supplies resulted in more fuel export, but more was never enough. World One's reserves were running out and they had an entire planet to supply energy to. Blackouts became a common problem everywhere except military bases and government centers. However, after the nuclear and fusion disasters, nobody dared to question the Chancellor and Senate.

3

Tremayne and many others saw through the emotional manipulation tactics. *"You must ship more fuel, or else many more will be unable to have heat this coming winter. Their lives* depend *on you."*

It was all nonsense. Not the struggles of the people, but the farcical notion that the colonists could do anything about it. Most people here knew that the fuel they shipped back was mainly supplied to the military and government. There was a reason those areas never had blackouts. Sadly, anyone who froze to death would still do so, even if World One had a hundred-year supply of fuel worldwide.

Regardless, the grip of the Alliance was slowly squeezing the necks of the colonists. They were not trusted by the powers-that-be, especially when the supply of resources did not meet the demand. They existed only to serve the needs of the Alliance. Needs, which could never be satisfied. There was no regards for the setbacks caused by violent wildlife and harsh landscapes. Just an insatiable desire for results.

Like a greedy hand reaching across the kitchen table, the Alliance utilized force to ensure their quotas were met. Security, they told the Governor, for the protection of the colonists and to ensure peace on World Two.

Peace at the end of a gun. The one part of humanity that did not change.

It was dusk, and the sun was minutes away from setting. Winston Tremayne stood on the hillside, his binocs raised to his eyes. Dome-shaped and encasing his entire head, his facemask was foggy and crusted with residue from the planet. Alas, it was the state of most standard-issue rebreather masks. It was the same with all of their equipment and attire. His dust jacket, originally tan in color, was covered in red dust and minerals. His black boots were cracked, showing signs of heavy use. This was the cost of frontier life on an unforgiving planet. Nothing stayed clean, and nobody was ever truly safe outside the domes.

World Two had been partially terraformed. Its gravity matched that of World One's and its atmosphere was in the midst of transformation. At this rate, it would be at least another ten years before people could breathe outside the domes without the use of masks.

Out here, the poisonous, mineral-filled air was the least of Tremayne's worries. This was the western edge of the Blackout Hills, a large stretch of landscape north of the established territories. It was a place that rightfully earned its name. Radio communications were garbled at best in this region, and navigational equipment often failed, leaving the colonists to resort to old-fashioned methods such as map reading. That was nothing compared to the real concerns.

At his feet were the markings left by what was likely a rhysec, a three-legged reptilian with sickle-shaped claws. So far, there was nothing around except his trusty steed. The onset of night heightened the dangers. In the past year, at least eight colonists from Espinosa, Schaffer, and Mayze had been killed by these beasts. This was the cost of drilling in the Blackout. Furthermore, it was the cost of serving an ungrateful Alliance.

Despite the challenges, Tremayne would rather be here than anywhere else. Here on World Two, he and many others had enjoyed their first taste of true freedom—freedom that was now being threatened for the supposed comfort of security.

He brushed the eyepiece with his sleeve, then raised the binocs. The rounded eyepiece was designed to complement the surface of his protective facemask. It too was dusty and had to be repeatedly cleaned. There was no shortage of dust anywhere on this planet, with the drilling and sporadic volcano eruptions that took place over the years.

Tremayne focused on the southwest and zoomed in. A quarter mile from the edge of the Blackout were the keepers of *peace*.

Tridents. Cannon fodder of the government, they were dressed head to toe in black, light-armored combat uniforms. The only color contradicting the black uniforms were three red electric bolts which ran from the shoulder down to the elbow. These three jagged lines met at the shoulder, like a trident pointing down.

The military had designed them to resemble lightning bolts. To everyone else, they resembled blood veins.

Their facemasks were like tinted windows, erasing the identity of these infantrymen. The Alliance did not embrace individualism, for such things slackened the flow of progress—a fancy word for government rule.

From afar, they resembled a colony of ants converging on an unlucky victim which found itself in their path. This victim in particular was a transport tanker. It was on route from the E-42 methane extractor, hauling fuel to be specifically used for powering Espinosa Colony.

The company of troops was supported by two Rhino-class combat tanks, seven personnel carriers, and a Viper Jeep equipped with a turret mount. The Rhinos were big hulking machines, capable of firing energy projectiles powerful enough to punch a gaping hole in the side of an Arbiter-Class star-freighter.

Three transport crewmembers stood outside the tanker, their hands raised. Tremayne could hear one of the tridents shouting orders at them, his voice mechanicalized due to his facemask apparatus.

In front of the Viper Jeep, a more relaxed trident observed the inspection. Even from this distance, his jacket was noticeably cleaner than his men. There was only one officer on this planet so pompous.

Tremayne had seen Colonel Segan on a few occasions, mainly during inspections. Ever since the young officer arrived, he acted as though he owned the place. His tridents did not hesitate to follow his commands, no matter how inhumane they were, and regardless of how often those orders resulted in their deaths. He was a slow learner at best, and failed to understand the hazards of World Two. To him, it was just another territory to be ruled.

Utilizing a scanner, one of the tridents approached the LED reader on the side of the tanker. Tremayne zoomed to the max, coming in just close enough to read the green digits. *100%*. They were traveling with a full payload.

Segan pointed to another group of tridents, who marched to the cab of the vehicle.

One of the workers stepped forward, finger pointed. His voice, though distant, was loud and clear.

"No! You can't take it! We'll be without power for a week!"

His shouts were cut short as the tridents standing guard sprang into action. The colonist was struck repeatedly, knocked to the ground, only to be lifted to his feet and held by two other soldiers, while the third ruthlessly beat him to a pulp.

His fellow workers stepped forward, hands clenched into fists. Their defiance was met with the tip of an electric rod. Like an expandable baton, it was drawn from a holster attached to a duty belt, the tip glowing blue upon activation. The trident wielding it jabbed the tip into one of the colonists, transferring a powerful charge which induced uncontrollable spasms. More infantrymen converged, viciously zapping the third colonist with their own batons.

All three workers convulsed on the ground, their attackers relishing in the torture they inflicted. This was part of the indoctrination—the *one* joy they were allowed to feel. Serve the Alliance, crush your enemies, embrace the suffering they feel, do not feel remorse, for this is all for the benefit of civilization.

"Keep at it. Let the fools learn their lesson," Colonel Segan said. "Take the tanker back to Hope Central. The rest of you mount up."

Without hesitation, the tridents returned to the carriers. Engines shook the landscape, their forward lights flashing the hillside.

Tremayne lowered his binoculars. He had seen enough. These soldiers were not doing an inspection. They were collecting fuel for export. The Chancellor had demanded they deliver every last drop they could obtain, and this clearly included colony reserves.

Espinosa needed to be warned.

He turned on his heel. His trusty steed raised its head, then extended its six legs. Scarabs, insectoid creatures as large as horses, were as gentle as they were ugly, so long as they trusted you. This specimen was fifteen years old and seven feet in length. Its abdomen was bulky like that of a spider, its carapace dark and scaly. Small mandibles frolicked, making up for the lack of expression in its eyes.

It leaned forward and slightly to the left, granting easy access to the saddle strapped to its thorax. Tremayne pulled himself aboard and slipped his boots into the stirrups.

"Let's go. Hee-yah!"

The creature turned around and raced east, disappearing over the hillside. It crossed a mile of rocky landscape with relative ease, scaling rocks that were otherwise impassible. With the battalion out of sight, they moved south, exiting the Blackout hills onto the relatively smooth Martian valley. From there, they continued east toward Espinosa Colony.

***

Espinosa Colony – outside the dome.

Night had set over the huge, transparent dome which sheltered two-thousand colonists from the elements. From outside, it resembled a disco ball, with lights shining from the building windows, streetlamps, and small transport shuttles moving within. The large tunnel-shaped atrium was brightly lit for easy access. Most of the colonists had settled in, for work outside the dome was too dangerous at night.

Parson Lerner watched from the guard tower's east window. Every night was the same. He would rather be anywhere but in this small, disc-shaped structure. Sure, it was sealed, thus enabling him to be maskless. That was the only positive aspect. He hated this assignment as much as he hated the shift. There were only a handful of other night workers, particularly maintenance crews who worked on the vehicles. He could see them in the garage lights outside the dome.

Most of the nights were spent admiring the small city inside the dome. Espinosa was smaller than most colonies, thus requiring a smaller dome. It was only twelve acres from west to east. Outside of the dome were less-impressive buildings, such as the maintenance shed, the scarab barn, and the refinery buildings on the north side. Each of them had cracked sidings from exposure, the exposed metal rusted and stained.

The entire system was interconnected with long pipes, which allowed for the transfer of electricity, water, waste, fuel, and recycled oxygen. Zipping throughout the area were small maintenance drones, which constantly inspected every aspect of the buildings. Like moths to a flame, they danced around the dome, checking for even the slightest hint of damage. In a place like this, even a microscopic crack could lead to total disaster.

Not in thirty years had a dome breach occurred. The worst threat, aside from the volcanos, was the subterranean—now terranean—wildlife. They were a couple miles from the Blackout Hills, but that did not mean they were safe from carnivores. Even now, new species were revealing themselves, and almost *always* at night. This was the purpose of the night watchmen: keep an eye out and be ready to protect the night workers.

BEEP!

His companion, a curly-haired twenty-one-year-old named Shaw Horton, leaned toward the monitor on the desk console.

"I think there's something out there."

Parson longingly watched the dome, disinterested in the reading.

"Probably just Martians again. They usually come out of their tunnels this time of night to scavenge."

Shaw put his mask on and approached the doorway to the balcony. The first set of doors led to a small atrium. He passed through, let it shut behind him, then opened the next set of doors.

With a set of night vision binocs raised to his visor, he scanned the mountainside.

Immediately, he saw movement. A single scarab carrying a rider. That rider was waving frantically and shouting. Shaw tried to listen, but could not make out what the guy was saying. However, the tone was distinguishable enough. Whatever he was trying to say, it was urgent.

Shaw activated the intercom. "Parson, get out here."

"What is it?"

"Just get out here, will ya?!"

Parson went through the atrium, groaning through the five-second process until he was on the balcony. Shaw handed him the binocs. Parson leaned forward and watched the rider galloping toward the dome.

"Is that…?"

"Winston Tremayne," Shaw said. "I think something's wrong."

"Hang on. Shh! He's saying something."

As Tremayne closed the distance, his words became clear.

"The blood-jackets are coming! Look alive! The blood-jackets are coming!"

CHAPTER 2

Espinosa Colony – inside the dome.

In all the years Moza served as the Administrator of Espinosa Colony, he never got used to the high-pitched ring from his bedside comm unit. Many times, it jarred him from a deep REM sleep. In tonight's case, it was worse, because he had just fallen asleep minutes ago.

Moza swung his legs out of bed, his senses hazy. His hands shook, as though the muscles had to learn how to move again. It felt as though he had been raised from the dead. It was the cost of being a leader, but that didn't make Moza dislike it any less. In fact, the night calls were the worst. If they were waking him, then whatever it was, it was urgent.

He punched the transmitter button with his finger. "Moza here. What's the matter?"

"This is the watchtower, sir. We have an emergency."

That word gave Moza a greater jolt than the comm's ping.

"I'm listening."

"Sir, Winston Tremayne has just arrived. There's a company of tridents on approach."

In the blink of an eye, Moza was wide awake.

"I'm on my way to the airlock. Alert my staff."

He touched another button on his nightstand, opening his closet. He approached and dug out his boots, grey tunic, and trousers.

If there was anything to be learned from this experience, it was to think twice before going to bed early.

***

Every time Moza stepped outside, his eyes naturally went to the dome ceiling. Only a hundred-and-twenty feet over his head, it always felt a little too low in his opinion. Some of the buildings were barely able to fit under it. A few inches lower, and the reinforced glass would be pressing against the roof of the hospital and internal radio tower.

Moza redirected his gaze from the dome ceiling to the shuttle waiting outside his residence. Usually, he balked at riding these small transports.

He never saw himself as royalty, and the colony was so small, he could walk its length in ten minutes if he hustled.

This time, he was grateful for the shuttle. He boarded the backseat and waited quietly while the driver sped toward the west end of the dome.

Colony Square was made to resemble a typical World One neighborhood—minus the pollution, garbage, decaying structures, and general apathy of its residents. Another thing it lacked was the sense of overpopulation. With a census of two-hundred-and-thirty-eight colonists, the small colony was fairly spacious. Tonight, however, Colony Square perfectly captured the crowdedness of World One.

If Moza didn't know any better, he would have thought the watchtower had alerted everyone in the whole damn colony. But he did know better. Somewhere behind that crowd was Winston Tremayne, and knowing him, he had already spread the word of advancing Alliance forces coming to strip Espinosa of their fuel supplies.

Well over a hundred colonists, most of them male, had gathered near the main atrium. Engineers, maintenance workers, off duty medical personnel, rover drivers, geologists, lab techs—the very blood of this colony stood before him.

"Oh, Lord. They've formed a militia," he said.

The streetlamps were lit, giving Moza a clear view of the rifles in their hands. Standard Plasma V-13 Rifles, often referred to as plasma muskets. They were not single-shot weapons, as implied by their nickname. However, they were not much better. After three shots, the plasma core would require several seconds of cooling before it could be fired again. These weapons were older models, mainly used for hunting or defense against wildlife.

They were the type of weapon that could be constructed out of scrap, for their mechanical structure was simple. All one needed was a Vescinium-13 plasma core, a triggering mechanism, something to serve as a barrel, frame, and stock. Most of them were factory made, though showing their age. Some were enhanced with scopes, which did little good. They were weapons of limited range, not suitable for boots-on-the-ground combat. Certainly not the most ideal weapon against a company of battle-hardened tridents.

To the colonists, it did not matter. They knew why the military was coming and what they would do. Though it had been two years since the last visit, the wounds were still fresh in their eyes.

The shuttle came to a stop. Moza stepped out and was greeted by his staff. He couldn't hear what most of them were saying due to the bombardment of questions from the crowd.

Moza raised his hands in an attempt to calm them.

"Everyone, I am aware of the situation. Please return home."

It only served to rile them up further.

"Not happening!" one colonist shouted.

"You going to do something about this, Administrator?!" another shouted.

A security officer approached the crowd. "Make a lane, please! Let us through!" The security officer walked a dozen steps ahead of the administrator, continuing to bark commands to the horde of colonists.

Moza, aided by six of his staff, slowly followed through the pathway, while doing his best to put the colonists at ease.

Another voice called from behind the crowd, demanding they widen that lane. The colonists complied, making way for Counselor Swan. He was a short figure, almost stereotypical for political figures these days, even if he was only a simple colony advisor.

He met with Moza, then did an about turn to walk with him to the atrium.

"I take it Tremayne's up there?" Moza said.

"Yes," Swan said.

"Obviously you've already gotten the scoop."

"Aye." Swan took a breath. He, like many of the colonists gathered here, was visibly unnerved. "Winston got a visual. Colonel Segal is on the way with a whole battalion."

Moza closed his eyes. *Just what I need.*

"How many tridents?"

"Two hundred strong at least," Swan said. "Armed to the teeth. They're riding with tanks, turret mounted rovers..."

One of the colonists stepped in their path. "The window is approaching! It's obvious why they're coming."

"Excuse us, please," Moza said. He and his staff walked around the colonist, only to be stopped by another.

"We provided them a shipment two weeks ago, Administrator. We haven't had enough time to refill the tankers."

"I know, I know," Moza said. "Please step aside. And please, keep your voices down. I can barely hear myself think."

For once, the crowd obeyed his instruction.

Moza reached into his pocket and dug out a packet of Excreed. He broke the cap and sucked in the liquid painkiller. By the time he reached the atrium airlock, his headache was starting to subside.

Awaiting him was Winston Tremayne. A middle-aged man of average build, he had transferred to World Two as a repairman. Tremayne personally preferred the word silversmith, due to his unmatched ability to form any metal on the planet into whatever shape he desired. On World Two, there was always a shortage of supplies, but never a shortage of scrap. His hands were calloused by years of hard labor, his attire stained by his exposure to the elements.

"Winston."

"Moza."

"Thanks for the wakeup call. I was having a good dream," Moza said.

Tremayne cracked a smile and approached the administrator. "Trout fishing on the shores of Lake Michigan?"

Moza chuckled. "The good 'ol days. Back before Gregorio dried it up."

Both smiles faded as both men recounted the last days of green on their home planet. Now, from afar, World One no longer glistened with a green and blue color. Now, it was a dusty grey. Only mass differentiated it from its moon. Sure, there were still oceans, but their gracious blue color was gone.

Now, Gregorio's grasp was choking the lives on World Two. The colonists of Espinosa could already feel the fingertips starting to squeeze.

"Segan's coming," Tremayne said.

"Swan updated me," Moza said. "You think they'll settle for what's in the containers?" He nodded at the five enormous tankers outside the northern part of the dome.

Tremayne scoffed. "What do you think?"

Moza nodded. *Yeah. Dumb question.* He glanced at the crowd, who were gradually starting to get riled up again, then sighed.

"How can you blame them?" Tremayne said. "Certainly, you remember what happened two years ago when Segan made an unannounced late-night arrival."

Moza exhaled slowly. "Yes. I remember too well."

"Not nearly as well as I do!"

The crowd went silent, then turned to give their attention to the towering figure who approached.

Moza held his breath, helpless to stop one of the most influential figures on World Two from making his entrance.

Dr. Douglas Warren had a powerful presence even when he wasn't speaking. His black beard was kept nicely trimmed, his blue eyes piercing whomever they gazed upon, and his body language maintaining military discipline. His voice had a smoothness to it, which even at age fifty-five, had a charming effect on the ladies. Despite this, Dr. Warren did not have a reputation for being a womanizer. His name was associated with his profession. He had invented over a dozen vaccines since arriving on World Two, saved hundreds of lives with his hands alone, thousands with his inventions. He was a gentle soul who was rough around the edges.

Tonight, those edges were sharper than ever.

Warren approached the atrium with his own plasma musket, equipped with a scope and a longer muzzle for increased range. The spring in his step was replaced by a purposeful strut. He was dressed in a battered jacket, black leather boots caked with Martian soil, and black trousers held up by a belt with a circular symbol on its buckle—a symbol of the Martian colonies.

Numerous colonists walked behind him like soldiers following a general into battle. As they approached, Moza felt his authority dissipate. The colonists were not interested in attempting peaceful methods for dealing with the tridents. Such things had been tried in the past and failed every single time.

Dr. Warren stopped a few yards from the administrator, his right hand holding his rifle by the barrel.

"We *all* remember," he continued. "We remember how they arrived in the dead of night and sucked the methane containers dry. That's fine, that's what they're here for, I suppose. But with a small window for shipment every two years, they justify to themselves that every last particle of fuel they can get. We remember what came next.

"They drained Espinosa's generators of every last particle of methane to be shipped back to World One. 'Generators will last you until you can harvest more fuel. Until then, rely on life support.' All surgical procedures were forced to shut down. We didn't even have lights. Patients barely had oxygen. Lost three the first night, four the next."

Warren pivoted to direct his attention to a man on his right.

"Davy Austin. I know *you* remember."

Davy nodded. "Damn right I remember."

"I was treating his wife for a mineral infection," Warren said. "I couldn't remove the particles because my equipment was forced to shut down. She died the following morning."

Moza said nothing. What could he say to that? Especially with the entire colony siding with Warren.

Hell, deep down, *he* sided with Warren. Moza wasn't blind to the truth. For a week, they lived on minimal life support. For a dome housing two-hundred-plus colonists, that was insufficient.

Tremayne stepped forward. "They're coming, Doctor. You can bet they'll do the same tonight. They don't come this heavily armed for nothing."

"Maybe we can hide some of our reserve fuel drums. They're smaller, easier to relocate…"

"No time," Tremayne said. "They're almost here."

"And they're thorough," Warren said. "They'll comb through this place and take whatever they want. *If* we let them. Frankly, I'm tired of letting them. We've *let* them get away with too much for my liking."

The crowd murmured in agreement, their voices soft, but filled with the same anger that fueled Warren. Many of them gripped their rifles with two hands, holding them at port arms while they followed Warren to the atrium.

"Like the time they ransacked the Raver Farms. Took every last crop because 'World One is facing a food shortage.'"

The crowd chanted again.

"How about the time they opened fire on the Martians? Apparently, it's not enough that we intruded on their planet, but apparently World One thinks we should bomb a shrine that's inconveniently located near a methane deposit. To hell with any locals who dare try to put a stop to it."

He and his followers put on their facemasks and made their way into the atrium. Moza slipped his on and followed, hoping to find some means to put an end to this.

The airlock opened, allowing for the first group to make their way in. When the outer doors opened, a crowd of forty colonists followed Dr. Warren outside the dome.

"They've taxed us to starvation, stripped us of our resources, and they're demanding we wreck this planet like we did the last one. They speak only one language: blunt force. And that's what will be necessary if they want to empty our generators."

He took a left and walked to the Espinosa generator units, located on the southwest side of the dome. A moment later, another group of colonists exited the airlock and joined him.

A human barrier surrounded the generators, each man facing west in the direction of the oncoming storm.

In the front of this blockade was Dr. Warren. In a steady, commanding voice, he instructed his people.

"Stand your ground. Do not fire unless fired upon. But if they want to have a war, let it begin here."

CHAPTER 3

Fifteen-hundred yards west of Espinosa Colony.

"We've got at least fifty colonists, armed with what appear to be V-13 Rifles," Major Remer said. "It does not appear they are taking defensive positions."

Colonel Segan made a rat-like sneer. It fit the description the colonists had given him. He had overheard the lowly workers refer to him as a rat. Colonel Segan was more amused than offended, for he thought of the colonists as little mice.

Better to be a fierce rat than a squeaky mouse.

"That's because they're not," he replied. "They're flexing their muscles. Unruly children. Squeaky mice."

The Colonel looked over his shoulder at the two-hundred-and-thirty-five trained tridents behind his Viper Jeep. The carriers were spread out, ready to deploy their troops at a moment's notice.

"Yellow alert."

The tanks armed their cannons. Each trident primed their gauntlets on standby-mode. The enormous tanker carriers remained in the back, following protocol. Though the tanker was heavily-armored, it was still standard practice to keep it far from any potential firefight. In this case, there was potential.

Segan wasn't too worried. He could see through the binocs that they were staging a protest. If they truly had plans for combat, then they were the dumbest lot on the planet. There was no strategic formation. By the looks of it, they were barricading the generators with their very lives.

They were pushing it. Segan's lack of concern did not override the personal offence he took by this protest. These people seemed to think they were separate from the Alliance. Nobody on World One would dare take such action. Nor would they be able to. It was a travesty that Governor Lovell allowed guns, even ones as primitive as the V-13s, in the hands of civilians. Only law enforcement and military forces were permitted possession of arms by the Alliance. This was the way of peace and prosperity.

Segan took his seat. "It may be for show, but it's not something we'll tolerate. We might have to make this planet a little redder." He looked to his driver. "Proceed."

The Jeep led the way. Behind it, the carrier and tank engines roared to life as they followed it to the dome.

***

Dr. Douglas Warren could hear the breathing of his fellow men intensify as the battalion closed the distance. White spotlights stretched across the landscape, touching the west side of the dome.

Already, the carriers were spreading out. This action, combined with their uncharacteristic stop fifteen-hundred yards out, indicated they had spotted the militia. Precautions were taken in the form of a pincer movement. The battalion was branching out in an effort to quickly surround the smaller militia.

The Viper Jeep and two tanks proceeded to the watchtower, where Moza stood with his advisors and a handful of other colonists.

Warren was close enough to overhear them trying to talk Moza out of this 'ridiculous bout of showmanship'.

"What good is this? What will it achieve?" Counselor Swan said.

"You talk as though I have any real power over the situation," Moza replied.

"You do. You are the colony administrator."

"Rank only carries your authority so far," Moza said. "These people here, they've lived on a hellscape for most of their lives. They don't respond to comforting promises. They respond to strength and courage. Something we in government often lack."

The engines of the mighty tanks shook the earth beneath their feet. The carriers came to a stop, their personnel immediately deploying.

Two-hundred tridents, faceless thanks to their pitch-dark masks—and soulless, at least surmised by Warren—surrounded the militia. Their black uniforms camouflaged them with the night, only visible thanks to the safety lights around the dome and outside buildings.

Proving Moza's point, Swan and the other counselors retreated to the entrance, quickly shutting the airlock door behind them.

A single Viper Jeep led the way, coming to a stop near the watchtower. The passenger door opened, and a human rat stepped out. At least, that's how any sensible person on this planet referred to Colonel Segan. It didn't help that his face was oddly shaped. His jaw was angular and his nose scrunched. Either he was injured in an accident or in combat, or he was spawned by the lowest gene pool. Warren suspected the latter.

The Colonel gave a glance at the doctor and the militia standing behind him. That rodent-like grin came over his face. He, like many Alliance authority figures, relished in their perceived superiority.

Moza summoned the courage he so desperately needed, then approached the Colonel.

Segan greeted him with a condescending look.

"Is there a point to this?"

Moza ignored the question. "Colonel Segan. What brings you here? The hour is late, and my office have received no notification of your arrival."

"Don't play the fool," Segan said. He strutted past the administrator in favor of speaking directly to the colonists behind him. "By order of the Chancellor and the World One Alliance, you will provide access to Containers One through Five."

"Had you contacted us beforehand, we could have prepped the containers in advance," Moza said. "You have full access to the tanks, but only One, Two, and Three are ready for transfer. They're all yours. Four and Five are still empty. We have not had sufficient time to refill them after the last collection."

Segan turned to face the administrator, his condescending expression withstanding.

"What a shame. You're aware you have not met your quota, Administrator. Correct?"

"I am aware. I'm also aware that World One has taken a large number of our workforce to assist in the construction of the Jupiter Orbital Refinery. In addition, most of the deposits in our location have run dry. We're branching out to locate new ones as we speak, but it's slowing progress."

"Looks to me that the only thing you've produced in mass are excuses," Segan said. He nodded to Major Remer, who gave the order to the tanker driver to bring the giant vehicle to the containers.

A three hundred foot beast built entirely from steel, it resembled a giant caterpillar tearing through the Martian landscape. Its wheels kicked up dust and splintered rock, its vibrations felt even by those inside the dome.

It lined up several yards from the containers. Like refinery tankers, they towered at the height of the dome. Each one was equipped with a mineral resistant hose to allow transfer of methane to the transport.

Major Remer joined the tanker driver by Container One. Pushing the colony engineer to the side, he performed his own readings on the control platform. Satisfied with the results on the computer, he moved on to the next, then the next, all the way to Container Five.

His voice came through Colonel Segan's transmitter.

"He's telling the truth, Colonel. They've slacked. Four and Five are empty."

"At least he admitted it," Segan replied. He lowered his transmitter and looked at Moza. "I don't care what difficulties you face. You still need to meet your quota."

Moza's next breath was a shaky one.

"I assure you we will meet our numbers next time."

"I can assure that too," Segan said. He turned and leaned into his transmitter. "Empty the generators."

Warren's fears had come to fruition.

A squad of tridents approached. Their M3 Gauntlets were primed and ready for combat. The newest phase in standard weaponry, Alliance infantry did not carry firearms, instead wearing them on their right forearm. It was always the right. Progression of the human race supposedly required order. Every living member was required to think the same way, eat the same foods. Not even left handedness was allowed. The only diversity, other than physical features such as skin pigmentation, were roles in the workforce.

Had it not been for his preexisting knowledge of these so-called soldiers, Warren would have mistaken them for droids. Even their voices were often mechanical, their humanity driven out of them during training and indoctrination.

A trident with a sergeant insignia stood six feet from the doctor.

"Step aside."

Neither Warren nor his supporters budged.

The Sergeant clicked a mechanism on the top of his gauntlet. The trigger mechanism extended to his palm. The muzzle ring expanded and took on a bluish glow.

The colonists began to quiver. Though brave, most were not combat tested. Their opposition, on the other hand, did not waver an inch.

Segan stepped toward the crowd, unfazed by their showmanship.

"Anyone foolish enough to keep up this charade will be zapped or shot. Depends on my mood. Considering you're stupid enough to brandish weapons in the face of Alliance troops, I'm leaning toward the latter."

Moza chased after the Colonel, visibly unnerved.

"Colonel, I must ask you not to do this. That's our fuel supply. If you do this, we'll lose all functions…"

"Except life-support," Segan said. "You'll be fine. If anything, this'll teach you and your people to hustle and siphon more methane. You know, like you're *paid* to do." He concluded the statement with a chuckle.

"Last chance," the Sergeant said.

The colonists kept their rifles pointed skyward, unprovoking.

Warren ignored him, instead looking to Segan.

"If you thieves believe we're just gonna stand by and let you take our fuel, you have another thing coming."

Segan studied him for a moment. "I know you, don't I?"

"We may have met."

"Dr. Warren!" Segan said. "How could I have forgotten?"

"Probably because of the humiliation," Warren replied. "I can't blame you. Thirty years on this rock, and you're literally the only patient I've had seeking treatment for a severe groin rash. I'd want to forget that too."

Some of the less nervous colonists chuckled.

In that moment, Segan wished he had a blackened mask. No way would a Colonel want anyone to see the look on his face.

His brief, but noticeable, discomfiture shifted quickly to anger.

"Sergeant, confiscate all weapons. Arrest every single colonist standing by that generator, and prep for incursion into the dome."

Now, the tridents were aiming their M3s at the crowd.

"Place rifles at your feet and place hands behind your heads," the Sergeant ordered.

Administrator Moza was fogging up his facemask with his heavy breathing. Though stricken by anxiety, he could not allow his people to suffer the tortures of the Umbrella Prison in Fremont Territory. There, they would face several months of hard labor at minimum.

He sprinted until he was standing in front of Segan.

"Colonel, if we may… AGH!!!"

A flash of light preceded his scream. The administrator fell to the ground, smoke billowing from the football-sized burn in his thigh.

Colonel Segan turned his gauntlet toward the militia.

Warren's rifle shifted from port arms to firing position. Years of resentment peaked at this very moment.

Fueled by rage, his aim was swifter than the Colonel's.

He fired the first shot, striking Segan in the right shoulder. The Colonel whipped to the side, then hit the ground.

The point of no return had arrived.

With his rifle needing several seconds to charge, Warren drew his energy revolver and fired from the hip, striking the trident Sergeant center mass before he could get a shot off.

All out chaos followed.

Plasma bolts, blue and red, zipped through the air like burning horizontal raindrops. The world outside the dome became a hurricane of heat and violence, as tridents and colonists exchanged fire.

The blockade broke formation, the limitations of their weapons proving a grave disadvantage.

Warren backpedaled, firing into the battalion.

Blue M3 projectiles zipped by his head. Some dissipated in the air, others found other targets.

In less than twenty seconds, over a dozen colonists were on the ground with smoldering craters in their chests.

Warren's revolver hit its limit, forcing him to holster it. By then, his rifle had recharged, allowing for another shot. Up to the left, he spotted a colonist and a trident locked in combat.

Preston Gosly, a droid chip repairman, tried ramming his rifle barrel into his opponent's facemask. His efforts backfired. Overpowered by the trident, the weapon was instead shifted into his own face. Preston fell on his back, then cringed as the trident aimed down with his M3 gauntlet.

Warren took the shot. The plasma bolt struck the target in the head, shattering the glass and charring the so-called human underneath.

He ran to Preston's side and helped him up.

"Your mask's fine, lucky bastard."

"Not sure lucky's the appropriate word in this instance," Davy Austin shouted as he approached the two.

His point was made by the explosions from tank shelling. Huge fireballs erupted along the south side of the dome, scattering the militia further.

The tridents advanced, taking no notice of their dead. Two of them took aim at a fleeing target, ready to gun him down until one ordered them to cease.

"He's the administrator. Don't kill him unless necessary."

Moza overheard that and was instantly relieved. He ran as fast as he could, hobbling on his injured leg until he neared Warren.

"Doctor, GO! You absolutely do not want to be captured, believe me! Take my speeder. East garage! Get with Lars! Go now!"

"Lars?" Davy said.

"No time to explain," Warren said.

The three of them turned around and raced along the dome, ducking as plasma fire zipped by.

Clinging tight to their weapons, they ran for dear life until ultimately arriving at the garage.

Warren punched in the entry code and opened the doors. Inside were two-dozen rovers, each parked in a single row. At the left end of the garage was a silver vehicle with six wheels, capable of carrying up to six passengers. The speeder was built with superior technology. Capable of levitating three feet off the ground, it was the perfect all-terrain vehicle. Less likely to get stuck in a rut, they were reserved mainly for the top administrative officers of each colony. Everyone else was stuck with the primitive rovers, equipped with two-inch tread tires.

The doctor climbed into the speeder and moved to the operator's chair. There, he punched in the ignition code, provided to him by Moza a year prior.

"You know how to drive these things, Preston?"

"Sure do, Doc," Preston said. "I just hope you know where to go, because those blood-jackets will be on our six the whole way."

"North," Warren replied.

Preston took his place, then waited a count of three to allow his passengers to strap in. A touch of the accelerator sent the vehicle speeding from its compartment. He turned it north, tripling its speed within a few seconds.

"We're going to the Blackout Hills?" Davy said. "Hell, we might as well have let ourselves get caught by the blood-jackets."

"Relax," Warren said. He dug into his jacket pocket, finding a square communicator. He pressed the transmitter, then silently voiced a prayer. "Please answer. Please answer..."

An alien language replied. A moment later, in a deep, soft tone, it spoke in English.

"I am here."

"Lars. It's the Doctor. Douglas. Please, we need your help."

"Hopefully he's willing," Davy said, pointing behind them with his thumb. "They've commandeered the speeders. They're coming after us."

"Just keep going," Warren said. "Take us all the way into the Blackout."

They crossed a half-mile of open landscape, which grew increasingly bumpy and rigid as they approached the vast mountain range that was Blackout Hills. It wasn't long before they entered a jagged landscape, full of twisted rocks, deep pits, random cliffs, quicksand, and flesh-eating fauna.

Warren could see the incoming speeders behind them. Unlike the colonists, the tridents were untrained in maneuvering through the rugged Blackout. Within seconds of entering, one of the speeders smashed into an obstacle at high speed, the implosion of metal and personnel heard for thousands of yards.

"Careful. Keep going this way," Warren said. He activated the forward spotlight.

"You sure this is a good idea?" Davy Austin said. "The Martians aren't necessarily too fond of us humans."

"I saved the life of Lars' brother after he was hit with gauntlet fire. Trust me, he's good," Warren said.

"I hope we're close," Preston said. "Because I don't think we're gonna go much further."

"Hug the left here... keep going... move around that pit... alright, here! Stop!"

Preston didn't have to slow the thing down—he smashed into a twisted rock tower. Luckily, only the engine suffered for it.

Warren opened the supply console and grabbed the emergency survival kit. It was a standard supply case, complete with binocs, basic medicine, cartridges for the rebreather masks, among other field items.

With weapons in hand, the three men dismounted and continued up the hill on foot, with the doctor leading the way.

"You sure you know where you're going?" Preston asked.

"Almost there."

"I hope you're right. Because I don't see any—" Preston gasped, then stopped in his tracks, "—Martians."

Lars was a tall figure, even taller than most of his counterparts. The species was humanoid, their basic shape almost identical to earthling species. His forehead was rounded, then crested on the back. There were more tiny crests and slits near the cheeks and neck, leading Warren to theorize they were once an amphibious species.

The Martian held something that appeared to be a Bo staff. Though primitive in its appearance, the weapon was as advanced as the first energy weapons invented by humans. Though Warren did not know the mechanics behind it, he had seen the weapon in action—unfortunately. It was simultaneously a projectile and melee weapon, and effective at both.

Lars stood emotionless, still as a statue.

Davy and Preston held still, unsure of what to do. Was this thing going to help them? Or kill them?

They turned to look at Warren.

He approached the figure and slowly raised his hand to chest level. With his hand straight, he initiated a motion, translated from Martian language to being the Circle of Peace. He held his hand flat, moved it inward a few inches, then in a high arching motion. Lars raised his own hand, then mimicked a similar movement, the arching movement low.

Two halves of the circle.

Lars looked past the trio at the distant lights behind them. The tridents were approaching fast.

"Come."

Warren, Davy, and Preston knew not to ask questions. They followed the Martian to a five-foot pit in the ground. Following his gesture, they crawled into the pit. Lars descended behind them, then drove his staff into a flowery mechanism in the wall.

The tunnel entrance sealed, the topside perfectly blending with the surrounding landscape.

They waited in silence, listening to the arrival of a dozen tridents.

"They're here somewhere."

"Fan out. Shoot on sight. They are armed."

"Their speeder is back there. They're close."

"No visual, sir."

Several minutes passed.

The platoon moved on, completely blind to the existence of the tunnel entrance.

Breathing a sigh of relief, Warren turned his eyes to the neck of the tunnel. The walls were covered by some kind of fungus which emitted an orange luminescence. Farther down the tunnel, he could see the hint of a purple glow from the *Lusah* orbs. The natural lanterns of the Martian lairs, they fed from an incredible power source deep below the ground.

A power source kept secret by the Martians. Dr. Warren was the only human to ever lay eyes on it.

"Come," Lars said.

They followed him into the depths. From the look of it, they were in for a long walk.

Not that it mattered. It wasn't as though they had anywhere else to go now. Returning to the surface world was suicide for them. That was the consequence for starting a revolution.

CHAPTER 4

World One.
Alaska.

There was once a time the auroras could be seen across the night sky. Andre Gardner would never know—he was just going by what his grandfather told him. What he did know was that the Alaskan nights were much darker than they used to be, and that the days were not nearly as bright.

Only four more weeks of summer remained. Andre, and all other staff at the Alaska refinery, knew to cherish that time. The nights had grown darker than ever before. The skies, which had once been bright and star-filled, were now grey and cold. Now, the surrounding forest looked grey instead of green. The Sitka spruce, paper birch, and Western red cedar trees looked sickly from lack of direct sunlight. To anyone under forty, this was how trees naturally looked. Only the older generations, and those with access to unapproved literature, had some insight into the past.

Andre had to be careful. He kept two books on trees and another on natural history in his quarters, hidden away behind a vent. Part of him wished he had never stumbled upon those books. For one, discovery by government enforcers would land him two years in the brig, and likely ten lashes for disobedience. Second, truth caused him to mourn for the world he inhabited. The world was green once, the oceans blue, the country vast and open. Now, the only speck of nature left on this planet was this little bit of grey, withering forest. At one point, there was white snow on the ground in the wintertime. Today, all they got was rain which smelled as though it came from a wastewater plant. Mankind had been given a tremendous gift, only to taint it through centuries of war and industry.

Even though Andre worked inside that speck of nature, he was still surrounded by industry.

The Alaska Methane Refinery was one of the largest on the planet. In 2098, a vast deposit of methane had been discovered in the Fairbanks interior region. In 2120, twenty-two years later, the station was constructed after a series of lawsuits and protests. The world was expanding to the north. Forests were being cut down to build and make space for living quarters. Then came the worldwide hysteria following the Tokyo Nuclear Meltdowns, which veered humanity toward fossil fuels for energy sources. Following the Fusion Wars and the eventual banning of renewable and experimental energy, production was ramped up. As the years went on, fewer people cared about the cost, even as the sun was blanketed out of view.

Surrounded by nearly a mile of concrete wall, the plant exported over five tons of refined fuel each day. Huge tankers stood forty-feet high and thirty-feet wide, each one connected to pipes, which were connected to more pipes, which were welded to different sorts of machinery—not one of which Andre understood the function of. He was just a simple security officer. He wasn't a dumb jock; he had his talents and his fortes, but engineering was not one of them. Unfortunately, he had to wait another year for his next aptitude test. Security was fine, but he craved other work, preferably in a quieter location. Not once in its twenty-four-seven operation cycle did the noise subside. There was always the buzzing of machinery, the roaring of twenty-four cylinder engines, the sparking of welders, and the ringing of alarm bells. Whenever someone communicated in this plant, they were nearly shouting. Only those who worked in Administrations and the operating centers were spared from the constant onslaught to their ears.

"South Gate to Operations."

"Operations. Go ahead."

"Lexus-One-Seven-Charlie-Niner is entering gate. Heading for High Service."

"Copy that. Ten-twenty-eight."

Andre watched from his station, a hundred yards southwest of the huge block of steel that was the Administration Building. He could see the south gates yawn open. The hundred-and-ten-foot tanker eased through the perimeter, then turned right at the fork to travel to High Service. On his first day, he swore he felt the ground shake under his feet when the first tanker rolled into the station. In all likelihood, the ground did shake. The only questionable part was whether it was the truck, for the ground was *always* shaking around here, from various mechanical causes.

A much smaller vehicle pulled up to his gate: a one-man transport shuttle, piloted by Myles Gautley. A six-year veteran of the Alliance 283rd Ground Forces, he still walked with a military swagger. Lucky for Andre, his temperament had lightened drastically since those days.

Myles wore the same beige-colored uniform, and had the same factory produced blaster model on his hip. They were nothing compared to military-grade firearms, but they served their purpose.

He approached the small post, carrying two coffees.

"Enjoying yourself?"

Andre stood up. "Same as usual."

"I like usual." Myles extended one of the coffees.

Andre accepted it. As *usual*, he did not say thanks. Myles didn't need him to; it was a normal habit of them to bring each other brew. The young security officer took a sip then looked at the cup.

Cups, one of the oldest inventions still in use in the age of space travel. The wheel was another. He had looked up their invention dates. The first drinking cup was invented somewhere around 1570 B.C. in Mesopotamia. It was in the same location where the first wheel was invented, over two-thousand years earlier. It was the potter's wheel, and while not used for transport, its design was realized for transport around 3300 B.C.

The first technology, leading to greater and bigger inventions. They set the precedent that humans could develop whatever they desired to suit their needs. The bow and arrow and the horse saddle turned into the gun and the combustion engine. People turned to firewood for warmth, then coal, then electric heat. The largest difference was not the technology, but the people. Back before the days of Christ, people had to have appreciated these new inventions, for they truly made life easier. Now, in the year 2176 A.D., these gifts were taken for granted.

To be fair, how could they not be? After all, nearly all of World One's landscapes were now completely covered by technology.

Andre took another sip, then looked to his friend. "Have you heard anything more about that explosion in the bay?"

Myles shook his head. "All I know is a lot of fuel was lost. Turned the sky black for miles."

"No word of the cause? Equipment failure? Fire? Sabotage?"

Again, Myles shook his head. "I don't know."

Andre looked to the western horizon. In all likelihood, he would not be able to see any of the smoke. The winds were blowing southeast toward Vancouver and Washington. Then again, a burning tanker produced a hell of a lot of smoke. Three-hundred-thousand barrels of fuel, gone in an instant. Not to mention the fuel supply for the ship itself. He was not sure how many people worked aboard those ships. A hundred? Two hundred?

"Any survivors?"

"No idea," Myles said. "Nothing's been reported."

Andre scraped his foot on the concrete floor. All the technology in the world, and yet important information failed to be shared.

"Any word from the military base in Vancouver?"

"You are just full of questions this morning, aren't you?" Myles said.

"I don't like it," Andre said. "An explosion in broad daylight? Sorry, something about this isn't sitting well with me."

"South Gate to Operations."

"Go ahead."

"Repair Group Delta-Three-Nine has arrived."

"Copy. Direct them to Pump Eleven. Fifty-yards past High-Service, near the yellow building."

"Copy."

Myles chuckled and looked at Andre. "You gonna start asking questions about Pump Eleven now?"

Andre smirked. "Well... it *did* break down rather unexpectedly. That said, what *doesn't* these days? Which is ridiculous. We can build colonies on neighboring planets. Build orbiting stations with technology to extract sulfur from Venus' atmosphere. Yet, we can't build freaking pipes that last more than a few years."

"Talking about here or your quarters?" Myles said.

That smirk flipped upside down.

"Bad plumbing and bad circuits. It's been two days, but I can't seem to get a maintenance guy. They're backed up with service requests from a hundred other units." He groaned, then finished his coffee. "Maybe I should relocate south. I hear the living quarters down there are somewhat more spacious."

"Not by much," Myles said.

The sound of metal gears drew their attention to the south gate. It was opening, making way for a large personnel carrier. It was a similar model used by the military, which could carry up to forty tridents. Or, in this case, repairmen.

Both security officers glared as they watched the vehicle miss the fork in the road. Instead of going to the east side of the refinery, it followed a road which led toward Administration.

"The gate guard did not explain the directions, apparently," Andre said.

"That, or the driver is an idiot."

The five-ton vehicle continued its approach, passing the guardhouse. The driver shot them a quick unconcerned glance, then turned his eyes to the path up ahead.

Myles' attempts to flag him down went ignored.

"Okay I'm going with the idiot explanation," he said. He tossed his coffee cup in a nearby trash can, then marched after the vehicle. It parked a few feet near the Administration's south entrance.

Already, a couple of refinery workers in small shuttles stopped a few yards away.

"Hey! They're not allowed to park right there!" one shouted to the guards, pointing at the carrier.

"Yes, yes! I know."

"You better make them move before the administrator finds out."

"Jeez. What does it look like we're doing?" Myles said, waving the busybody away.

Andre lagged behind, studying the carrier's tailgate. He could see the men inside. There were at least twenty of them in there. Maybe even thirty. Some of them were looking in his direction, which unnerved him slightly. Not a single one of them looked happy to be here.

What looked the most bizarre were the crates in the aisle between the seats. Thirty men, with that much equipment, all for *one* flow pipe repair? And why did they come to this side of the plant?

By the way Myles was glaring at the vehicle, it was clear he was thinking the same things. He approached the driver's side window and waved to the driver.

"Excuse me! You're not supposed to be over here. The pipe's on the opposite side of the plant."

The driver did not say anything.

Andre quickly caught up with his partner. "Maybe we should…"

"Hang on." Myles' patience was quickly growing thin. He grabbed the door handle and opened it. "Listen, pal. You need to back up and…"

By the time Myles recognized the blaster pointed at him, three red blaster bolts had burned deep into his chest.

Andre jumped back, his hand desperately yanking at his holster. Panicked clumsiness caused him to fail to unstrap his weapon in time.

The tailgate opened, making way for the thirty passengers. In their hands were second generation plasma carbines, with range and a rate of fire tripling that of the plasma muskets.

Energy bolts flew across the plant. The nearby refinery workers turned around and fled. Some were shot in the back, dead before they hit the ground.

All Andre could do was run for the Administration building, and pray that he would make it in time. Red bolts, nearly as hot as the sun, zipped by his head. Several yards ahead, the doors opened up. Two security officers peeked outside, alarmed by the sound of gunshots. One was immediately struck in the chest.

"Get inside! Get inside!" Andre shouted.

By the time he reached the building, the area had become a war zone. The group of terrorists had branched out, shooting at anyone who came near. Twelve of them swarmed the building, forcing Andre and the other guard back with blaster fire.

"This way," the other guard said. They ran down the corridor and took a right at the next juncture, pulling an alarm as they turned the corner. The guard raised his comm mic. "All units, we need backup immediately. We've got blaster fire in the courtyard. Numerous casualties. Roughly thirty hostiles…"

Several explosions rocked the outside of the building. Screams pierced the air, many of them silenced by more blaster fire.

The south admin doors opened. The next sound were footsteps of the invading force.

Andre unholstered his blaster, then took a deep breath. An armed group invading a methane refinery station?

It suddenly became pretty clear what caused that tanker explosion.

CHAPTER 5

"Yeah, we read you. We're adjusting orbit by seventeen degrees. Headed toward Alaska."

"...I repeat! Shots fired. Multiple casualties! Forty-nine-one, do you have any update?"

"This is Alaska Refinery Security, confirming they have taken the civility. At least twenty-two personnel have been taken hostage."

"Perimeter Command to Fort Bennett. We've secured outer perimeter. We've got friendlies exiting through the north gate. Surveillance drones have been dispatched. Looks like Administration has been overtaken. Some of those bad boys might've gone to the sublevels."

"I don't like it."

"What's the Governor's call?"

"Standby, Perimeter Command.... Perimeter Command, use landline code three-seven-three."

"Copy that."

While riding aboard the Whirlybird C-208, there were only three things for Vince Caparzo to do: Review the objective with his team, stare out the window and watch the world below, or listen to the radio transmissions.

His fireteam of a dozen tridents were experienced professionals. Though their blank facemasks concealed their faces, he knew there wasn't an ounce of apprehension. They waited in their seats, machine-like in their demeanor. This wasn't their first rodeo. While individual nations did not exist anymore, there were still sects that needed to be neutralized. A thirty-man group of environmentalist extremists was nothing they couldn't handle.

Looking out the window did nothing but present the same basic view. The landscape was concealed under a carapace of technology. High-speed rails extended in all directions, the veins to the ever-growing Alliance. Drones, often referred to as droids these days, hovered in the air like tiny satellites. They were like an alien species working with the human workers, conducting many of the same tasks. With so many tall structures, there was more maintenance than the population could handle.

Vince chose to focus on the transmissions. Between satellite surveillance, refinery security, trident forces surrounding the perimeter, and the regional government's office, there was almost too much to keep up with.

Too much information was better than none. Thirty armed men had taken control of the Alaska Refinery Station. Currently, the staff were being evacuated, mainly through the north gate. Explosions and blaster fire had rocked the south side of the station, making escape through the south gate extremely difficult. Security was reportedly making a last stand in the administration building, though at this rate, they wouldn't last long.

Insufficient fools. Trained only to the minimum standard. They certainly were not tridents.

The landscape took on a leafy shade of grey. All of a sudden, there were trees, swaying in the downdraft from an abundance of military aircraft flying above them. Military and first responder vehicles sped down the roads toward the destination.

Beyond those trees was a big circle of concrete wall surrounding the Alaska Methane Refinery Station. Huge tankers towered on all sides of the facility, connected to a tiny city of pipes, conductors, pumps, and other technology. In its center, a huge shaft dug into the earth, suctioning the liquid methane from the bowels of the plant.

It was no secret why this group had infiltrated the plant. Ideologists known as the Greenland Crusaders, they were dedicated to returning the world to its natural state. Technology and pollution had ruined the planet. Mankind was a disease, blackening the skies with his thoughtless exploitation of the earth.

The voice of their so-called leader occasionally entered the radio feed.

"I'll repeat! We have hostages! We have total control of the plant. Any attempt to infiltrate this facility will result in their deaths. If you dare use explosives, you risk destroying this entire facility. Airstrikes won't save you this time. We are monitoring perimeter. Security cameras are still functional. If anyone breaches the gates, there will be consequences of biblical proportions."

"Yadda-yadda," Vince muttered. "Yeah, we get it."

"Thinking of doing the negotiations, Captain?" the medic said.

"That's what we're here for," Vince said. He put his hand on his M4 Gauntlet. "To deliver our terms."

***

The world around the perimeter wall was alive with movement. Vehicles were moving in and out of the area. Surveillance drones were zipping in every direction, attempting to get a view of what was happening inside the plant. The north perimeter entrance was the busiest, as several staff were making their escape.

All the while, the terrorist leader continued making his threats on the radio. It was the usual spiel, warning the military of deadly consequences should any action be taken.

The Whirlybird C-208 set down on a clearing roughly two hundred yards beyond the south wall. The bay door opened and the fireteam filed out, Vince Caparzo in the lead. They marched to a radio tent which had been hastily set up near a few emergency transport vehicles.

Major Thomas Jern, the perimeter commander, was leaning against the table, eyeing the footage on a computer monitor. On the screen was an aerial shot of the north side of the plant.

Blaster fire strobed in the lens before the screen went black.

"Damn it," the major said. "Lost another one."

"They're definitely in the administration building," another officer said.

"And probably below," Major Jern said. He turned to face Vince. "Captain, I don't imagine I need to waste speech telling you how critical this situation is."

"I can use my imagination, sir," Vince said. "Is there a plan in place?"

The major's expression soured. "In all likelihood, a chemical drop. After what happened in the bay, we can't risk these people destroying this plant."

"Have you confirmed they brought explosives inside?" Vince asked.

Jern shook his head. "Not visually, and most of the staff that escaped did so through the north gate. The ones that were near the truck when it arrived are either dead or still in that plant."

"They cut off our link to the security footage," the Lieutenant said. "We can't use the plant's system to monitor their movements. There's too much fire ablaze to use infrared. They're shooting our drones out of the sky. Clearly, they're monitoring the gates. If we go inside, they'll see us."

"Not necessarily," Vince said. He walked to the computer and tapped on a few keys. "I've studied these plant designs. There's a way in that they may not have considered." He brought up an underground blueprint of the perimeter. A jagged blue line streamed under the wall into the plant.

"Catacombs," Jern said.

"Built two-hundred years ago for water transport," Vince said. "My team and I can sneak in through there without being detected. We'll use a laser cutter attached to a decoy drone to cut through the soil."

More transmissions came through the radio. Blaster fire echoed in the distance.

Major Jern watched the monitor, shaking his head slightly. He was a man conflicted. He knew the regional governor would issue a chem strike, an order that was likely passed down from Rome. Protecting and preserving this refinery was critical, especially with the looming energy crisis.

Another drone feed appeared on the screen.

"Zoom in on the admin building," he said to the Lieutenant. A closer view of the building showed small flashes through the south side windows. There was a firefight taking place in that corner of the building.

Vince saw it too.

"Major, at the very least, I can maybe get those staff out of there before we make the drop."

Jern did not have the luxury of time to think over all of the details.

"Fine. Go in at your own risk, Captain."

"Understood, sir." Vince looked to his sergeant. "Prep a decoy drone. Cut a hole in the tunnel."

"Ready in thirty seconds, Captain," the Sergeant replied. He returned to the Whirlybird and hauled out a large metal case. He opened it, revealing what appeared to be a surveillance drone. He primed its systems then tested the controls. It hovered in the air like a mosquito, then slowly glided a meter over the ground until it found the catacombs. It latched onto the dirt, then fired a hot red laser. With smooth precision, it formed a three-foot-wide hole in the ground. There was a sound of falling metal, rock and dirt.

Vince approached the smoking gap in the earth and shone a light inside.

"Don't mind the smell, gentlemen."

He was the first to descend.

CHAPTER 6

Andre Gardner shook his hand. His blaster had run hot, near to the point of singeing his palm. Moving down the corridor with him were two other security guards, Mackey and Winslow, both men of equal experience and training. None of them ever believed they would have to draw a weapon on another armed individual, let alone endure the anxieties of evading incoming projectiles. The few times any of them drew their weapons was against unarmed individuals, usually protesters or disobedient workers.

Now, they were dealing with hardened men with better equipment and training. Aside from the supervising officer, who quickly retreated to the north gate to 'escort people out', they were the only security staff still alive in the plant. Even through the haze of nonstop blaster fire, they could hear the security transmissions slowly die down. In some cases, they got to hear the death throes of their fellow guards as they were gunned down.

The three of them backed down the corridor, guiding nearly a dozen drill team workers to the south exit. They had evacuated through the stairwells after the elevators were shut down. According to one of them, several gunmen had already made their way to the sublevels.

Mackey and Winslow kept firing at the hallway juncture up ahead, ducking as plasma bolts zipped in their direction. Surrender was not an option, not because of bravery, but because they had no choice. These terrorists did not seem like the type to take many prisoners. Only a small handful of staff, likely the higher-ups, were being kept as leverage. It made sense, as those people typically had political connections and knowledge of plant functions and layout.

"Where do we go?" one staffer said.

"Out that way," Andre said. "Out that exit, then make a run to the southeast maintenance door."

"What if there's more terrorists out that way?" another staffer said.

Winslow looked over his shoulder, his pistol smoking in his hand. "Shut up and GO!"

It was the last thing he would ever say. His body danced in place as numerous blaster bolts cut into him. Smoke billowed from his many burn wounds as he hit the ground, eyes half shut, jaw slack.

"Go! Go! Go!" Mackey said, returning fire.

With great haste, the workers fled for the exit. Luckily, the doors were unlocked. Andre pushed one of them open and held it with his back, allowing the workers to file out.

The landscape outside was one of hot fire and metal. Several vehicles had been exploded, as well as a few transport tankers. There were only a few narrow passageways through the lake of flame that led to the wall.

"To the left. The maintenance door!" Andre said.

The workers zigzagged between fire and debris, quickly making tracks from the administration building.

Andre held the door open until the last one was out. Soon, it was just him and Mackey.

The guard was backtracking, firing his scalding hot pistol at the gunmen. Compromised by fear, adrenaline, and the overheating weapon, he missed every shot.

One of the gunmen turned the corner, rifle shouldered.

Mackey sprinted for the door, eyes wide, teeth clenched. Almost there. Five steps. Three. One. He was out the door... when one of the blaster bolts struck him in the back.

Yelling out, he fell down the concrete stairs.

Andre rushed to his side. Mackey was still alive and was already pushing himself to his feet.

"Come on, man," Andre said. "Just a little further..." He jumped back after a blaster bolt zipped by his brow. There was no time. Three terrorist gunmen were advancing with murderous intent.

Mackey scampered on all fours, taking cover behind a disabled shuttle. With his back to the front wheels, he put a new magazine into his blaster pistol.

"Get to the gate!" he said to Andre. Hearing the gunmen advance down the steps, he emerged from cover to fire a shot.

Their rifles were already aimed at him. Before he could squeeze the trigger, a dozen blaster bolts tore into his body.

Andre looked back just in time to see Mackey hit the ground. Running as fast as he ever had in his life, he weaved through burning vehicles down the path the other workers followed. He ran for hundreds of feet, tucking his head down as several blaster bolts zipped past him.

The workers were grouped by the maintenance door. A one-man entrance, it was designed for maintenance crews to access the outer part of the wall without having to go through the main gates.

More blaster bolts whooshed across the air, splattering into a burst of flame after striking the wall. The staffers ducked down, hands on their heads as if that would somehow protect them from the little plasma balls of death.

Andre hurried to the door. There was a scanner on the right for authorized personnel, mainly maintenance staff. Security should be cleared for this exit as well, for the guards had access to most of the plant.

He scanned his badge, then felt as though he shrank ten inches when he saw the dreaded red flash of rejection.

"No… no…"

He scanned his badge again. Same result.

"What's happening?" one of the workers said.

Again and again, Andre scanned his badge. After the fifth try, he had to face reality: they were trapped.

That reality hit with sweltering force. Andre whipped to the side, then fell to his knees. His pistol fell from his grip. The blaster bolt that struck his arm had burned all the way to the bone, smoldering his triceps.

The small group of staffers knelt and put their hands on their heads. With nowhere to go and nobody to defend them, they were reliant on the hopes that the terrorists would be merciful.

Three men, dressed as refinery workers, approached with rifles in hand and grins on their faces. One of them had a security radio on his collar, through which everyone could hear their glorious leader telling off the Alliance forces outside the gates.

"We have hostages. Any attempt to enter this facility will result in agonizing pain, and eventually death."

A whirring sound overtook the radio. The three criminals looked to the sky at the surveillance drone hovering a hundred feet above them. Without hesitation, they opened fire on the machine, exploding its battery core. Pieces of metal rained onto the panicking crowd, who still refused to move from their position.

"Don't kill us!" cried a worker.

The terrorists looked at each other and chuckled.

"Could use them as leverage," one said.

"Not the guard," another said. "Best to waste him."

Before they could follow through on that decision, their eyes were drawn to yet another drone that flew over the wall. It descended to fifteen feet and turned its lens toward them.

One of the terrorists shook his head. "Another stupid surveillance drone. These perimeter guys can't seem to take a hint."

Chuckling, he raised his muzzle.

The drone tilted up slightly. Under its nose, two small ports opened up, making way for a pair of blaster muzzles. An automatic burst of hot energy projectiles spewed from the guns, cutting down the three terrorists in the blink of an eye.

Andre uncovered his head, shocked and relieved to see the lifeless bodies of the gunmen laying on the dirt. He and the staff watched the drone in awe as it flew over the smoldering corpses, then lowered itself to the ground. Like a housefly, it searched the area until finding its desired spot.

A steady laser fired from its underbelly, cutting a large circular hole in the earth. After completing the cut, it moved away from the black crater.

The tip of a grappling hook secured itself on the corner. A mechanical zipping sound followed, hauling the first of many tridents to the surface. Most of them wore the usual head-to-toe black outfits. The only one whose face was visible was the leader. Judging from his insignia, he was a captain.

His face was one of intense experience and misery. There was mild scarring along the jawline, both from previous combat, and from injuries inflicted during training. Andre had heard that the special forces divisions physically beat their trainees to further toughen them up. This guy was living proof.

The Captain checked his surroundings for other hostiles, then secured the terrorists' weapons.

"Surveillance drone flying at fifteen feet? I think it's *you* who didn't take the hint."

Vince Caparzo's team ascended from the tunnel and formed a small perimeter. The team corporal knelt by the two gunmen and confiscated their radios. While the Sergeant and team monitored their surroundings, Vince and the team medic approached the injured guard.

"Good morning. Captain Vince Caparzo. Sorry we didn't get here earlier."

"Officer Andre Gardner. No apology necessary."

"Medic, see to his injury," Vince said before activating his comm unit. "Southeast corner secured. Got seven friendlies. Sending them out through the catacombs."

Andre sat up and winced as the medic tended to his injury.

"Just hold still," the medic said.

"I'll do my best," he said.

"Are you people among the twenty-two hostages they claim to have?" Vince asked.

"No," Andre said. "One of the other guards told me they're holding people near Storage and in the upper levels of the admin building."

"Who are they?" one of the workers said. "What do they want?"

"They're an environmental extremist group," the medic said. "Apparently, they're out to stop World One from extracting the lifeblood of the earth."

"It's not just here," Vince said.

"Let me guess, they're the ones who hit that cargo ship in the bay," Andre said.

"Correct."

At that moment, Major Jern's voice came through the comm.

"Command to Delta-Niner."

"Delta-Niner. Go ahead, Command."

"Extract now. Argo is en-route. The regional governor has officially ordered the chem strike on the plant."

"Sir, there are still twenty-two hostages in the plant. A chem strike will kill them as well as the hostiles."

"We're well aware, Captain. Out intelligence believes those men snuck a truckload of explosives into that refinery. It's highly likely they intend to suicide themselves in an effort to destroy the entire facility. A chem strike will eliminate the threat without risk of damaging the equipment or setting off the charges."

Major Jern spoke with the laxness of a seminar speaker. Like most of the inhabitants of this planet, there was little concern for the human cost of progress. The needs of the many outweighed the needs of the few, and the needs of the Chancellor outweighed the needs of the many. The Chancellor needed working government centers and military to prolong his reign, and for that, he needed an endless supply of fuel.

"We cannot afford the loss," he continued. *"We have no choice but to assume those hostages are already dead. This is the way of things. Now extract your men."*

"Sir, we have leads on the hostages' location," Vince said. "These environmentalists are sloppy. There's only a little more than a couple dozen on site. My team and I will make easy work of them."

"That's an awful big risk, Captain. Those people are replaceable."

"Ten minutes. That's all I need."

A short pause followed. The only reason a commanding officer hesitated was when he was considering something.

"Not a second more."

Vince faced the group of civilians. "Officer Gardner, please lead these people out of the plant. Go through the breach into the catacombs. Keep heading south for a quarter mile, and you'll find an opening. There will be personnel there waiting for you."

The civilians fled, then lowered themselves one after another down the fast rope. Andre Gardner was the last to depart.

"Thanks, Captain," he said. He didn't wait for a reply. The Captain needed every available moment to plan the next course of action. He lowered himself into the tunnel and led the personnel to safety.

The fireteam assembled around the Captain. Using the sergeant's drone control module, Vince brought up a 3D image of the refinery.

"We'll split into two teams," he said. "I'll take Team One into the admin building. Once that's cleared, we'll head down and take the fuel storage area. Sergeant, you lead a team to High Service and the north tankers. Neutralize all targets." He shut down the module, then knelt by one of the dead terrorists. He stripped two of them of their radios, tossing one to the sergeant before clipping the other to his belt. "Monitor their chatter. They're probably on the same frequency. Time's a wast'n, gentlemen. Get to work."

The team split in two, with the Sergeant leading Team Two northward along the perimeter.

Vince, leading five of his tridents, cautiously followed a path through the burning south landscape. The gunfire had ceased for the most part, leaving only the sound of radio chatter echoing from various comm units scattered throughout the refinery.

Team One arrived at the admin building entrance and took breach formation. Each trident crossed their arms into firing position, gauntlet hand on top of the left. A trigger rod, like a bicycle handle, extended to the palm. A squeeze of the small lever mechanism—the trigger—was now all that was required to generate an energy-based projectile nearly as hot as the sun.

Vince took point.

The first-floor hallways were empty. Taking a right at the next juncture, they came to the eastmost corridor, where two elevators were located alongside a stairwell. They were inoperable. It didn't matter, taking elevators was tactical suicide. However, they needed to make their way up the building fast and didn't have time to carefully apply grappling gadgets. The most appropriate option was to take the stairs.

The Corporal took the lead, then slowly opened the stairwell entrance.

Clear.

Vince took point again, keeping his gauntlet aimed high as he quietly ascended. Directions located at the second floor confirmed that the administrative offices and radio tower were located on the top floor.

He turned the corner, trotted up the steps, then arrived at the third floor. He held up a fist, halting the team in place. Leaning to the side,

Vince looked up the next couple of levels. The muzzle of a blaster rifle swung over the stairwell railing two floors up. The handler was not acting with any haste, therefore was likely unaware of the team's presence.

Vince leaned further, far enough so he could tap his fist on the wall. "Psst! Hey, you! Down here!"

The gunman, thinking one of his comrades was calling for him, peeked over the railing. Instead of his fellow environmental extremists, he saw a black-uniformed trident, then the blue flash of energy streaming right at his head. His facial identity and life were simultaneously stripped away.

Vince watched as the body slumped over the guardrail, then waited for any others to come out. Moments passed, and nothing happened. Fortunately, the gauntlets were not overly loud when firing, and additionally, the stairwells were tightly sealed, which sustained the noise level. This building, designed for blocking noise so the higher-ups could work in relative peace, was perfectly suitable for a stealth operation.

They ascended to the top floor, then took breach formation by the doorway. Silent as the grave, they listened to approaching footsteps coming from the other side. Peeking through the window would allow the hostile to see him and alert any others on the top floor.

The trick was dispatching him quietly. Firing in the hallway would alert the others and possibly result in the death of hostages. This was a job for close-quarters weaponry.

He reached along his belt and unsheathed his tactical knife. One of the oldest weapons in human history, second to stone, it still played a valuable role in combat even in the age of space travel and energy weapons.

The tridents knelt out of sight as their captain unclipped the enemy radio from his belt. He spoke in a low, gravelly voice.

"Southeast stairwell, third floor. Got a straggler. Might be someone important. I need one of you to come down here and help me drag him to the top floor."

The ploy worked. The gunman quickened his pace and arrived at the door. He opened it, pushed the door open, and was immediately met with Vince's wrath. With one hand cupping the sentry's mouth, he plunged the blade into his heart, ridding the world of one more terrorist nuisance.

After gently lowering the body to the floor, Vince led his team through the doorway. Quiet and swift, they soon arrived at a juncture. The intersecting hall led west in the general direction of the two hostiles detected on the scan.

Vince pointed to his corporal, then pointed at the corridor, directing him to inspect the rooms on that side of the floor. Meanwhile, he and the medic proceeded north to the main offices.

No longer was the radio needed to monitor their chatter. He could hear the so-called negotiator up ahead, barking his usual tough-guy talk through the radio.

With caution, he arrived at the radio room. The door was propped open. Two gunmen were inside. One stood at the opposite doorway, facing the adjacent room. The other was at the console, his hands animated as he addressed the Alliance forces outside the gates.

"We have hostages! Withdraw your forces, or they will die. We have operational control over the security functions of this plant! We have eyes everywhere, know every move you make, are two steps ahead of you in every turn…"

Vince couldn't help but smirk.

"Well, this is awkward."

The terrorist turned, wide-eyed. Those eyes were even wider as Vince planted a plasma bolt in his chest. He adjusted his aim and fired on the other, killing him as he attempted to aim his rifle.

Vince and the medic passed through the room, cleared the next one, then went through to the next hall.

There, three other gunmen were rushing in the direction of gunfire. They were met with a slew of plasma bolts. The terrorists attempted to return fire, only managing to squeeze off a few clumsy shots before the two tridents cut them down. The clash resulted in the three men on the hallway floor, their flesh seared where the projectiles had landed.

Blaster fire on the west end of the floor signified the clash between the Corporal's unit and the two terrorists in that direction. Only a few shots were exchanged before silence took over. Vince, incredibly confident in his team's capabilities, already knew the outcome.

"Sweep the floor. Regroup at the administrator's office."

They went room-to-room. To their surprise, there were no hostages on this floor. After a thorough sweep, they regrouped in the plant administrator's office.

"No hostages," the Corporal said. "They must be holding them in a different part of the plant."

"Damn. I was sure they'd be up here," Vince muttered. He checked the time. "Only six minutes left. Proceed to storage."

They found the nearest stairwell which led them to the sublevel beneath the admin building. From there, they followed a long corridor northward to the objective.

The storage area was a large underground room, consisting of a giant spiderweb of metal pipes connecting rows of cylinder-shaped containers. The deafening sounds of whirring machinery and warnings were not enough to dull the verbal exchange between environmentalists. Just from listening to the voices, Vince knew there were at least six down in this level. Possibly more.

One of them was on the radio, barking to the team situated in the admin building.

"Whitmer. Troutman. Marcelli. Respond. What's going on up there? Why have the transmissions stopped?"

The fact that these men were down here gravely concerned Vince. These pipes and containers were designed for separating the methane from other liquids, sediments, and gasses that were drawn up from the earth. It was a room full of caution signs reading *Explosive material.* Not even a match could be lit down here. The LED lights were equipped with extra barriers, which dimmed the illumination, while reducing the risks of an accident. Likewise, electrical panels and conduits were doubly protected to prevent any chance of an exposed circuit setting off an explosion.

The plant took this area seriously, as though the air could be set ablaze. Then again, if one of these pipes ruptured, that would very well be the case. That meant every gauntlet shot had to be precise.

Vince would have to rely on close quarters yet again, but also be prepared to use the gauntlet. If these thugs were desperate to destroy the refinery, then they likely would have no issue with discharging weapons in here.

"Shoot if necessary, but make sure you damn well hit your target," he said. With that understanding, they pressed into the maze of pipes. Sneaking under the first row, they entered a clear aisle. Vince took a left, the Corporal going right.

At the next turn, the latter came upon a sentry. There was no choice. He fired off a fast shot, striking the hostile at point-blank. Immediately, another converged on the Corporal. He and another trident fired off a few shots, all of which hit their mark just in time. The terrorist reared back, his gun muzzle pointing at the ceiling right as he squeezed the trigger to fire. Blaster bolts harmlessly peppered the ceiling, missing all pipes and cylinders.

"Keep going," Vince spoke into the comm. "Locate any explosives. Double-time it."

He went in his own direction. Past a large container was an intersection leading westward into the storage unit. Three terrorists, armed with blasters, were charging in his direction. All three stopped, alarmed at the abrupt arrival of the trident Captain.

Their anxiety was justified. Three consecutive gauntlet blasts dropped all three targets before they could get a single shot off.

Vince checked the area around them. No explosives.

What he did find was another terrorist on the other side of a section of pipes. The contact saw him, then yelled to his comrades.

"Got one here!"

Vince's first instinct was to shoot him, but with a row of piping in the way, he had no choice but to close the distance. He sprinted as fast as he could, sliding under the pipes and taking the contact out at the knees. The terrorist's back hit the floor. In a frenzy, he tried to aim his rifle at the trident imposing on his group's grand plan.

With lightning-fast reflexes, Vince planted one knee on his chest, and grabbed the gun by the barrel, redirecting it skyward. Blaster bolts stung the ceiling.

"Whoa!"

Hearing the exclamation, Vince looked up the aisle at the additional terrorist that had just arrived.

Oh, crap.

Like cranking a lever, Vince shifted the rifle forward, pointing its muzzle at the new arrival. Two shots struck center mass. The terrorist spun on his heels, dropped to his knees, then fell on his face.

The fun didn't end there.

Still pinning the terrorist to the floor, he looked over his shoulder just in time to see two others appear from seemingly out of nowhere. As usual, he had a split second to take action.

That action began with stunning his opponent with a blow to the face. He dismounted, grabbed him by the collar, lifted him to his feet, and held him between himself and the two gunmen. Several blaster bolts cut into the terrorist's back, turning him into literal dead weight.

With a mighty shove, Vince launched the fresh corpse into the duo. The impact briefly knocked them off balance and shifted their aim.

The Captain closed the distance. A front kick struck the nearest one in the chest, knocking him backward. Vince pivoted left to confront the next terrorist. Hammering his fist, he knocked the rifle muzzle downward. Before the opponent could retaliate, Vince landed a kick to the knee and an elbow to the face.

The terrorist dropped his weapon and staggered backward. He was stunned, but not yet out of the fight. He attempted to land a haymaker, which Vince deflected with a block which fractured the elbow joint. A kick to the ribs doubled the terrorist over. A knee to the face knocked him unconscious.

Vince turned his attention to the last terrorist, who was getting up after being floored. The man attempted reaching for his dropped rifle, only to resort to close-quarters methods when he saw the trident coming at him.

The two men collided, the terrorist attempting to lock Vince in a chokehold. The attempt backfired, and he was thrown over the trident's shoulder. He quickly rolled to his feet and spun to face Vince. A clumsy kick was thrown and easily deflected, causing the terrorist to stumble off balance.

Vince lunged, plowing a fist into his ribcage, before landing a second into the jawline. He turned, pivoted on one foot, then threw a heavy kick with the other.

For the terrorist, it was like being struck by a freight train. The kick knocked him off his feet straight into the ribbed side of a methane cylinder. The terrorist slumped, jaw slack, killed by the blunt meeting between skull and metal.

After taking a moment to catch his breath, Vince glanced around to study the next direction to search. He went further west past a row of storage tanks. The next turn took him northward toward the central circulation machine units.

Here, the signs were larger and more frequent.

Warning! Highly Explosive.

There, he found one last terrorist kneeling by a piece of equipment the size of a briefcase.

It was a brief interaction, initiated and concluded with the throwing of Vince's knife. The terrorist turned around to shoot, not realizing he was exposing his jugular for the trident. He clutched his neck, then slumped forward.

Vince pulled the body away and knelt by the device. The Alliance's suspicions were confirmed. This was indeed an explosive device. An accelerated timer had been set and was rapidly counting down to zero.

"Team One, converge on my location ASAP. DeMarco, I need your expertise this instant." He set off a laser flare, which fired a harmless strobing light onto the ceiling.

Within seconds, his team arrived at his location. DeMarco, the explosives ordinance technician, knelt by the device. He was already shaking his head with unease.

"We've got problems."

The Sergeant's voice echoed through the comm. *"Team Two to One. What's your status?"*

"Hostiles eliminated in Administration and Storage," Vince said. "We've located one of the bombs. Anything by the generators? Have you located the hostages?"

"You available for video comm?"

That question alone indicated bad news.

Vince looked to the Corporal, who removed his tablet and held it flat. He connected with the Sergeant's frequency, bringing up a holographic image of Team Two.

The Sergeant did not have to say a word. He simply panned the camera to the left, revealing several dead hostages on the floor of the generator area. It was evident from their attire that they were the staff from the admin building.

"Twenty-two of them, at least," the Sergeant said. *"We've got explosives near each generator unit. One of my guys just found one by one of the tankers."*

"They were being thorough," the Corporal muttered.

"And they planned to attempt an escape," Vince added. It made sense. Why else would they set off a timer when they could have simply used a remote trigger?

DeMarco stood up. "Captain, there's no stopping this. Timer's been accelerated, probably after they realized a strike team had infiltrated the room. I'd need at least three minutes to deactivate this. We've got *two minutes* before this blows."

"Same here," the Sergeant added.

Vince pointed to the exit. "Everyone, double-time it to the east lot. Move! Move! Move!"

The video comm ended, and all members of the fireteam raced for the exit. Through the comm, he could hear the Sergeant relaying the orders to Team Two. Everyone ran as fast as they could, sliding under pipes and weaving around containers until they reached the exit.

Vince switched the channel to link with the Air Force unit.

"Delta-Niner to Bravo-Six-Three. I need immediate extraction on the double. Set down on east lot, two hundred meters from the northeast corner of the main building. Be ready for fast takeoff. Perimeter Command, get everyone as far back as possible. Code Black. I repeat, Code Black."

There was a lot of credit to give to the dropship units. Bravo-Six-Three, a personnel carrier and bomber with a design similar to the Whirlybirds, was already lowering to the lot.

Team Two ran from the north, joining Vince's team as they raced for their ride. The hangar door touched the pavement.

One-by-one, the tridents filed inside and quickly strapped themselves in. With a rapid takeoff, nobody wanted to be standing.

Vince was the last one inside. He peeked at the timer on his wrist unit. Fifteen seconds to go.

He hit the button to close the hangar door, then threw himself into the nearest seat. Clipping his harness, he shouted to the pilot.

"Punch it."

The dropship boosters engaged. Like the afterburners to a space shuttle, they pushed the ship skyward, high over the perimeter wall.

The timer reached zero.

Even high above the sky, they felt the shockwave of the monstrous blast. The Alaska Methane Refinery, a mile-long industrial power-station responsible for a sixth of the world's fuel, had been turned into a glowing mushroom cloud. Like sprinklers from Hell, the extractor units burst, causing burning streams of methane to shoot high into the air. Black smoke filled the sky and dropped hot ash onto the surrounding forest.

Vince leaned against his headrest, debating whether or not to state the obvious into his comm. Unfortunately, it was protocol. There was no sense in screwing up even further, even at something this small.

"This is Captain Vince Caparzo of Fireteam Delta-Niner. Could not deactivate explosives. Mission failure."

As the ship turned, the cargo shifted, drawing his attention. It was a large package dressed in a black protective tarp. A large yellow label read the words *Chem Drop. Use with caution.*

CHAPTER 7

World Two.
Centauri Colony.

From a flying elesoar's point of view, the colony resembled a tiny speck in the middle of a red portrait of hell. It was surrounded by a slew of conundrums that threatened the population within. To the north was the eastern side of the Blackout Hills, and the mysteries that lay within. The west was a vast landscape, stretching for miles, and roamed by herds of horned ollubs. Though their diet consisted mainly of mineral buried in the dirt, they were still highly aggressive. The south was ravaged by cliffs, ravines, and uneven valleys that were almost just as unpredictable as the Blackout.

After four years on this rock, Dr. Anastacia Drucus thought she was finally getting used to the hazards. At thirty-one years old, she was already the lead geologist in the region. It was only by default—her superior officer was killed by the same explosion that left her husband hospital dependent. When the accident was reported to Hope Central, there was no condolences. Only, 'We're going to need you to fulfill the duties of Dr. Lawrence Platt.'

Standing at the atrium at the west side of the dome, Anastacia felt as though a giant hand was squeezing her. Her bones felt brittle, her heart beating as though about to burst. In her hand was her newly issued badge, reading *Dr. Anastacia Drucus, Head of Geological Research Division – East Territories.* The congratulations were hollow. It was a job title nobody wanted all the way out here. In the few colonies scattered on the outer rim, there were only a handful of geological research personnel, and a freighter-load of duties to be carried out.

Her world had changed so much, so fast. Her responsibilities had tripled, all while her personal life was falling apart. How could one run such an important operation when her husband was in the hospital, suffering from mineral damage to his lungs?

It took several frantic radio calls to Hope Central, demanding a shipment of DZ-5. After two long, sleepless days and nights, the transport was en-route. It was not out of the goodness of Colonel Segan's heart that the Whirlybird C-235 was making the twelve-hour flight. The fact was that there was already a pickup planned to collect the colony administrators and science officers from the outskirt colonies and bring them back to Hope Central for an in-person conference with Rome. Simply put, it was easier to have everybody in one room, rather than worry about fluctuating signals between two-thousand-plus colonies.

"Dr. Drucus?" the atrium monitor said.

She looked up from her badge. "Yes?"

"Everything okay?" He immediately felt stupid for asking. How could everything be okay? Everyone in the colony knew about Patrick and the accident. Patrick's condition was the tip of the iceberg. Three research personnel were dead, over thirty-million dollars' worth of equipment damaged or lost. He cleared his throat. "Pardon me. I meant, uh…"

"No, no." Anastacia put her hand up in a peacekeeping way. "Things are about to get a little better. For now at least." *Who knows what will happen in the coming weeks, though.*

She put her facemask on then scanned her badge. The inner hatch opened, and she passed through a twenty-foot tunnel comprised of twelve-inch bulletproof glass. There were two inner doors she had to pass through before arriving at the outside airlock. She waited for the scans to complete before the doors finally opened. It took effort not to be impatient. The computers always ran scans on people, making sure the masks were air-sealed. It saved a life on more than one occasion.

Outside, she could see the Whirlybird on fast approach. Huge twin rotors, powered by four dragonfly-class turbo engines, kicked up clouds of sediment as the metal beast initiated its descent.

The scarabs in the corral went nuts, as did their handler, Ed Burger.

"Do these wingers have any respect for the working class?! Eh, who the hell am I kidding?" The balding animal handler tended to his herd. There was no calming them down until the aircraft made its landing.

Anastacia marched to the vehicle, becoming a silhouette in the cloud of dust until she arrived at the fuselage door.

"Open up," she said. She hit her fist against the door. The cowards inside were waiting for the dust cloud *they* created to subside. She pounded again. "Open the door."

It slid open. As she figured, it was not a colony worker on the other side, but a trident. Like the worker ant he resembled, he stared at her with his seemingly blank expression.

"Is it here?" she said. "The DZ-5."

"I am only authorized to deliver it to medical personnel," the trident replied.

"I've been sent by Dr. Carlos LaFonte," Anastacia said, her tone increasingly impatient. "We need that medicine *now*."

"Only to medical personnel. You are geological division." The trident's manner of speaking was as mechanical as the words he said.

That patience was paper-thin, and it had only been fifteen seconds.

***

Centauri Medical Center

After what felt like forever, the supplies had been unloaded and delivered to the hospital. Anastacia accompanied the official transport to the hospital's main entrance. On the way, she alerted the inventory team and Dr. LaFonte's head nurse, all of whom were ready and waiting.

Once everything was signed, the DZ-5 was officially in the hospital's possession. The nurse did not require a formality from Anastacia. She handed over the first case without question.

"Go."

Anastacia was up the stairs to Med/Surge. Every time she entered the room and saw her husband Patrick lying on that bed, it was a punch to the gut. There was always a naïve hope that one day she would walk in and see him sitting up, the doctor greeting her and stating it was a false alarm. She knew the truth. Regolith Lung Rot had claimed thousands of lives throughout the colonies in the three decades since Man's first arrival. The only sign of hope was *Dethrohydroxaphine Zincloride-Five,* a medication developed in Year Six by the colonial medical and chemistry divisions. Originally designed to combat parasitic species such as Eolian Dune worms, it was discovered that DZ-5 was capable of stalling the effects of Regolith Lung Rot.

Only stall. A cure was yet to be invented. With the mineral physically embedded in the tissue like ticks on a dog, there was no way to undo the damage. The DZ-5 quelled the burning residue, but like tiny little suns blazing in the depths of space, the particles were always pulsing, releasing tiny flares that destroyed flesh during prolonged exposure.

Dr. Carlos LaFonte, a senior physician in his late sixties, turned when he heard the door open up.

"It just came," Anastacia said.

"Thank goodness."

He took the case from her, opened it, and removed one of the pouches. Anastacia winced as she watched him fill a huge syringe with the blue fluid, then lean toward the patient. She helped the nurse roll the unconscious Patrick onto his side, wincing again as the huge needle entered his back.

"Don't worry. He'll be able to breathe with this stuff in his lungs. Though he's unconscious, I can assure you he's feeling better already."

"Thank you, Carlos."

"You don't have to thank me," he replied. "I just wish I could do more." He looked at the remaining DZ-5 medicine. "This will help the Regolith mineral from damaging his lungs further."

"What's left of them," Anastacia muttered.

Carlos put a hand on her shoulder comfortingly, then looked at the monitor. "He'll be fine for now. Let him rest."

He walked out into the hall with Anastacia.

"How much time does he have left?" she asked.

"Don't be so defeatist," he replied.

"How much time?"

Carlos sighed. "With that shipment, I can stretch it out to three weeks. But unless we find a cure for Regolith Lung Rot, that's all we'll be able to do for him."

It was the answer Anastacia was expecting. All she could do was look away and stay silent. Can't break down now, not with the meeting tomorrow.

With another sigh, Carlos turned away. "I'm sorry."

"Stop being sorry. You didn't cause the accident."

"No, but I used to be in research. Hell, that was one of the reasons I volunteered to come to this planet. Yet, I'm stuck running a hospital, treating an endless flow of patients." He shut his eyes, embarrassed at his poor wording. "I mean, with no time to make an expedition."

"It's all right. I know what you meant," Anastacia said. Now, it was her putting a hand on his shoulder. Carlos had no gripes toward helping people. It was his calling, after all. The catch was that many of the physical ailments the colonists on World Two faced required new research in order for cures to be produced. There were some trailblazers, such as Dr. Douglas Warren.

With him now in hiding, finding a cure for Regolith Lung Rot seemed practically unobtainable.

"We're in Centauri, where there's no shortage of setbacks," Anastacia said. "We appreciate everything you do, Carlos."

"Maybe I can put one of the other doctors in charge temporarily," Carlos said. "Then, I could go out on an expedition. Maybe we'll find something in a dig."

"No, you're needed here," Anastacia said. "But thank you." Her communicator chimed. She unclipped it from her belt and raised it to her lips. "Dr. Drucus."

"Forgive me for intruding, Doctor." She recognized the voice. It was Bill Cook's administrative assistant.

"He's leaving now?"

"Correct. They won't wait much longer."

"Thank you. Tell him I'm on my way." She ended the call and clipped the comm to her belt. "After I grab my bag, that is."

"I'd say enjoy your flight, but then again, I know better," Carlos said.

"You want to go in my place?"

"I thought you said I was needed here."

Anastacia managed to chuckle. "That was before I remembered I had to suffer through a conference with the almighty Chancellor Gregorio." She turned around to leave. "See you when I get back."

Carlos waved goodbye. "Don't get yourself in too much trouble."

"Cross my heart."

***

Bill Cook glanced between the atrium and the trident guard standing by the fuselage.

Come on, Dr. Drucus. Where are you?

He didn't judge too heavily, for he knew the importance of delivering the DZ-5 straight to her husband. Still, it did not make him any less antsy being near the blank-masked infantryman.

It was a pathetic feeling for a colonial administrator. This grunt, the lowest on the totem pole in the Alliance military, had more real power than him. It only went to show greatly the Chancellor depended on his tridents, even the cannon fodder.

Fifty-five years old, twenty of which spent on this planet, Bill Cook was now realizing his influence was on the decline. Like many of his fellow colonists, he had grown to detest government reliance. It was human innovation and compassion that got them this far. Even the technology, though supplied through the Alliance, was implemented differently. It had to be, or else survival would have been impossible. He watched through the dome glass at the city within. Despite the difficulties, despite this horrible location they were subjected to, his people managed to flourish. They extracted metals from the ground and built real houses, not condensed living quarters like those on World One. It was years of hard work, which only managed to be complete because there were no government officials spying on them at every turn.

That was about to change. Hence, the meeting.

The airlock opened up. Bill Cook saw the thirty-one year old, blonde-haired geologist strutting for the Whirlybird. He walked over to greet her, and accompanied her to the fuselage.

"How's Patrick?"

She shrugged. "His best bet is a constant supply of DZ-5 until we figure out some kind of cure."

"I'm confident we'll find something." He looked at the large aircraft, and the horizon behind it. They were on the verge of a twelve-hour trip that would take her eleven-thousand miles from the man she loved. "Anastacia, you can stay here with him. You don't have to come to Hope Colony."

She resisted her laundry list of quips. Bill was a good-hearted man with everyone's best interests in mind. Unfortunately, best interest and reality sometimes were different things.

"Thanks, but let's be real. You seriously think Gregorio would actually grant me leeway? With the departure window on approach? Besides, I have something I need to share with him."

He pursed his lips. Anastacia, especially after the accident, was not one to mince words. It was a good quality in a person... until it got them into trouble. Here they were, about to be electronically face-to-face with the most powerful person in the solar system.

"Don't push it too hard," he said. "You've heard what happened at Espinosa Colony. Things are getting tense right now. Word is, we're looking at full military oversight. This will affect all colonies, including ours."

"I suppose that's what happens when you push back against a bully," Anastacia said.

She entered the vehicle and took a seat. Bill Cook sat down across from her and strapped himself in.

The doors slammed shut and the vehicle lifted off the ground, generating another massive dust cloud.

Anastacia looked out the window at the colonist workers, trying to get the residue off of their rovers, while Ed Burger tried to calm his scarabs yet again. Segan's forces truly were a hindrance, even in their arrival and departure.

It would only get worse from here.

CHAPTER 8

Hope Colony.

It was a multi-mile settlement, comprised of numerous domes interconnected by tubes, pipes, and underground conduits. At its center was a massive dome, the largest the Alliance had ever constructed. Underneath that half-globe was Hope Central, the capital of the World Two colonies.

The only true city on this planet, it was home to nearly a million colonists, and too many partymen to count. Due to the latter, it was awarded the largest military presence, something many of the colonies only saw during harvest time. Lift freighters kicked up dust to the southeast beyond the airfields, delivering methane to the enormous transport freighters. The departure window was about to open, and Governor Lovell was seeing to it that every last available molecule of methane made it to the freighters.

It was a futile effort. The Alliance was *never* satisfied.

As Anastacia Drucus and Bill Cook departed the Whirlybird, they took notice of the other aircraft arriving and departing. Over two-thousand colony administrators were arriving with their experts and assistants. They were to be transferred by shuttle to the ironically-named Liberty Hall, a gargantuan structure in Hope Central designed specifically for mass gatherings such as this.

They filed into the nearest station, where they were loaded onto express shuttles.

Anastacia managed to keep to herself while they waited in line. It was nice just to be standing up. The flight was long and her legs were stiff. To top things off, they were going straight to the conference. There was no quartering, no offering of sustenance, just 'go, go, go.' Meanwhile, the aircrafts would refuel in preparation for the return trips.

Sore, drowsy, and irritable, the last place she wanted to be was in this fortress of elites.

She had to check that line of thought. Not everyone here was an elitist. In reality, the majority of Hope Colony's citizenry were everyday blue and white collar workers. The technology and resources were greater here, but at the same time, increased surveillance. Ever since the first regiment of tridents, led by Colonel Segan, first arrived on this planet, Hope Colony began to function more and more like a typical World One city. Ironically, it was the settlements on the dreaded outer rim that enjoyed the most freedom these days.

As Bill Cook often reminded her, those days were coming to a swift end.

**

Hope Central, Hope Colony.

After exiting the transit station, they followed the escorts to the Capitol Building. The path was a simple paved street, regularly maintained and patched. For much of the trip, Bill Cook watched the top of the dome. This one was designed to mimic the skies of their home planet. The image panels did not often work, leading to dull blots of clear glass in the middle of grey skies and clouds.

Anastacia took more interest in the big building in front of her. The Capitol Building took up six more acres of space than it needed. The Governor's mansion was undoubtedly spacious, as opposed to the living quarters of most of the citizenry. Governor Lovell was not a bad-hearted man, but he had the spine of an invertebrate. He supported colonists' rights, even the freedom to be in possession of weaponry, until the Alliance cracked down on him. Now, virtually everything was a debate.

They arrived at the front steps of Liberty Hall. Anastacia watched the conference members ascending the steps. Each one had the same dreary look in their eyes. It was as though the building drained the very soul from their bodies.

"Look at these colony administrators. Not one of them wants to be here. They'd rather be somewhere else. *Anywhere* else."

"Shh." Bill glanced back and forth. There were guards posted everywhere, and knowing the indoctrination of tridents, they would surely report any sign of treasonous language. Even the slightest hint of wrong thinking led to imprisonment. Even if one was caught reading unapproved literature, they could spend two years in a labor camp.

"The Chancellor is not happy. That incident at Espinosa changed everything."

"It was bound to happen."

"Shh." He glanced around, then leaned in toward her. "Anastacia, please… just give your report, state your concerns, but for Heaven's sake, do not rattle the cage. Please? For me?"

Anastacia thought about it for a moment, then shrugged.

"You know I would *never* disappoint."

She trotted up the steps.

Bill hesitated a moment before following her.

"Right..."

Liberty Hall – Conference Stadium.

There was a time when such a structure was designed for entertainment. In the center of the conference stadium was Governor Lovell and Colonel Segan, whose arm was wrapped in a sling. Even from afar, Anastacia could see the look of humiliation in his eyes. Such an injury did not fare well for the projection of authority and power. It was a surprise he was here at all.

From where she sat, they looked like referees for a major sporting event. In years past, people would watch teams of sports players compete to win the all-important score. Anastacia would happily trade places with anyone from that period of time. She would give anything to watch a well-meaning sports game than stare at the pompous so-called leader of humankind.

She was hoping for technical or signal error. Sadly, she and the rest of those in the building were subject to see Chancellor Gregorio's pudgy face in full, unabashed detail.

His Highness was well into a drawn-out, sleep-inducing speech. Only those who feared him the most managed to pay attention. The disillusioned, of which she believed there were many, had to project the illusion of investment.

"Your failures cannot be overstated. My faith in you has never been lower. Now, it is clear there are those who would lead an uprising. How many more have this mindset, I wonder."

In typical fashion, Governor Lovell clicked his transmitter to calm the aggravated lord.

"Chancellor Gregorio, my Lord, I can assure you that this was an isolated incident."

"You've also assured me your colonists would reach their fuel quotas," the Chancellor said. *"We've gone over the tally. You're short five-thousand containers, Governor."*

Another High-Counsel member entered the holographic projection.

"It seems your people are not focused on the task they were sent there for."

"I will push them harder," the Governor said.

Anastacia had to look away at that pathetic attempt to pander. There was not even the slightest bit of pushback. Lovell certainly cared for the well-being of his people… just not enough to risk sacrificing his own position for them. To think he was one of the better career politicians was enough to make Anastacia lose faith in the system.

"Given the risk of further uprising, I am granting the World One Alliance Military full authority to oversee colony operations. Each colony will house a security team that will ensure safety and order. The colony administration will fall under the authority of the oversight officer, who will work to ensure each colony maintains an adequate function of operations."

"Because of the destruction of the Alaska Refinery, it is imperative that each and every colony doubles their export," the High Counsel member said. *"There is an ongoing energy crisis here on World One, and it's quickly getting worse."*

Another High Counsel member approached the lens. *"Thanks to our planets' elliptical orbits, and the fuel capacity of our space freighters, only one shipment can be made every twenty-six months. Launch is in two days. The next shipment twenty-six months from now will require one-hundred-and-sixty thousand containers."*

Anastacia's jaw dropped.

"Shh," Bill Cook immediately hissed. He saw the look on her face and knew she was seconds away from blurting something out.

She clenched her teeth and crossed her arms. *Double the payload. Lovely. And Lovell's going right along with it.*

"It will be done, my Lord," the Governor said.

Right on cue.

The Chancellor looked at his tablet, likely studying a list of the subjects of today's conference.

"Now, let's hear the report from the head of Centauri Colony's research division. Dr. Lawrence Platt, we direct our attention to you."

Anastacia stood up and approached the podium.

Bill Cook swallowed. "Doctor," he whispered through gritted teeth. "Where are you going?"

Hundreds of eyes turned toward her as she followed a stairway to the main podium. When she arrived on the stadium floor, she was met with discerning glances from the Governor, Colonel, and the Chancellor.

"I'm the head of Geological Research Division, East Territories," she said, sparing herself from the 'who are you' questions. She extended her badge.

"Doctor Anastacia Drucus," Governor Lovell read from the card.

"Where's Doctor Platt?" one High Counsel member said.

"Deceased," Governor Lovell said.

"And this young lady was put in his place?"

"You want the job?" she replied.

The room went quiet. The crowd members exchanged glances. Those who were barely awake were all of a sudden perked up and watching with heightened interest.

Colonel Segan's right arm shifted, bringing his gauntlet closer to his other hand. He kept one eye on the screen, waiting for the word from the High Counsel to make an example of this woman.

"Pardon me," Governor Lovell said loudly. He approached Anastacia. "You do realize you are to make your presentation from your platform."

"Sorry, I need to present some visual aid."

She brushed past him on her way to the podium.

"First of all, I need to address the increase in manpower my colony, and many others, require. In all fields, but especially geological research. After we used explosives at the sites assigned to us by the 'brilliant' World One Geological Commission—who never once set foot on this planet, may I add—we hit chemical pockets, yet to be identified. The result was a blast equivalent to ten-thousand pounds of TNT. Our team was showered by dust and debris.

"Three of our team members were killed, including the late Dr. Lawrence Platt. Three others had their protective masks damaged exposing them to minerals. One case resulted in Regolith Lung Rot, a condition that deteriorates the tissue..."

"I'm not interested in your setbacks, Doctor Drucus," Gregorio said. *"I want to know if you have found any new methane deposits."*

"It was *your* advisors who sent us to that location and issued instructions to use explosive charges," Anastacia said.

"Your point?"

Another man stepped forward. Judging by the grey attire, he was likely a senator. Regardless, he was equally as determined to remain in the Chancellor's favor as the High Counsel members.

"Doctor, you are wasting the Chancellor's precious time."

"Aww." Anastacia at least resisted the exaggerated pouty face. "Does he not have enough of it? Running out of age enhancers? It would be a shame to stop at one-hundred-and-thirty years of age."

There was a sound of running footsteps. In the corner of her eye, she could see Bill Cook running over to the podium.

"Excuse me, Governor, Colonel, my Lord..." He leaned in toward the doctor's ear. "For the love of Heaven, Anastacia, *stop!*"

"In a sec." She dug her thumb drives out of her pocket. "The other issue I need to bring to your attention is this." She raised the thumb drives for the Chancellor and High Counsel to see, then plugged them into the podium.

A detailed image of a fragmented structure hovered in front of the podium. On World One, the Chancellor and his counsel had their own image projecting in their conference room.

It resembled a huge gravestone. It was rectangular in shape and carved from rock that appeared to be thousands of years old. On its front side were inscriptions, none of which resembled any language from the thousands of years of human history.

"It is my belief that this was a valued shrine that belonged to the Martians. Shortly after its destruction, the nearby colonies reported sightings of Martian gatherings on the surface, usually at night. Contact with the indigenous has been sparse since…" She looked at Colonel Segan, "…an unfortunate encounter. We have not been able to communicate with them regarding this issue."

Gregorio hit a button on his own podium, ridding his chamber of the projection.

"Why would they want to?" he said, dismissively. It was clear from the tone of his voice that there was zero interest in her findings.

"Well, for one, they might be able to tell us what it is."

"So, you blew up some sacred rock that was boobytrapped with a heavy load of flammable chemical."

"Possibly a sacred shrine."

"Have the indigenous come forward and offered to have a little chitchat about this? 'Hey, you idiots blew up one of our churches.' None of that?"

"As I said, they're refusing to speak with us at all. Might have something to do with the fact that we screwed with the planet's gravity, air, and temperature. Not to mention all the seismic activity we caused. A lot of them have succumbed to illness. We're lucky only a few tribes have retaliated… so far."

"Then it's irrelevant," Chancellor Gregorio said. *"I'm going to overlook this irritation you've caused me, since we're short on science staff at the moment."*

"I assure you, Chancellor, that Dr. Drucus is the best geologist in the region," Bill said.

"Who asked you?" Chancellor Gregorio said. Bill Cook backed away, struck by the sheer power exuded by the lord's presence. *"Dr. Drucus, I will remind you of your purpose—not just yours, but World Two as a whole. You are there to locate, extract, and process methane to be delivered to World One. In addition, you will seek out possible alternative energy sources and test them. Then there's the Jupiter mission. The assembly of the Jupiter station and the launch site is crucial to the survival of our species. Those five words sums up your priority:*

the survival of our species. Not making friends with underground scavengers who run around with sticks."

"We're well aware of our duty, Chancellor. My husband is in the hospital, fighting for his life, for having done his."

"Excuse me..." Governor Lovell cut between her and the podium. "Chancellor, honorable counsel, we understand our duties perfectly. I guarantee there will be no further problems."

"General Pyre will see to that."

The Chancellor activated a device on his podium. There was a blinking signal on the holographic receiver, as a new signal was detected.

The image that appeared was one of a military general, dressed in full uniform, his white beard neatly trimmed, his hands behind his back. Right away, Anastacia took notice of the many scars on his face, and the interesting fact that his right hand was gloved while the other was not. His presence alone demanded arguably more respect than the Chancellor. The only difference was that this man looked like a human weapon, having experienced more than the average soldier. There was no hint that he was a career man for the cushy benefits. This was a general who looked as though he chewed nails for his entire life, and would gladly do so even if offered a filet mignon.

"General Pyre, are you with us?" the Chancellor said.

"I am, Chancellor," the General said.

"To all Administrators, this is the officer who will be in charge, starting in twenty days."

"Let's hope any civilians with thoughts of treason have a change in attitude by then," General Pyre said. *"There will be thorough investigations starting the moment I arrive, Governor."*

Lovell exhaled slowly, his hands twitching slightly. "Understood."

"As for the rest of you... your necks belong to me now. Get used to it." With a press of a button, his image disappeared.

"Colony administrators, prepare quarters and offices for your security staff. Any failures will guarantee you an unpleasant meeting with General Pyre. This meeting is adjourned."

The transmission ended.

***

The recycled air outside Liberty Hall felt better than ever. Anastacia marched down the steps, agitated for a number of different reasons. The first was the uselessness of this meeting. There was no reason to require all of the colony administrators to physically attend this one meeting. A visual message could have been relayed to each of the colonies. It was yet another example of the powers-that-be throwing funds around. It was no wonder they gave Lovell plenty of reminders of the 'wealth-transfer' before moving on to talking about fuel. Wealth-transfer, as though anyone had any significant wealth. It was just a new way of saying tax.

"You have no idea how lucky you are," Bill Cook said, struggling to keep up with her.

"Someone needs to stand up to that old potato."

Bill chuckled nervously, noticing stares from a few guards.

"She's referring to, uh... Martin Grovis! The geological supervisor on Quincannon Colony." He sprinted to catch up with Anastacia. "He's a little hefty. Then again, he *is* a government official."

It was going to be a very long flight home.

CHAPTER 9

World Two.
Rome.

Quintus Julio, Custodian of the Faith, was the last to leave the conference room area. Nobody, not even the Chancellor, seemed to share his concerns. It was as though they had all forgotten the scriptures of centuries past, heeding the warnings of the Great Conquerors. They were real. There was physical evidence supporting this. That evidence was the basis for the development of human space travel. As usual, time had a way of reducing concerns.

Dressed in the golden robes of his sacred position, he stood at the Chancellor's conference podium. Fast-forwarding through the conference recording, he finally came to the slab of rock presented by Dr. Drucus on World Two.

He studied the markings on the so-called shrine. At its top were five specific lines, angling upward at different angles, almost mimicking a sunrise. Below it were inscriptions that almost resembled octopus tentacles. To the laymen, they were nothing more than illustrations or random markings. Only the wisest knew the truth. This was not Martian scripture, and Dr. Drucus truly did know what she had come across.

The damn robes always concealed his comm device, which was tucked below the belt. He dug the square piece of plastic and metal then clicked the tiny red switch.

"Chancellor, I need to speak with you."

The response came from one of his assistants. *"Chancellor Gregorio is currently in a meeting."*

"Where is he?"

"If you wish, I can arrange a meeting..."

"Just tell me where he is. This is the Custodian of the Faith, and I have important information to relay to him."

There was a pause, followed by, *"Excuse me. One moment."* There was no urgency to her voice. Custodian of the Faith—a title only Quintus Julio took seriously nowadays. When the voice came back, she delivered the message Quintus expected. *"He is not available right now. I will leave a message with the assistant currently accompanying him if you wish."*

Quintus switched off the comm. There was no sense in any more useless interaction. He ran down the east hallway, quickly spotting one of the senators at the nearest junction. There was a look of loathing when the senator looked in his direction. Before he could step away, Quintus managed to approach.

"Senator."

"Yes?"

With everyone Quintus encountered, he was met with the same tone. They looked at him as a government sanctioned freak, less normal than even the Martians. Nobody read the scriptures anymore. Today, it was seen as a formality, a fading homage to the founding of the Alliance.

"Which way did the Chancellor go?"

"Why do you need to know?" the senator said.

"Senator, I am his advisor. I need to share something with him. All I'm asking is that you point the way."

The senator sighed. "Hallway Twelve. He's in a meeting with the General. I don't think he'll be pleased if you barge—"

Quintus hurried past him, taking a left at the next hall. A hundred feet down was Hallway Twelve. When he turned the corner, he spotted Chancellor Gregorio in his red robes, walking beside one of his assistants, two advisors, and a hovering droid with a flat-top which contained a holographic projector image. It was of lesser quality than the one in the conference room. The General stood at eighteen-inches and was shrouded in blue light, but it was enough to get the job done.

"Colonel Segan is yet to locate the traitor: Doctor Douglas Warren," Gregorio said.

"The Colonel reports that Warren and two accomplices have disappeared into the mid-west section of Blackout Hills," the General said. *"It is dangerous terrain, full of nasty fauna. IF he's alive, it is because he has help."*

"The Martians."

Pyre nodded. *"Once I arrive, I might have to delve into the underground lairs and smoke him out."*

"Good. Then we can put our excavation equipment to good use," Gregorio said. "We've always suspected the Martians are hiding some kind of power source down there. They're not typically advanced, but they do have access to energy weapons. It is possible their colonies have sustainable energy, provided by something in the subterranean..."

Quintus Julio ran to catch up with the Chancellor. "My Lord! I must speak with you."

All eyes, full of disdain, turned to him.

Immediately upon making eye contact, Gregorio hung his head down. "Oh, great."

"Is this something I should be concerned with, Chancellor?" General Pyre asked.

"Give me a break, General," a bemused Gregorio said. "This is Quintus Julio, Custodian of the Faith. Spends a little too much time in the archives." Fighting through his contempt, he turned his attention to Quintus. "You do realize you're intruding on an important meeting?"

"Forgive me, Chancellor. But I have important information that could not wait."

Gregorio's interest was slightly heightened. Slightly.

"What, exactly?"

"The markings on the debris that Dr. Drucus revealed…"

"Dr. Drucus?"

"Uh, yes… Dr. Platt's successor?"

"Oh, her!" Gregorio said. "The woman geologist with the attitude. Something about a dying husband."

"Y—yes. But the debris, my Lord… the markings on them, I know what they are."

"The debris… you're referring to that useless slab of rock? Of course you know what it is. We all do. It's a Martian shrine. Was. Now, they might as well break it into pieces and line a campfire with it."

"It's not Martian," Quintus said. "It's Vallachian."

Gregorio dropped his hands and looked to the heavens. "Oh, for God sake."

"Excellency, I recognized the inscriptions," Quintus said with heightened urgency. "They match those that were found during the digs in South America."

"When the crashed vessel was discovered in the limestone," Gregorio said.

"Correct."

Sighing, Chancellor Gregorio began searching the pockets in his robes. After a minute of futility, he turned to his assistant, who already had her hand outstretched. On her palm was a sweet, watermelon-flavored, wrapped in foil. Gregorio snatched it from her palm, unwrapped it, and tossed it into his mouth.

It was a sign of other things on his mind. Worse, his lack of interest in Quintus Julio's testimony.

"And like the ship in South America, this shrine was empty," Gregorio said. "Except for some kind of chemical, apparently."

"I don't think it was a shrine," Quintus said.

Gregorio started to turn away, then stopped. "What?"

"I don't think it was a shrine. I think it was a garden. Planted by the Vallachians a hundred, maybe two hundred years ago. The seeds emit fumes when they are on the verge of sprouting. Those fumes are flammable. *Explosive.*"

"OR, the team hit a methane pocket. There's plenty of them across World Two," Gregorio said.

Quintus shook his head. "Chancellor, the holy scrolls tell us everything we need to know about the Vallachians. How they seize worlds, corrupt landscapes and oceans, bend the populace to their will…"

"And how they never show up except in text," Gregorio muttered. "Let it go, Quintus."

It was like telling a bird not to fly.

"Excellency, I strongly suggest we analyze Dr. Drucus' findings. Halt all methane operations until we know for sure…"

Gregorio's eyes lit up. "Halt all methane operations?! Are you out of your blasted mind, Quintus?"

Several guards arrived in the hall, alerted by even the slightest hint of distress in the Chancellor's voice. He waved his hand, telling them to stand down. Facing Quintus, he took a moment to quell his temper.

"Maybe… *maybe*, we'll look into it. But if you make one more idiotic suggestion like that again, you'll be back on the block where your grandfather begged for scraps. Unlike him, you won't be able to marry your way out of it."

Quintus Julio, a man of great faith, was a man who feared only the wrath of divine spirits. As scripture stated, there was no greater wrath. Only when Chancellor Gregorio was angry was that certainty tested.

Quintus stepped back, head down, yielding.

Gregorio pivoted to face General Pyre's projection. In the blink of an eye, his focus was back on the original issue at hand.

"Right now, our concern is rebellion and the energy crisis," he said. "General, what's to be of the incompetent fool who allowed those heretics to destroy the Alaska refinery?"

"I have plans for him, Excellency," Pyre said.

"I'll leave you to it then," Gregorio said. "The freighters leave in two days. I understand you have much to do."

"We'll be in touch." With that said, General Pyre ended the transmission.

Gregorio immediately relaxed, the way one did when a large task had been completed.

Quintus, hoping to take advantage of this shift in demeanor, approached a second time.

"My Lord, if I may…"

His words went unheard as Gregorio walked away with the others, taking a turn at the next hall.

"It's been quite a day. Is the ballet ready?"

"That, and refreshment awaits," his assistant replied. "Mediterranean sea bass, topped with fresh lemon from Minori Gardens."

"Ah, my favorite." Gregorio rubbed his hands together. "I feel like I haven't eaten in days."

Their voices faded as they approached the entertainment auditorium.

Quintus Julio stood alone in the hall, staring at the electronic image of the inscriptions on his tablet. The itch of obsession demanded to be scratched. Perhaps more knowledge would help convince the rest of the counsel of the dangers they faced.

That knowledge lay in the vault of scriptures.

CHAPTER 10

World One.
Seattle.

"Nuclear reactors. Wish they'd install one of those on my end of town. Tired of the constant blackouts."

"I'm sure the people of L.A. would have something to say about that. There's still fallout from those meltdowns. Makes Chernobyl look like a picnic."

"It was the Fusion Wars. Nothing was safe. That's where the Captain's father served, right?"

"Shh. It's Lieutenant now. They busted him."

"Hmm. Lucky he's got his daddy's name. If it were any of us in the same predicament, we'd already be strung up for target practice."

The pilots' attempt to lower their voices was fruitless. Vince could hear every word exchanged. Even with his decreased rank and ravaged reputation, he could easily have them written up for insubordination. Instead, he kept to himself. What was the point of potentially ruining more lives. His failure had cost him command of his team, his status, possibly his pension, and his good standing with the Alliance. Forty-two complete combat missions throughout the planet, suppressing riots, neutralizing extremists and pirates, and protecting security interests—all successful.

This was his first taste of failure, and it was a mouthful.

He kept quiet, looking out the aircraft window as he was flown over Seattle. It was considered a sector, not a city. The entire continent was a city, as were the others. There was not a speck of nature beneath him. Trees, for the most part, were a thing of the past. Power plants spit fumes into the atmosphere, adding to the grey color in the sky.

On the ground, people moved about, many of them wearing electronic rebreathers over their mouths and noses. Only in recent years were such devices issued out. Some areas were better than others. For Vince, Alaska had literally been a breath of fresh air. Now, following the explosion, the air quality was probably worse than the densest of sectors.

South of the Seattle sector, they arrived in a 'gap' in the city. This clearing was the Seattle Alliance Military Base. To the west was the training center, where new cadets were being put through rigorous exercises.

Watching them brought Vince back to his training days. To this day, tridents were shed of their humanity and were given new purpose. New identities. 'You are not human, anymore. You are something more. You are *Tridents*. Literally means Three Teeth. For us, that means control over air, land, and sea.'

To the north were the outdoor firing ranges, where live targets attempted to evade gauntlet fire. Somewhere in the distance, explosions rang out. Grenades, RPGs, tanks, proton bombs—everything was tested around here, or out at sea.

After flying over the base, the pilots steered the ship to the landing pads.

"Charlie-237, request permission to land."

"Copy that, Charlie-237, you have clearance to set down on Pad Four."

"Copy that."

The pilots found their location and lowered the ship. Vince stepped outside, where an escort awaited.

"Lieutenant Caparzo, I'm here to escort you to General Pyre's office."

"I know the way," Vince muttered. He brushed past the escort and marched into the building.

Toward an uncertain fate...

***

"Lieutenant." There was emphasis on the rank. Vince Caparzo knew very well that when General Pyre emphasized anything, there was definitive meaning.

The mere sight of the General displayed experience and provoked fear. Being a trident, Vince had to contain that fear. Those who displayed fear were, at best, forced from the ranks into supporting roles. To the layman, that seemed to be a relatively tame consequence. In the military, dropping out from combat training was dishonorable and led to life-long scrutiny from their physically and mentally superior counterparts.

The desk, consistent with Alliance standards, was well kept. Even more so was Pyre's uniform. The left breast was decorated with honors rarely seen, some dating back to the Fusion Wars. Given his age, it was clear this man lived and breathed combat. Such men often didn't do well behind a desk. It was that thought that made him notice how most of the shelves had been cleared out. Such things only happened when someone was retiring, or was being relocated.

With his hands behind his back, Vince stood straight, his eyes forward. Good discipline was all he could do to retain what little honor he had left.

"General."

There was a slight hint of amusement in the General's eyes. Yet, there was also disappointment, almost like that of a parent who thought their child had turned out to be a failure.

"Lieutenant, I'm sure by now you've heard the high-profile demands from numerous senators urging me to put you on a public firing range," Pyre said. "I imagine you're wondering who it was that convinced the tribunal to let you off with a demotion."

Vince merely nodded. The calls for his execution were immediate and passionate. There was no sleep that first night after the explosion in Alaska. The hypernet was flooded by the grave news, and quickly followed by the demands of government officials across the planet. Their sentiments were parroted by the populace, many of whom were simply interested in remaining in good standing with the Alliance. Certain death seemed inevitable. Except, it wasn't.

Only a man of great influence could sway such a decision.

"I believe I'm looking at him, sir," Vince replied.

"Is that your way of saying thank you?" Pyre said.

"More like 'why'?" Vince said.

There was a look of elevated interest by the General. A lesser man would be on his knees, thanking him for having his life spared. Vince Caparzo knew better, at least.

"Do you not know who I am?"

"Yes, General," Vince said. "I know who you are."

Pyre tapped his fingers on the desk, studying Vince heavily. He stood up and pushed his chair in.

"I don't normally allow personal feelings to affect my judgement, Lieutenant. Doing so tends to halt progress. Sometimes, it even leads to disaster." He began to walk around the desk. "That said, I'd be remiss if I allowed the son of General Caparzo to be put on Hangman's Pier."

There was a slight tilt in Vince's jawline, simultaneous to a small twitch in his eyebrows. The Fusion Wars Victory Medal on Pyre's jacket breast, his age… The L.A. Beach Invasion Medal.

"You served under him, sir?"

"I did," Pyre said. "In the Fusion Wars, if it wasn't obvious enough by now. You wanna talk about great leadership, your father was it. He didn't command from a big office from afar, safe from enemy gunfire with hot Joe in his hand. No, he was with us on the frontlines of L.A. Even the Chancellor thought it was a doomed mission. But General

Caparzo knew what was at stake. It was because of him that we were able to prevent the Southern States from launching a satellite strike which would have glassed Rome and much of Europe. We would not have succeeded if it was anyone else leading the charge."

The General leaned on his desk, the look in his eyes shifting to disappointment.

"What a shame. I guess good leadership is not genetic." He allowed a moment of silence for Vince to feel the impact of that statement. Afterwards, the General's tone grew harsh. "You failed your mission, Caparzo. I know you know this, but I'm sure as hell going to keep hammering it in."

"Aye, sir."

Pyre leaned in. "What's that?"

"Aye, sir."

Pyre began to walk circles around him, like a shark monitoring its prey.

"You've been reassigned, Lieutenant. Operation Oversight on World Two."

"World Two?"

Pyre stopped near his right shoulder. "That a problem?"

"Negative, sir."

The General watched him for a moment, then returned to his desk.

"If I can handle it, you certainly can," he said. "The colonists are forgetting their place. World Two is now under complete military jurisdiction. It should've been that way since Day One as far as I'm concerned. Once we arrive, you will oversee the operations of one of the colonies. It's a second chance at leadership, though nothing compared to what your father has done."

Pyre pulled his chair back and took a seat, his eyes never shifting from his guest. "But I think we both know there's no hope for that anyway."

Such words were considered worse than the firing line, particularly to those who dedicated their lives to the service. In Vince's case, it had been nearly twenty years since he first joined at eighteen.

"It's an honor to serve, General." There was nothing else for him to say. It was a sentiment he would have to remind himself of every single day. At least he was still being given a command.

"At least you have the right attitude," Pyre said. "This is likely to be a permanent assignment for you. Considering Alaska, I doubt you have any complaints. Or am I mistaken?"

"Negative, General."

Having received the answer he wanted, Pyre turned his eyes to his desk computer. Final arrangements were to be made, both business-wise and personal before his departure.

"Report to Fort Cobra, Hangar Twelve in thirty-six hours," he said. "Only pack what is absolutely necessary. Anything left behind will be taken by the district. Any questions?"

It was a lot for Vince to process, all while exhibiting the basic disciplines that were expected of a trident officer. He was no stranger to far-off assignments and long tours, but this was something different. This was a complete and total life change, all in the span of a couple of days. The words 'permanent assignment' echoed in the depths of his mind. Everything around him, everything he had ever known, would never be seen by him again. Regardless of how dull and metal this planet had become, it was familiar. He knew he would etch out a halfway decent retirement, possibly enough to purchase better living quarters to live out his later years. Now, everything was uncertain.

Uncertainty was all he had now.

Despite his question, the General was not one to receive a long list of personal requests. Only one thing mattered to Vince enough to be said here and now.

"What of my next of kin?"

Pyre looked up from his device. "The choice is yours, Lieutenant. You can take her with you to live on World Two, or she can remain here. The district administration will assign care for her in that event. But you'll have to decide now."

The General watched the Lieutenant contemplate the options.

"Hell of a choice," he continued. "Either don't see your young one ever again, or commit her to a life on that hellhole. Remember what I said about personal feelings, Lieutenant."

"Aye, sir."

"So, what's your decision?"

CHAPTER 11

Waterville District - previously known as Douglas County, Washington.

The crunch of the grape was so pure and juicy. It was Lucy Caparzo's second time eating authentic fruit. The synthesized stuff always had a leathery texture to it, and the flavor was a shadow of the real thing.

Seated at the kitchen table of the small living quarters, she had already gone through half of the bag. They were so addictive, a sharp contrast to most available foods.

"Be not glad at the misfortune of another, though he may be your enemy," she read aloud from her book. Days Gone By, by William Glayson, published in 2043. Like the grapes, it was a miracle she came across this piece of literature. Most other people would have turned it over to the authorities, who would surely have it incinerated. And like the grapes, it was a sharp contrast to the required literature of Alliance schooling. Full of quotes from then high-profile figures of the Western hemisphere, this book was banned from existence, along with many others.

"'Freedom is never voluntarily given by the oppressor, it must be demanded by the oppressed.'" She read the rest of the page, then flipped to another section of the book, titled *The Duty of The People.* The first quote on the page was from Thomas Jefferson. 'If a nation expects to be ignorant and free, in a state of civilization, it expects what never was and never will be.'

Ignorant. Lucy thought on her classmates and teachers. Never once did she hear a descending voice, not even in the public sector. It was all the same. They recited quotes such as "we are in this together" and "the price *we* pay"—words almost strictly used by officials.

Officials, many of which were over a hundred years old. Age enhancers were said to be a limited commodity and were supposedly needed to be given to the government class, for their experience and wisdom was too priceless to lose. That was the justification provided, at least.

She flipped to the introductory chapter of the book.

Aristotle wisely said 'be a free thinker and don't accept everything you hear as truth. Be critical and evaluate what you believe in.'

Lucy frequently came back to this quote. She felt as though this Aristotle fellow legitimized her internal nature. Lucy liked to ask questions about the state of things and why they functioned the way they did. What stuck in her mind the most was how some questions were not allowed to be asked. Accept official reports, follow the instructions of your superiors, accept the wisdom of the High-Counsel.

Lucy perked up. There were footsteps outside the door. Minutes prior, she received notification that her father was returning home.

She shut the book then put her study tablet atop of it. She activated it and brought up the required text. *The Need for Order after the World Experienced so much Chaos.* Unlike many of the other students, she got hung up on the ridiculously long and wordy title. She slid the bag of grapes over the spine, then leaned forward to resume her school-sanction studies.

When the door opened, she turned and smiled at her father.

"You're back!"

Vince stepped through the doorway, holding a small backpack over his shoulder. He was utterly exhausted and seemingly in a haze.

"That tends to happen when I finish an assignment," he said.

"Well, I heard the refinery blew up. There was a lot of talk going around. I didn't know…"

"Where's your temporary caretaker?" he said.

Lucy gestured at the door. "She left twenty minutes ago on another assignment. Babies need watching." She smiled at the thought. Babies, small animals, anything young and innocent made her gush with affection.

Vince stepped to the refrigeration unit and pulled out a small, tin beverage. He took a small drink, then pressed it to his forehead.

"They are indeed work."

"And adorable," Lucy added.

Vince shut his eyes and groaned. "So you say."

Lucy scoffed as she turned her eyes back to her tablet. "I guess we're adding babies to your collective dislike of people."

"I was in combat with over thirty green-grass murderers, recently. They killed multiple people and accelerated our world's energy crisis. They were babies once. Those 'adorable' little creatures eventually went on to kill innocent people and decimate our way of life."

"Wow, Dad. Is that what you thought of me when I was born? Missed you too, by the way."

Vince decided to keep his trap shut. He was tired, frustrated, and still processing his new circumstances. He checked the time, then reached into a compartment above the refrigeration unit.

Lucy watched as he pulled out two large duffle bags.

"You leaving again already?"

It took her father a moment to answer. She knew the look. Whatever the answer was, he didn't like it, and feared she wouldn't either.

"We both are." He put one of the bags on the chair beside her. "Sorry, kid. You're probably not going to like this. We're being relocated."

"You're getting reassigned?" she said. Excited, she stood up. "To where? Is it Hawaii? The beaches are still nice and tan…"

"World Two," Vince said firmly.

"World—" Lucy's voice trailed off. It was the last thing she expected him to say. "Mars?"

"If you'd rather go by the old-fashioned names," Vince said. Lucy sat back down, processing this sudden change. Vince pulled a chair and sat beside her. "Listen, kid. There's no time to discuss it. There's no way out of this for me. But, if you'd rather remain here on World One, I can make arrangements to—"

"No!" she said. She chuckled shyly, both at her father's reaction and at the realization of how she felt. "We're going off planet?"

"Yes. Likely will be permanent."

A fresh energy began to flood Lucy's veins. This was something daring and new.

"Actually, I'm feeling excited about this," she said. "I've been doing lots of reading on frontier life, how people lived hundreds of years ago, and such. That's what this will be like, just with better tech."

Vince looked to the bag of grapes conveniently placed next to the tablet, which was interestingly elevated.

"Reading, huh?" He pulled the book from under the tablet, glanced at its title, then gave her a look of horrors. "Doesn't look like this is about frontier life."

Lucy made a nervous, toothy smile. "Wait a minute… that's not about the adventures of Davy Crockett?! I feel so robbed!"

The joke had no effect.

"Where'd you find this?"

Lucy groaned then tilted her head to the northeast. "They tore down some old living quarters a few blocks from here. The caution barriers weren't put in place. The items were free for the taking." She pushed the bag toward him. "I found some real grapes in there."

"Real fruit and contraband. By the way, they *weren't* free for the taking. They were for the district to collect."

Lucy put her head on her palm. "What's so bad about a book?"

"Let's start with how this is illegal to have," Vince said.

"I was just curious."

"Curious about conspiracy theories about the danger of world order? About the so-called fall of individualism?" He put the book down. "They burned these for a reason. Hopefully nobody saw you with it."

"Are ideas really that bad?" Lucy said.

"The wrong ones are."

Lucy smirked. It was the exact answer given by everyone at her school.

"Okay." She picked up her duffle bag. "When will we be leaving?"

Vince checked the time. "We'll have to depart from here in thirty-one hours."

"Gosh, I can't believe we're going to Mars."

"World Two," he reminded her.

"World Two, right," she said. "What ship will we be on?"

CHAPTER 12

Space freighter *Crimson Nova*.
Day thirteen of travel.

Lucy shifted in her bunk, reading the holographic text from her study tablet. It was unbelievable. Humankind was able to construct mile-long starships, design huge, pressurized domes over large settlements, build huge satellite refinery stations to orbit Jupiter and Venus… and yet, they couldn't install a decent mattress to a tiny bunk.

Back on World One, she thought the Alliance was testing the human condition by enforcing such small housing. Now, she would give anything to be in a habitat that size. Their quarters on this ship was a single room with two crummy bunks. The only luxury they installed was a narrow treadmill for exercise. There was a mess hall on the aft part of the vessel and restrooms in the same direction. Aside from that, there was no reason to leave their quarters, and nothing for her to do inside except study.

Once in a while, she explored the ship. Technically, it was not allowed, but nobody on the vessel really cared, including Vince. At least once every twenty-four hours, Lucy took a long stroll through the ship. Each journey took her past the tanks, aircrafts, digging equipment, dome supplies, and other supplies. This was a cargo freighter, designed specifically for hauling equipment. Though it was a giant ship, it had a very small crew of a few dozen people. With the Caparzo being last-minute additions to the next World Two voyage, they were unable to get bunks on the personnel carriers, each of which carried hundreds of thousands of tridents and new staff. General Pyre, through his many connections, was able to get them in the vacant crew quarters on the *Crimson Nova.*

Whenever Lucy was not stretching her legs, she was on that bunk doing her required studies for life on World Two. Vince was doing his routine exercise on the treadmill, content with remaining in the room as opposed to walking with her through the ship. He had his own study device set up, which he listened to while he walked.

"Five more days, and we'll finally be there," Lucy said. "I'm ready to stretch my legs and be liberated from this coffin."

"I'm looking forward to being liberated from your snoring," her father said.

Lucy sat up. It took nearly two weeks, but that sense of humor the military seemingly stamped out of him was finally peering through.

"Look at that; a joke. *And* projection."

Vince cocked a smile. "How's the studying going?"

"Only took you thirteen days to ask," Lucy said. She had thought two weeks being hunkered down with her father would lead to all new conversations. Strikingly, he somehow managed to bury himself in his work, even when he was only six feet away from her.

"You prefer I be on your case during the entire trip?" he asked.

Lucy shook her head and grinned. He had a point there. Every parent was pressured to monitor their child's education progress like a vulture watching a dying critter. Though she did not care for the loneliness his line of work caused her, she enjoyed being self-sufficient.

"It's very fascinating," she said. "I've heard other people complain about the mandatory studying on Mars, but I like it." *Though I wish I had something else to do to break up the monotony.* "I will say, I'm not sure if I'm going to like the six-hundred-and-eighty-seven day year."

"That's why we'll be relying on World One's orbital cycle for calendar time. Luckily, World Two has a twenty-four-hour rotation, so day and night will be the same."

Lucy scrolled through various digital pages, each of which were decorated with photographs of the early colonial process.

"I never knew all of the details that went into colonizing and terraforming Mars… World Two." More than once, she was chastised by her father for her use of out-of-date names. "Here's a question: Why didn't they call the moon World Two? We colonized it first, didn't we?"

"Probably because it's a moon, not a world," Vince said. "It's considered part of World One."

"Hmm." It made enough sense. "Regardless, in colonizing the moon, we learned a lot of lessons that made colonizing World Two much easier. That's how we perfected planet mass alterations, so we don't have to live in low gravity. Did you know low gravity can have all sorts of negative effects on health? Like muscle atrophy, calcium balance, decreased plasma volume, shifting of bodily fluid, cardiovascular issues…"

"Whoa, kid." Vince put his hand up. "I was just asking how the studying was going. Not for a lesson. If I wanted that, I'd attend school with ya."

"Heck, I've given thought to becoming a teacher," Lucy said. "I love explaining this stuff."

Vince resumed walking on the treadmill, scrolling through his own digital pages. "Well, when you're old enough, apply for an application to pursue course study. You should have no problem getting one through, as long as you don't goof up on your aptitude tests."

"I wish that wasn't the case."

"Wish what be the case?"

Lucy shrugged. "Aptitude tests. Shouldn't people pursue things they want to do?"

"Only if they prove themselves capable, and if those things they pursue are even of worth." Vince stopped the machine and looked her in the eye. "Self-aggrandizing is dissolute."

Lucy placed her tablet down. On its screen was a wide-shot of Mars, surrounded by the solar panels, docking stations, and satellites. It was an image that brought to mind why humanity went there in the first place, and what was becoming of the world they left behind.

"Some say aptitude assessment leads to unqualified people in places they shouldn't be working. Chernobyl, the 2084 Marker Shuttle Explosion, the Tokyo reactor meltdown..."

"How much of that book did you read?" Vince said.

Lucy chuckled. "Have we not been in the same room the last two weeks? I've been reading all of these books nonstop."

"No, the *other* book," Vince said.

Lucy suppressed the urge to roll her eyes. The book that shall not be named, which her father destroyed prior to their departure. Two weeks later, she wondered if it was done out of his patriotic duty, or fatherly love. Even someone her age would have faced serious consequences had anyone else known she was reading William Glayson's work.

"Just a little."

"It's in your best interest to forget its so-called lessons," Vince said. "Now, back to studying, kid." He resumed walking on the treadmill.

"What about you and mom?" Lucy said. "Was that self-aggrandizing, or just service to the Alliance?"

Vince immediately stopped the machine again. Holding tight to the handlebars, he stared into his tablet. There was no notice of the text projecting from it or the audio in his left earbud. He was a man searching for something to say.

"You know how things are supposed to happen, Lucy," he said. "The Alliance allows people to choose their partners. If they don't by a certain age, arrangements are made for pairings in order to... well..." He shrugged, then gestured to his daughter, the result of his arranged pairing.

It was the way of things. The population was vast, but it was the belief of the High Counsel that such numbers were necessary. A planet-wide city was difficult to maintain, and such a task required intense labor from many, *many* workers. The large population was maintained through a strict one-child system. After birth, the fathers were sterilized. The paired couple were free to remain together if they wished. However, the labor duties took precedence over personal relationships, and in most cases, couplings did not last. As long as the young were cared for and the labor performed, the obligation was met.

Vince turned his eyes to his tablet. Perhaps it was better to have said nothing. The truth only reminded Lucy that she was an obligation, not a choice. Vince justified it to himself, saying there was some degree of choice in the matter.

"We had conversations about giving permanent pairing a try, but reality wouldn't let it play out that way. I had my military post, your mother had her research assignment in Sydney. Duty got in the way. The district gave us a choice for primary guardianship over you. That's how you ended up with me."

Lucy gave no reaction. A smart girl, she knew the demands of researching star-energy harnessing and transmission. It was the one field that was probably more demanding than a career infantry officer. True solar power, drawn straight from the source, it would be more than a thousand nuclear and methane plants combined.

"Duty," Lucy muttered. "You'd think if people had greater ability to choose their profession, they could obtain lifestyles suitable for family life."

"We do have choice, hence the aptitude tests."

"Choice between approved options provided by officials."

"Lucy…" Vince clamped his jaw, stopping himself from providing a long, drawn out lecture. That damn book was destroyed. After some time, she would forget the indoctrination within it. There was no point in chastising a tired kid who had been couped up in a starship for thirteen days. "There is choice. I *chose* to bring you with me. Is that worth anything to you?"

A few moments of silence filled the room. Lucy looked to her father and rewarded him with a small smile. She knew he could have reassigned guardianship if he wanted to, and was certainly given the opportunity. Yes, it was enough.

For now.

The smile provided Vince with the answer he needed. He switched his treadmill back on and resumed his exercise.

"Now, back to your studies, or you'll be eating slop rice for the remainder of the trip."

CHAPTER 13

Blackout Hills, North of Espinosa Colony.

Being underground was no life for a human. Even a trained physician like Dr. Douglas Warren underestimated the toll never seeing the sun would have on one's mind. Even on planet, it was essential. After only a few days, he and his companions lost track of whether it was day or night. With their tell-timers broken or lost topside, they had no clue what time it was. Sleep was difficult and the air was stale.

Deep in the tunnels, there was no need for facemasks. There was something down here that purified the air. It was a fact first learned when Dr. Warren started practicing medicine on the Martians. Aside from the grace and hospitality of the Martians, it was the only thing working in favor to the fugitive.

Dr. Warren watched the cave walls. Bioluminescent lights, which he referred to as torches, lined the Martian colonies and the passages to the surface. There wasn't much else for him to do at the moment, except tend to his companions.

Davy Austin was in a cot, dozing here and there. It had been sixteen days since the conflict at Espinosa. Fourteen of those days consisted of nothingness. The fifteenth day was when things started to go wrong. After two weeks with moderate sleep at best, the only way to keep sane was to explore. Davy, being a man who kept close to the dome for most of his colonial life, was unfamiliar with the telltale signs of violent wildlife. He didn't even realize he was close to the worm's burrow until it stung him.

Spiked worms—the umbilical to Satan, as Warren referred to them— possessed a cruel, slow-moving venom. Twenty-four hours later, his veins were discolored, and the poor colonist was overcome with fatigue.

From the tunnel's incline came the sound of footsteps. The torch lights shined upon Preston Gosly. Covered in dirt and mineral, he was wearing his protective facemask, which was now at a quarter capacity.

"Take that off," Warren said. "How many times should I have to remind you?"

"Sorry." Preston took the mask off. "Force of habit."

"What's happening up top?" Warren asked.

"No luck," Preston replied. "Blood-jackets are crawling like roaches. They must want us bad to be scouring the Blackout two weeks after our escape."

"Damn." Warren tossed a stone into the depths of the cave, then stood up. "I was hoping they would've assumed we got devoured by some large animal."

Preston nodded at Davy Austin. "That's somewhat the case for one of us."

"He's lucky he didn't run into a bigger one," Warren said. He put his head against the cave wall. "So much for getting him to the infirmary."

Davy shifted in his thin little cot. "I'm fine, Doc."

"No, you're not," Warren said. "Shut up, Davy. You're not impressing anybody."

He knelt by Davy's right arm and peeled back the bandage. The veins near the puncture wound were very discolored, some almost black near the source. Davy made the mistake of looking at it. His pale face was a stark contrast to the infection.

"Gonna say I told you so?"

"I could if I wanted to," Warren said. "I could say 'that's what you get for wandering away from the sanctuary of the colony, right near a spiked worm's nest'."

"Hey, at least some of your Martian buddies ate well that night—day, whichever it was." Davy looked at Preston. "Hey, when you checked the surface…"

"Judging by the position of the sun, it's mid-evening," Preston said. "My guess, it's around nineteen-thirty hours."

Davy leaned his head back and smiled. Something about knowing that basic fact was comforting.

Warren covered the wound and stood up. Preston knew him well enough to know that he was concerned. Dr. Douglas Warren, the dedicated medical officer, could not stand to let a patient die, especially when he knew there was a cure for their ailment.

"I suppose you're making plans in that head of yours," Preston said.

"That stupid worm stung him good," Warren said. "Espinosa has the right medicine in their infirmary, but we won't get within a hundred yards before getting shot."

Preston knew the look in the doctor's eyes. Warren was not the type to sit around and do nothing. That quality was what led them down here in the first place.

"Any ideas in that big brain of yours, Doctor?"

"I'm working on it," Warren said.

"Work fast, because the Martians don't have an antivenom that'll work on human anatomy."

Warren turned around, resisting the 'you think I don't know that?' response. He strolled through the bend of the tunnel and gazed at the mass opening it led to. It was a cavern with many tunnels which went for miles in all directions.

Travel was the only way.

"We need to try and get him to another colony. Preferably one that isn't swarming with tridents."

Preston exhaled sharply. It was the answer he feared Warren would give. Once he overcame his personal anxieties, he was able to acknowledge that it was Davy Austin's best chance at survival.

"Which colony?" he asked.

"Centauri," Warren said. "They're furthest on the outskirts. I doubt there's any military presence there at the moment." A sigh of apprehension followed the statement. "We'll have to leave now. It'll take us days to get there."

"You think Lars will escort us?" Preston asked.

"Only one way to find out."

They each took one of Davy's arms and lifted him to his feet.

"Oh, knock it off you two. I can still walk," he said.

"You're starting to get a fever," Warren said.

"It's low. I'll cling to my dignity for as long as possible. I'll be damned if I let Carlita see me this way." Davy pointed up to Heaven.

How was Warren supposed to argue with that? He let Davy go, though he still made a point to keep a close eye on him as they walked into the Martian colony.

What a sight it was.

They entered an incredibly vast, open area. For the colonists, it was as though they were staring into the Grand Canyon, if it had a ceiling. Large pillars of earth stretched high, holding up the thick layer of rock and soil above them. From where the colonists stood, those pillars resembled massive red skyscrapers in a city sector.

Yellow lights filled the ground area. Hundreds of Martians moved about, each one tending to his or her duties. Like most of the animal kingdom, they operated in a hierarchical structure. There were the hunters and warriors, the nurses, carpenters, builders, among many other roles. Though they had the warrior-class, every Martian was trained in the art of self-defense and survival.

Each family lived in mushroom-shaped huts. Not only did their shape remind the colonists of the fungus, but their texture did as well. Whatever it was, it provided ample shelter to each family. Inside each hut was an orb-shaped object which gave off a light similar to those on the cavern walls.

There were at least three children to each mated pair. The female Martians were slightly shorter and slenderer than their male counterparts, with small, bony crests lining the sides of their heads. Many of them performed as blacksmiths, developing new staffs and digging for the deep hearts—purple crystals harvested from caverns deeper than this place. The deep hearts, as the Martians called them, provided power to the staffs. From what Dr. Warren observed, the staffs never required a replacement. Those crystals provided a lifetime of power.

It was Warren's belief that the lights on the walls drew some kind of power from the deep mines. There was enough in one pit to last a hundred colonies a hundred lifetimes, for only a tiny crystal was required for their weapons.

They did not use vehicles for transport. Scarabs, Dragos—giant caterpillar creatures—and triceratops-looking creatures called Ergits carried them for long distances. The corrals were stationed to what Warren believed to be northeast. It was hard to judge direction after two weeks underground.

Martian warriors stood guard, staffs in hand, motionless as statues. They were a species of discipline, honor, and peace. Peace did not mean they would allow themselves to be conquered. They preferred to avoid conflict, even against foreigners from a neighboring planet who altered their soil, atmosphere, gravity, and caused a myriad of ecological disasters in the process. They understood intent, even in the wake of tremendous loss. Though there was some carelessness in the colonialization of World Two, the humans did not intend genocide. At least, the colonists did not. The Alliance, however…

Warren led the trio to the colony's temple. It was a tall, holy structure, stretching nearly as high as the rock pillars. Inscriptions, glowing red, revealed the symbol of Circular Peace.

Two Martian warriors stood at the entrance. They moved their staffs from a vertical pose to a semi-hostile horizontal position. The humans stopped, each holding their hands up in terms of surrender.

Preston gulped and took a step back. "Sorry…" He cracked a smile and pointed at Dr. Warren. "His idea."

The Martians cared not for his quip. Nor did Dr. Warren, for that matter.

A voice boomed from deep within the temple. The guards promptly returned to their stationary pose, staring straight ahead with machine-like patience.

Orange orbs shined upon the figure emerging from the temple. Lars, staff in hand, stood on the top step and gazed on the three humans. He studied them, his large eyes blank and emotionless.

Dr. Warren put his hands behind his back and stood straight, as though addressing a military officer.

"Doctor Warren," Lars said in his slow, deep voice. "I sense apprehension."

He sensed right.

"Lars, I need your help. Davy Austin's condition is worsening. We need to take him to Centauri Colony, or he will not survive."

Lars turned his head slightly to look at the sickly colonist. "That, Doctor, is the least of your problems."

Warren could feel both of his companions burning holes in the back of his head with hard, concerned stares. As Lars correctly sensed, there was apprehension. It was a feeling that consumed Warren as well. Seeing Lars appearing... *fearful*, was something he was not used to.

There wasn't a tremor in his voice or anxious body movements. It was his deliberate use of words that only a trained ear would detect.

Lars looked into the tunnel, then at the humans.

"An emergence has begun. Malevolent eyes have opened. They are watching, preparing to make their return."

Warren felt Preston's elbow nudging his arm.

"Is he usually this wacky?"

Warren ignored him, keeping his attention on Lars. "The Watchers?" Lars nodded. Warren shook his head. Whatever Lars was referring to, it would have to wait. "Right now, my concern is getting my friend to the infirmary in Centauri Colony. Staying here means certain death for him. Can you please spare some scarabs?"

Lars nodded again.

From the darkness came another Martian. He was younger and shorter than Lars. Warren smiled when he recognized the plasma scoring on his neck.

"Godon!"

Preston nudged him again. "Is that..."

"Lars' brother. The one I saved," Warren replied.

"Godon. Finally! A Martian name that's actually pronounceable," Preston said.

"It's short for Godonellisfycus."

Preston stared blankly, then shrugged. "Rolls right off the tongue."

Godon and Lars communicated in their Martian language. A barrage of strange, warped syllables filled the humans' ears. None of them, even

Warren, understood what was said. All they could read were the tones of the younger, less disciplined Godon.

Like a teen on the brink of military boot camp, he was naïve and relatively eager. By human standards, he may as well have been a corporal. Even the youngest and most untrained Martians had an endurance the toughest trident could only wish for. It was fortunate that they were a benevolent species.

The exchange of words came to an end. Godon pivoted to face the humans, while Lars stood aside.

"I will take you," the younger brother said.

"There is danger," Lars said.

"Yes, dear brother," Godon replied. "Is it not my time?"

Lars hesitated to answer. "It is."

Davy Austin leaned towards the doctor. "Time for what?"

"Every Martian goes on a solo mission. It's their first step into adulthood. Manhood, whichever you want to call it." Warren glanced at one of the distant tunnels. "We're traveling under the Blackout. The area in the northeast is particularly dangerous. This is Godon's opportunity. The *Gojya*, his passage to the first echelon. Essentially, he becomes a man."

Godon bowed to his brother and the two performed the Circular Peace gesture.

"I accept the risk," Godon said. After clasping hands with his older brother, he looked to the humans. "We must go. We have a long ride ahead of us."

Preston shrugged again, then leaned to whisper to Dr. Warren.

"Well, I hope the *Gojya* doesn't turn into a 'gotcha', considering all the hungry things that are waiting for us over there."

"Relax," Warren said. "Follow Godon's lead and you'll be fine."

"Hope so," Preston said.

"I agree with the doc," Davy said. "I doubt there's anything over there worse than what we've already encountered."

CHAPTER 14

Blackout Hills. Two miles north of Centauri Colony.

Maya Napier checked the time. It was near twenty-one hundred hours, fifteen minutes from the curfew. Before long, the Blackout would visually be true to its name. It was bad enough being out here during the day. Night was a different matter entirely. Even her dedication to the task at hand wasn't motivating enough to keep her out here any longer than necessary.

Following her orders, most of the construction crew had already returned to the colony. Only she and four other construction workers remained. William Byrant, a thirty-five-year-old digger, operated one of the rusty rock-breaker machines. Like a massive bulldozer with forklift arms, it broke down one of the rock formations bit by bit.

He, like her and everyone else, was not enthusiastic about working out here. Frequently, one of them would mutter, "Why did Dr. Drucus have to find a methane deposit out here?" One would think the Blackout Hills would be off limits. Had it not been for the doubling of World One's demand, it probably would have been.

Three other workers, Matteo, Guillermo, and Richard, were wrapping up the groundwork for the extractor unit installation.

"I don't get it," Richard said. He looked at the base unit compartment which needed replacing. The big, semi-circular piece of steel was bent out of proportion, with large grooves lining its surface. "There has been plenty of high winds lately. More than enough sandstorms for my liking. But these things are supposed to withstand all of that. I don't understand how this thing ended up so heavily damaged."

"Sandstorms can blow rocks," Matteo said. "The thing probably got banged up over the course of the night."

"No, I'm not buying it," Richard said. He and Guillermo finished installing the replacement unit, a process which took much of the day. It was a heavy unit which needed to be fitted and installed in the crater they had drilled. Cleaning the cavity in the ground was an aggravating process in and of itself. Every time the wind kicked up, more residue would be blown into the cavity, which would then have to be cleared out with suction hoses, which frequently broke down.

William pressed the rock-breaker machine into another stone tower, busting its narrow top with explosive force. Bits of residue spat in all directions, one of which nicked the back of Guillermo's knee.

The construction worker turned around, arms waving high. "Hey! You mind watching what you're doing?!"

"Sorry!" the clumsy William replied.

"Ridiculous." Guillermo turned around and looked to their forewoman. "Mind smacking him for me?"

Maya Napier kept her eyes on their surroundings. "Maybe another time." She looked over her left shoulder in the direction of their trusty steeds. The scarabs were hissing and digging at the ground more than usual. Ed Burger, the colony animal handler, had informed her that such actions were usually done under duress. Something had the big bugs stressed. They were no strangers to the Blackout. Night did not scare them. Not much did. So, if the scarabs were uneasy, then so was Maya.

"Let's pack it in. The sun's going down. We ought to know better than to be out here after dark. Besides, the scarabs are getting antsy."

"Not only them," Matteo said. He, too, was glancing in all directions. It was as though he could sense there was something behind the howl of the wind. This area of the Blackout had not been thoroughly studied like the western regions. Already, one crewman had disappeared out here. The fool had wandered off during a scouting mission, and never reappeared. Search efforts failed to produce findings, of him, or anything else lurking in the area. Some believed it was a flying species that got him. It made sense, considering no remains were found. Most carnivorous species used teeth and claws. Even if venom was involved, the process of devouring the human victim always left shredded clothes, boots, and masks to be found. In this case, there was nothing.

Except a sense of dread.

William took his sweet time parking the rock-breaker in its spot. Guillermo and Matteo pulled the large tarp from the case and extended one end to William. He walked to the rear of the vehicle and knelt down to plant the stake.

A gust of wind stripped the corner from his grasp.

"Oh, crap!" He reached up and tried to catch it. Like a flag waving in the wind, the tarp pulled against the other two workers, who were standing in front of the spiked grinders. It was the worst place to be in that moment of time. The huge tarp pulled them into the pointed barbs. The sudden prodding sparked pain in each of them, causing them to lose their grip on the tarp. It flew away like a grey magic carpet, setting down several yards beyond the clearing.

"Nice going," Richard said.

"Didn't see you helping," William replied.

"He's got a point there," Matteo said.

"Will you guys quit bickering and hurry it up," Maya said. She looked at the scarabs again. Their mandibles were twitching and their forelegs were scraping the ground. A couple of them were tugging at their tie-up lines. Something wasn't right. She kept one hand on her plasma pistol.

Guillermo noticed it too. He picked his V-13 plasma rifle and held it close.

"Yeah, guys. Let's get going. She's right, we're pushing the time as it is."

"Well, we can't leave the thing uncovered. This metal isn't designed for nonstop exposure, especially with the wind tossing residue around like it is now," Richard looked to William. "Come on. Let's go get the tarp."

"I gotta put away this other gear," William replied.

"Relax. I'll go," Matteo said. He grabbed his rifle and followed Richard into the maze of rocks.

In the meantime, Maya got the scarabs ready. Once the rock-breaker was covered up, they would be on their way home.

When the tarp fell, it looked as though it only went about thirty feet. As luck would have it, it went well beyond that. It seemed as though they went two hundred feet before they found the thing. Adding to their misfortune was the fact that it was snagged around a big rock.

"Great. Just great," Richard said.

Matteo went around the back of the rock and found one of the corners. He peeled it back, gradually unwinding it from its snag. Richard walked alongside him, trying to look for one of the corners on the opposite end. He kept backing away as Matteo walked around the rock.

"You just gonna stand there?" Matteo said.

"Every time I try to grab the other end, you walk by. Not like it makes a difference anyway. The rest of the tarp is around it. I can't really pull it until—"

A gust of wind picked up, nearly yanking the tarp from Matteo's grip. He tucked his face down to protect his mask from any rigid particles flying through the air.

Through the howl was a grunt and the scraping of feet against the dirt coming from where Richard stood. He was behind Matteo, who couldn't see whatever it was that was going on. He clung to the tarp. Good thing, too. The other end unwound and began to wave in the wind. There was no forecast of a major storm. That was the trouble with this place. It seemed that things happened spontaneously and without warning. That was one of the many costs of frontier life.

Matteo nearly laughed as the wind settled down.

"What the hell you doing back there? The wind carry you away?" He turned around. "Or did you feel you had to…"

He realized he was talking to empty space. Matteo looked left and right, then turned in every direction.

"Richard?"

He wasn't there. It was as though the wind had indeed carried him away. Of course, that wasn't possible. It wasn't *that* strong a gust.

Turning to look where Richard had been standing, he paid attention to the ground. There were strange markings in the soil which he was certain were not there before.

Matteo's heart rate climbed.

"Richard? Come out, man. We gotta go." The lack of response made his throat tighten. "Rich! Where the hell are you?!"

A scuffling motion made him turn to the northeast. A blockade of rocks separated him from whatever was making that noise.

Matteo rolled up the tarp and stuffed it under one arm before unslinging his rifle. He flipped the safety switch, readying the weapon for use.

"Rich, I've got my rifle. I don't want to accidentally shoot you. Don't…" He moved around the nearest rock and laid eyes to the mass of uncoiling legs behind it. "Oh, God!"

With lightning-fast motion, he was knocked to the ground. Matteo kicked and screamed, his rifle shot flying uselessly into the air. A sharp piercing pain filled his gut.

Numbness followed. He was stiff as a billboard, but still alive, staring at the darkening sky as his attacker dragged him up the hill.

"Oh, no."

Maya, Guillermo, and William saw the blaster bolt soar high into the darkening sky. Like a military unit, they ran through the blockade of jagged rocks.

"Richard?! Matteo?!" As she feared, her calls went unanswered. She tried the comm. Same bad result.

"It came from this direction," William said, pointing ten degrees to the left. They ran for another hundred feet, ultimately coming upon a series of rocks shaped like a dragon's teeth.

Guillermo went up ahead to the left, weaving behind a large boulder. "Maya!"

She and William caught up with him. At their feet was a dropped V-13 rifle lying next to a rolled up tarp, gradually unfolding in the wind. The ground between them was disheveled by some kind of violent motion.

Richard and Matteo were nowhere to be seen.

"Let's evacuate," Maya said.

Guillermo and William did not need to be told twice. They turned on their heels and ran back the way they came.

Maya was right behind them. Right now, her job was keeping her remaining staff alive.

At the camp, she mounted her scarab and followed her workers southbound down the hill. As they neared its edge, she activated her long-range comm.

"This is Napier. Tell Bill Cook to come to the atrium. I require an emergency meeting. Something is in the Blackout."

CHAPTER 15

Crimson Nova.
Docking Platform Charlie-One-Four, World Two.

It was day eighteen. After millions of miles of travel, the shipping vessels had finally arrived at their destination. Now, the frantic hustle to deliver personnel and equipment from the docking stations to the planet had begun.

The red planet's atmosphere was like a busy highway, with dropships boarding new arrivals.

A semicircular docking station formed a half-ring around the star-front side of the planet. The freighters placed themselves in their designated berths, attaching themselves with clamps and umbilical passageways.

Vince Caparzo was in uniform, mask and gauntlet on, ready to set foot on his new home. With Lucy at his side, he followed the ship's crew to the starboard umbilical, which gave passage to Docking Platform Charlie-One-Four.

The check-in area was surrounded by large exterior windows, giving the Caparzos a grand view of the planet. They could see the length of the docking station arching around the western hemisphere. Freighters resembled tiny flies in the distance as they neared their destinations. Hundreds of ships, carrying thousands of people and millions of pounds of equipment. There was much to be done in the coming months. The construction of the Jupiter Orbital Refinery was underway near the starboard end of the station. The huge facility resembled a giant refinery in space, similar to the model being prepped for the upcoming Venus mission. The individual components were constructed on-planet, then delivered to the orbiting station to be assembled.

The idea was simple. Each station would orbit inside the planets' atmospheres and use complex equipment to suction the necessary elements from the gas clouds. In the case of the Jupiter mission, the station would suction hydrogen from the atmosphere. The Venus one was more complex, due to the violent atmosphere. In addition to the shielding, the Venus station needed to be able to separate the sulfuric acid from the carbon dioxide. That sulfuric acid would then be transferred to a processing station, where it would be mixed with water to produce hydrogen gas.

These were projects all in development. For now, the hope for mankind rested on the mining stations here on World Two.

A blinding stream of light pierced through the window.

Vince put a hand over his eyes, straining as if he was staring directly at a nuclear blast.

"Incompetent fools. It'd be nice if I could keep my eyesight."

"They're just readjusting the reflector panels," Lucy said. "They're big machines. They don't move gracefully. Usually, they're not worried about huge ships taking up their orbit."

Vince goaded her forward. "Yeeeesss, kid. You think I don't know that?" The solar panel completed its turn, liberating him from its excruciating glow.

Lucy had a spring in her step. Every opportunity she had, she glanced through the window at the planet. Vince dismissed her enthusiasm as pent up energy. They had been stuck in that small room for eighteen days. Even he was getting antsy toward the end.

"You know, World Two's original temperature was negative-sixty degrees on average," Lucy said. "If it weren't for those solar panels, you'd have to wear a full bodysuit with a built-in insulator. You should also be grateful for the planetwide radiation treatments during terraforming. If you were caught outside without a suit, you'd be dead in minutes."

Vince smirked. "I don't think you have to worry about that aptitude test. For crying out loud, they might make you a schoolteacher the moment we get down there."

"I'd be a nice one," she replied. "Nicer than Ms. Hendrickson."

"It's not about niceness," Vince said. "It's about standards and discipline. You picked the wrong planet to be soft. Wrong *species*."

They arrived at the processing area. A guard wearing a blue-collar outfit scrolled through digital pages full of colonial files. Without lifting his eyes, the hazy-eyed worker opened a fresh page.

"Name?"

"Caparzo. Vince and Lucy."

The guard went through the files, then shook his head. "Looks like some documents were not processed." Still not looking up, he pointed to some chairs on the far end of the room. "I'm gonna need you to take a seat over there. I'll have someone prep the documents for you to fill out."

"Documents?" Vince hissed. "What documents? My base handled all of that back on World One."

The guard shrugged. "I'm sorry. They're not showing up. Now please,   take   a   seat."

"How long will this take?" Vince said.

Another shrug. "Not sure, I'm afraid. As you can see, it's veeeery busy."

Vince read between the lines. Busy meant hours of waiting. Half a day, judging by the slow speed and incompetence of this staff.

"Not acceptable."

"Nothing I can do, sir."

Vince put his fist on the table, his gauntlet's LED reader shining bright. "I suggest you reconsider."

The guard finally lifted his eyes, gulping when he saw the angry trident officer standing before him. Up until now, he had dealt with a nonstop flow of colonists.

"Oh… excuse me," he said with a heavy studder. He adjusted his posture and with elevated energy and enthusiasm—or rather, the illusion of enthusiasm—he typed several keys. "You said Caparzo, correct?"

"Correct."

"Lieutenant Caparzo… alright, your shuttle is in Bay Seven. It's about to leave, but I'll tell them to wait. Thank you for your service."

The Caparzos moved down the next corridor, passing through crowds of confused and nervous new arrivals. Vince could feel Lucy's eyes on him, passing judgement on his methods.

"No room for softness," he said.

"He was just doing his job."

"So am I."

***

Bay Seven

At first glance, Lucy wasn't sure if she wanted to board the dropship shuttle. The seventy-foot machine's original silver color was completely lost. Now, the hull was shaded with red and brown scuffs and scratches, all due to constant exposure. The engines were starting up and had a crunchy sound that made her uncomfortable.

One of the crew members stood in front of the open fuselage. He had his hands clasped before him, his eyes conveying scorn for the late arrival, until he saw who that new arrival was. He straightened his stance, heels touching like a military officer.

"Sir. Ma'am. A pleasure to have you join us. Please take a seat and strap yourselves in. We'll be underway in a moment."

They stepped inside, seeing a crowd of anxious passengers. Each face conveyed uncertainty. Some had been drafted for this assignment, while others volunteered. In every case, an aptitude test was required. Physical fitness, math skills, work history, and social credit was evaluated. There was emphasis on that last one for this latest trip. The Alliance was not keen on another mutiny.

Lucy and Vince took the two remaining seats on the forward side and clipped their harnesses.

The crewmember closed the fuselage. "All hands aboard. Ready for takeoff."

The rumbling of engines intensified. Clamps detached and alarm bells rang out. As soon as all deck crew cleared Bay Seven, the hangar door opened. Now, there was nothing but empty space separating the ship from World Two.

The crewmember remained on his feet. A seasoned pro who had flown to and from the planet hundreds of times, all he needed was a handle on the overhead to cling to. He looked at the group of passengers like a tour guide about to take them on a daring safari.

Like all tour guides, he had an opening line.

"Welcome to hell."

That was a good way of separating the men from the boys. The more nervous passengers turned pale.

"That said, despite the red surface, it won't be nearly as hot," he continued. "In fact, be grateful you weren't part of the first settlements. Let's just say, it was more than a little brisk. But thanks to the surface warmers, those solar panels you probably saw out the window, you will be able to walk outside wearing normal attire. It will be a little chilly, like an autumn day in New Jersey, but tolerable. As long as you have your rebreathers."

He held his mask up.

"Without your rebreathers, none of what I just said will be worth a damn. Have yours on you at *all* times. Should you find yourself outside one of the domes or vehicles, you will find yourself out of breath. If you inhale the Martian air, your blood will be poisoned. Infectious dust will eat away at your organs. Parasites lurking in the air like microscopic floating jellyfish will enter your nasal passages and latch themselves to your muscles and organs. Then again, all of that will be the least of your worries, because you'll go into cardiac arrest and die in four minutes."

All at once, the passengers fastened their rebreather masks.

"Good boys." The crew member looked to the youngest member seated on his left. "And girl."

Lucy gave a thumbs up. Of all the passengers on this bird, she was the most eager to set foot on the planet.

So long as this rusty bird held together until then.

***

Hope Colony.

The dropship shuttle pierced a barrier of thick volcanic clouds. The windows turned dark grey, without a speck of light penetrating. It was here where Lucy's upbeat image began to falter. There were a few dry heaves from the passengers, though none dared to lose control. Each one was wearing a pressurized facemask, which would make for a very uncomfortable experience should one lose their cookies.

After ten-thousand feet, the windows cleared. The ship leveled out and turned to port, following a semi-circular path.

Lucy turned to look out the window. "Dad, we're here."

Vince pivoted in his seat and beheld his first sight of the planet's surface.

From high up here, Hope Colony resembled a spiderweb of glass and mechanics. However, it was a beautiful spiderweb. As its name suggested, it was the beacon of hope for humanity's future.

The colony extended for miles. As they got nearer, it began to resemble a glass mountain range rather than a giant spiderweb. In its center was Hope Central, an enormous dome covering three miles of civilization. The thought of constructing such a facility, let alone installing it on a hostile surface, was headache-inducing even for Vince. The other domes were smaller, though fairly large. All of them were interconnected through tunnels, which allowed shuttle stations to transport people throughout the colony.

Drones, both terrestrial and flying, conducted nonstop maintenance and inspections. Every inch of glass was consistently monitored. Any weak spot was reinforced with a gel patch that, when solidified, was as tough as Kevlar. Rovers and Whirlybirds delivered workers to their destinations. The outer perimeter was lined with vehicle garages, maintenance sheds, and watch towers.

To the north was a massive elevation, essentially the side of a cliff, overlooking the gigantic settlement. A massive ridge, it extended for miles, separating the colony from the eastern corner of the Blackout Hills. Numerous watchtowers lined the edge of the cliff, as did one enormous radio tower. It was one of two, the other stationed near the landing zone, southwest of the colony.

The dropship slowed, its bottom thrusters preventing it from smashing into the landing pad beneath it. The pilot eased it onto the platform and shut the engines down.

The crewmember opened the fuselage door. "You have arrived on World Two. Good luck."

The Caparzos followed the crowd onto the platform. The mass adjusters had done their job well. Walking on World Two felt as normal as when they were in North America.

They took their first breath on their new world. The air was rich and pure. Only now did they realize how dirty the air on World One was. For a brief moment, Vince found himself wishing he had one back home.

Home. He needed to stop thinking of World One as such. General Pyre had made it loud and clear that his new assignment was permanent. Permanence was one word that was never altered by the government's constant corruption of human language. When one was *permanently* relocated, it truly meant to the end of his or her days, including the retirement years.

His mental conditioning would take a while. It was a change that happened fairly quick. During the flight, he devoted himself completely to studying this new world. During that time, however, it still felt like just another assignment. Only now, it was truly hitting him that he was millions of miles away from everything he knew.

Almost everything.

Lucy spun around on her tiptoes, completely enthralled.

Together, they gazed upon their red surroundings. The skies to the south were dark and murky. Mountainous landscapes dominated the region. One particularly large one caught Vince's attention. He had read about the increase in volcanic activity following the installation of mass adjusters. Though he had not yet memorized the location of each active volcano, he suspected he was looking at one. Had he been in charge, he would have placed the flagship colony further away from such a hostile location. Then again, he understood why it was here. The largest methane deposits were discovered in this region. These deep wells could be mined for decades, nearly a century according to some experts. Not only were the colonists mining to ship fuel to World One, but they were mining to power their own homes.

He stepped off the platform onto the barren soil. It felt like the rough landscape of Death Valley, a name he now found more suitable for this region.

"Whoa!" Lucy pointed to a huge gorge far in the distance. It was a mile further southwest, visible only because of its enormous size. It stretched far to the west and hooked to the north past some drilling stations. "What is that?"

Vince turned to look. "I'm not sure."

"That's the Ice River. Not so icy anymore."

Vince rotated to his right as two individuals wearing standard uniforms approached. One was a male, close to his height, well-built and straight-forward in his attitude. The other was a female, much smaller in height and build, of Asian descent.

Both had the trident insignia on their shoulders.

"Basically," the man continued, "it originally was a large stretch of ice, which cracked during the planet warming process, forming the crevice. Over time, it melted completely, forming the Ice River." The man finally offered his salute. "Lieutenant, Corporal Tarseas reporting for duty. I've been assigned to your unit."

Vince looked the trident over.

"Where's your armor and helmet?"

Tarseas lifted his bag. "Pardon me, sir. We're not on duty yet."

"You're a trident, Corporal. You may not be on shift, but you're always on duty."

Tarseas nodded. "Aye-aye, Lieutenant."

Vince looked to the woman. "And you are?"

She saluted. "Private Nellen Yasutake, sir."

"That's it?" Vince looked around. "You two are all I get?"

"Us, and thirty-four others," Tarseas said. "It's a babysitting job somewhere on the outskirts. At least, that's what our Whirlybird pilot told me."

"Alright," Vince said. "Stand by. Lucy, hang with these tridents. I need to go to Command Central and retrieve my orders."

"Do you have time?" she asked. She had the look of someone running late for their flight.

Vince chuckled. "Kid, I'm the commanding officer. They can't leave without me. Follow these tridents to the launch pad and I'll catch up with you."

"She'll be safe with us, sir," Tarseas said.

Vince returned his salute, then took a small shuttle to the transit station. There, he boarded a transit shuttle which set course to Hope Central.

It operated like an old fashioned subway, except that instead of traveling through grimy tubes constructed from concrete, he was traveling under thick glass. He could see the sky above. The clouds were as red as the soil. The sun's rays appeared to be as bright as on World

One, though that may have been due to the reflectors. The sun itself was definitely smaller. A hundred-and-fifty-million miles made a hell of a lot of difference.

Everywhere he looked, there were colonists. Inside the domes, they were dressed in their normal attire, not requiring a rebreather. One thing he noticed right away was the cleanliness of the place. On World One, there was hardly a corner of the planet-wide city that didn't have some kind of litter blowing in the wind. Here, there was hardly a speck. Even the people themselves looked clean, except the ones coming in from outside. There was a sense of dignity and order. Perhaps Governor Lovell had a better leash on these people than everyone thought. Then again, petty details like this were not important, except for government and military personnel.

Twelve other people occupied the shuttle car. Whenever Vince wasn't watching out the window, he was observing those around him. It was quiet in here. Everyone minded their own business. A few eyes wandered in his direction. If there was any disturbance to the calm, it was due to the sudden increase in military personnel. Project Oversight had begun and it was clear most of the colonists were not pleased about it.

Vince found himself eyeing a gentleman in the corner. He was just an average-looking colonist, reading a morning article on his tablet. What stood out to Vince was how the man operated the thing. Almost every motion was with his left hand.

Maybe Lovell was indeed being too lenient on the colonists. It was taught from the first days of schooling that everyone be right-handed. It was about maintaining order and discipline, to weed out what the authorities considered mutations to the human state.

Vince looked at the others. From what he could see, everyone else appeared to be right-handed. Perhaps there was nothing to it. He took his mind elsewhere. The Alliance had never conjured up left-handedness as a criminal offense. It was simply eliminated from one's tendencies.

The shuttle passed through the first dome. Lights flashed up ahead for people near that section of the transit station, warning them of the approaching shuttle. He got his first view of a dome's interior.

This section of the colony had everything: living quarters, an emergency response station, local businesses including restaurants. Tridents patrolled the streets on foot. Interestingly, he saw plenty of firearms in the hands of civilians. The reports had stated this was an issue with the World Two colonies, and that the administration had been lenient on workers operating outside the domes. It was not so bad here in Hope, but elsewhere, there was still the threat of wildlife. That was part of Vince's mission. He was not only to police the colonists, but to provide protection. Peace and Prosperity was a phrase commonly used by the Alliance, and his World Two post orders were filled with it.

Considering the incident at Espinosa and the civilians' collective unease toward the influx of tridents, Vince suspected Code C-42 would soon be in effect.

After passing through three domes, the shuttle arrived in Hope Central. As he observed from the outside, it was the largest dome. From inside, it was impressively large. Better yet, the inner layer of glass was equipped with visual transmitters which imitated World One daylight. The setting was Hawaii, particularly Kauai. Like Alaska, it was one of the few areas with some shred of nature intact. It was one of the few areas on that planet where golden sunshine managed to appear in its full glory.

Drones cruised along the ceiling like houseflies trying to escape through a window. Like the ones outside, they inspected every square inch of the structure.

The buildings were tall, some stretching near to the dome's ceiling. Despite the abundance of people and buildings, there was a remarkable amount of open space. Like the other domes and the transit tunnels, everything was remarkably clean.

This was especially true in the block surrounding the Governor's mansion. There was always a cleaning crew nearby, polishing the front steps, applying a fresh coat of paint, or otherwise maintaining the area. Unlike the rest of the colony, this was a clear instance of government enforcement. It was consistent with the government buildings on World One. The Alliance, despite claiming otherwise, were never strict on the appearance of their inner cities. Their own facilities, however, were constantly being tended to.

Down the street was a fairly large gathering headed by three military officers. They sat behind a large plastic desk set up on wobbly legs. Behind them were several large containers loaded with assignment pucks. Each puck contained the specific details to the individual assignments, detailing population, inventory, layout of defensive operations, as well as top-secret information.

Vince stood in line behind a few other officers awaiting their puck. As he waited, he heard a familiar voice nearby. He looked to the Governor's mansion. Down the steps came General Pyre, walking beside Colonel Segan and Governor Lovell. Since his private meeting in his office, Vince had a decent sense of Pyre's temperament. Currently, he was expressing displeasure with the Governor and Colonel.

The exchange that followed confirmed that suspicion.

"It has been nearly twenty days and your people have still not located the traitors," Pyre said.

"It is dangerous territory, General," Lovell said. "The Blackout Hills are full of dangerous fauna. I'm sure you understand…"

"I understand three men have evaded your efforts. Or lack thereof," Pyre said.

"With all due respect, it's highly likely that those men are dead," Lovell said. "We've lost many people in the Blackout. We're still discovering new species, many of them highly dangerous…"

"Spare me, Governor," Pyre said, raising his hand commandingly. "How is it that I've been on this planet for five minutes and yet I somehow know it better than you? He's in league with the Martians. You know it and I know it. *That* is how Dr. Warren has evaded capture. But he can't stay down there forever. He and his companions likely return to the surface periodically. If patrols were more thorough, you might've caught him by now."

"Sir, it's a large area…"

Pyre stopped in his track and turned to look at him. "Is running this planet too much for you, Governor?"

Lovell clasped his hands over his belt, breaking eye contact with the General.

"We… we shall increase our efforts."

The General pivoted and continued walking. "You've had almost three weeks to do that. It's my turn. Once the excavation equipment is ready, we will head out to the Blackout Hills where they disappeared and dig them out. Any Martian gets in the way, we'll dig them out too. The nice thing about living underground is that your home can double as a grave."

Pyre looked straight ahead at the Lieutenant. Vince broke eye contact, only to immediately reobtain it.

"General."

"Lieutenant." Pyre tilted his head towards the table. "You make habit of holding up lines?"

Vince looked in front of him, realizing the tridents ahead of him had retrieved their pucks. Several others bunched up behind him, waiting their turn. He stepped to the table and gave the desk officer his name. After typing a few notes on the keyboard, the officer reached into one of the storage containers behind him and pulled out a black puck.

Vince signed off on it, then stepped out of line. He pressed a button, triggering an electronic voice from its speaker.

"Centauri Colony. Report to Flight Three-Thirteen."

Pyre and Segan approached. Behind them, the Governor gladly went about his way in hopes of avoiding further chastisement from the General.

Pyre looked at the puck, then at Vince. "You look disappointed."

"Never," Vince replied.

"I would be," Segan said with a laugh. "Centauri Colony. Have fun with that one."

Vince had half-a-thought of telling the Colonel off. This was the same guy who allowed himself to be humiliated by simple colonists armed with inferior single-shot guns.

Who am I to talk?

"May I ask why?" Vince said.

"It's the least desirable location," the Colonel said. "They've had three reported casualties in the past week alone."

"Hostiles?" Vince asked.

"Occupational hazards, by the looks of it," Pyre said. "Wildlife, accidents, disease."

Vince made the mistake of breaking eye contact again.

Pyre snapped his fingers, keeping the Lieutenant's attention on him. "Would you have preferred I not have pulled any strings?"

There was only one answer to that.

"Negative, sir."

The General was satisfied with that answer. "Colonel Segan, we'll reconvene later."

"Aye, sir." The Colonel stepped away, leaving Pyre to speak with Vince alone.

Pyre's stance softened, much to Vince's surprise. The stern look in his eyes shifted into something a little more comforting. Vince had heard of his reputation. He was a hard man who demanded nothing but the very best from his men, but he still cared for their well-being. Unlike the government, Pyre did not see his tridents as simple cannon fodder. Being a general, he was perfectly willing to make the tough calls which often sent hundreds of men to their deaths, but he never did it arbitrarily.

"It's the best bet you're gonna get after Alaska, son."

Vince nodded. At least Pyre didn't give the illusion that this job would be a walk in the park. The Lieutenant exhaled, ridding himself of all anxiety and disappointment. Perspective was key. The General saved his life from the firing squad. With that in mind, a babysitting assignment at a hazardous colony did not sound so bad.

"I lied before, sir," he said. "I *am* disappointed... that I can't personally hunt down the rest of those green-grass scum back on World One."

"That's a job for someone else," Pyre said. "Bury those feelings, Caparzo. You have a more important mission ahead of you." The General brought up his own puck. From a projector in its center rose a blue-tinted region map. On this holographic image were markers labeling several colonies. He scrolled farthest to the east, settling on the one labeled Centauri.

"These colonists are already giving pushback to this exchange of hats," he continued. "Segan has managed to keep the people in Hope and the inner-circle colonies in check. A place as far out as Centauri has not had much government oversight. Sure, they have administrators, but let's face it, they're installed by the citizenry. They made up a lot of their own rules over the decades, many of which have been deemed outdated. Bottom line, they think they're self-sufficient, meaning they won't take well to you showing up."

"Sounds like a personal problem," Vince said.

"Indeed. Put them in their place. Use force if you have to. More importantly, figure out if they know anything about Dr. Douglas Warren. I plan to use the excavation equipment to dig him out, and I will if I have to. That said, it's a large area to cover. So, any data you obtain that leads to his capture might grant you favor from myself and those on World One."

Vince nodded. He understood the hidden meaning behind that statement. Promotion, reassignment to an inner-circle colony, and in time, maybe even reinstatement to World One.

"You should be a motivational speaker, General."

Pyre cracked a smile. "I once heard someone say that to your father." The quick moment of levity came to an end, and the General was back to being all business. "You're in charge out there, Caparzo. Anything goes wrong, report directly to my command. Understood?"

"Aye-aye, sir."

Pyre did an about-face and began walking back to the Governor's mansion.

***

Flight Three-Thirteen was a large Whirlybird, similar to those he rode on World One. Despite its heavily marked exterior, the superiority of this model was plain as day. It was equipped with four dragonfly-class turbo engines, which would manage the eleven-thousand kilometer trip in twelve hours. It was a flight that would make four stops, the last being Centauri Colony. Seated inside the Whirlybird were over a hundred other tridents, ready to be transported to other colonies on the outskirts.

Standing outside the fuselage were thirty-six tridents, all of whom looked in Vince's direction as he approached. Most of them were in full gear, their faces obscured behind their masks. Others wore utilities, like Corporal Tarseas and Nellen Yasutake.

One trident saluted. "Sergeant Elias, at your command, Lieutenant. I've assembled your unit."

Vince returned the salute. "At ease." He gave his unit a casual lookover. "It's Centauri Colony for us. Once you arrive, you'll get quartered. During the flight, I will work on providing post-orders to all over. I expect you to study them and know them by heart. In the meantime, strap yourselves in and enjoy the ride. We're on duty the moment we get there."

"Sir, yes sir!" the tridents replied.

They boarded the Whirlybird, taking their seats in the back. Lucy was already seated in the final row, looking out the window.

Vince took a seat behind her. She made sure to offer him a salute as well, with a smirk on her face, of course. He decided to play along and salute her back.

"Should have a good view," she said, thumbing the window on her left.

"Won't see much other than red sand," Vince said.

"Might see more than that," Lucy said. "Maybe herds of ollubs. You know? Horned buffalo-looking things?"

Vince said nothing. He read about them in his documents. They didn't sound like anything he should concern himself with. As long as they were left alone, they typically did not cause trouble.

A dull echo reverberated from the west. Immediately, several tridents were peering out the portside windows.

"Whoa!" Tarseas exclaimed.

The ground shook. Little crackling sounds popped off like fireworks in the distance.

Vince had to nudge Lucy aside for a good look. What he saw was a mountain of fire encompassing one of the drilling stations. Several workers fled the explosion, many of them ablaze.

"Oh!" Lucy covered her mouth.

"What just happened?" Nellen Yasutake asked.

One of the flight crew looked to the window and shook his head. "Ha! Dummies."

Nellen shot him with a hard stare. "That funny to you? People are on fire."

The crewmember shrugged, not even batting an eye.

"Private, when you've been here as long as I have, you'll find it funny too. A methane geyser formed there about a month ago. They've popped up everywhere since the gravity alteration. All it takes is a little flame to make them go boom. Those idiots out there should've installed a placeholder container before attempting to pop that pimple."

Lucy looked to her father. "Should we help them?"

Vince continued watching the chaos unfold. Drones rushed in to assist, pulling bodies and body *parts* from the burning wreckage. Debris fell all around as the extractor unit broke apart.

Fire, bodies, chaos. It was something Vince had grown all too familiar with. As the situation unfolded, more injuries became evident.

Alarms rang out throughout the west side of the colony. Moments later, response teams were racing to the scene.

"No," he replied. "As you can see, their own people can handle this." He centered himself in his chair and clipped his harness. "Enough chit-chat. We've got eleven-thousand kilometers to cross. Hope you don't get airsick." He leaned over Lucy to activate a comm unit under the window. "Pilots, get us moving."

The order was swiftly followed. The Whirlybird lifted off the platform and flew east. In a few moments, the blazing fire appeared no bigger than a candlelight.

CHAPTER 16

Centauri Colony.

Anastacia awoke every thirty minutes or so. The hospital cots were several years old and rock hard. The chairs were a little better. She would have preferred them if they reclined. Sadly, they didn't. Between the uncomfortable mattress, the blinking of hospital monitors, and the storm that was her concerned mind, Anastacia Drucus struggled to find sleep.

Dr. LaFonte had put Patrick in a medically-induced coma. The few times he had awoken were thankfully brief, for they were moments of intense agony and confusion. Having your lungs partially broken down by minerals was no small thing.

The past few weeks had been an onslaught of personal responsibility and personal grievances. It was difficult for Anastacia to focus on work while her husband was clinging to life. Making the situation even worse was the fact that the DZ-5 supply was nearly depleted. Dr. LaFonte had managed to stretch the two-week supply for an extra week by giving partial doses. All in all, it seemed to work in Patrick's case. Perhaps he wasn't exposed to the mineral as badly as they initially thought. Regardless, it was still bound to get worse once the meds ran out. What would follow was immense pain. With each breath, Patrick would feel as though a razor wire was wrapped around his lungs. He would be on morphine, the one drug everyone had plenty of, for the rest of his life. All two weeks of it, at most.

Anastacia moved to the chair and scooted it to be by Patrick's bed. There, she leaned to the side, using his thigh as a pillow. Though her back complained, she liked it better than the cot. Being near her husband was comforting. She liked to believe that, though he was unconscious, it was somehow comforting for him as well.

She dozed in and out for another hour before the door opened. Hazy-eyed, she looked at Dr. Carlos LaFonte. He wasn't surprised to see her, nor was she to see him at this hour.

"Don't you have a home to go to?" she said. It was a variation of the same old joke. Truly, it felt as though Carlos lived in this hospital.

Usually, he would offer a response such as 'I practically do live here, it seems.' Today, he went straight to the point.

"Anastacia, go home."

"I want to be here," she said.

"I know, and that's a good thing," he replied. "But you're exhausting yourself. The situation is obviously stressful beyond words. Combined with the fact that your job responsibilities have increased, you're pushing yourself to burnout. Go home. Get a couple hours of decent sleep. You're gonna need it. The 'new arrivals' will be here in the morning."

Anastacia rubbed her eyes. "I do. Has there been any word on our 'overseer'?" She made sure to make air quotes.

"I spoke to someone from Cook's office. Some guy named Caparzo."

"Yeah?" Anastacia waited for the rest of the answer. Carlos was a hard-working guy, whose only free time was spent reading news on the solar-net. News from World One traveled faster than the freighters. Carlos, being a curious type, undoubtedly looked up any public information available on this Caparzo guy.

"He was a special forces captain. He has quite the resume, actually."

"Great," Anastacia muttered. "Apparently not that good. Not if he's being sent all the way over here. Which means he's both a hard ass and a screwup. That's the most dangerous individual to put in a leadership position."

"Anastacia," Carlos' voice had a gentle, fatherly touch, "I want you to go home. Please. Get some semblance of rest. Don't worry about Patrick. I'll take care of him."

The instinctual urge to debate crept into her throat, but Anastacia suppressed the words. Carlos was right. A lot was riding on her shoulders. The Alliance commander was here to oversee progress, and a large aspect of that included geological reports. Personal contact with him was inevitable. It was best she not be hazy-eyed for their first meeting.

"Okay."

She gave her husband a kiss and went out the door, thanking Carlos by affectionally squeezing his arm on the way.

***

It was oh-seven-fifty when Anastacia arrived at the lab. She wondered if sleeping in her bed was a mistake. Being in that familiar and much comfier mattress, the exhausted geologist had fallen into a deep sleep that was nearly impossible to awaken from.

It was just another stone that formed the mountain of frustration. Any other day, she would have called the office and said she would be in late, allowing herself an extra few hours of rest. Not today.

One thing was for sure: this morning would require a trip to Antonio's café. Coffee was demanded and *needed* on World Two as much as anywhere else in the universe. With the planet lacking the soil necessary for growing coffee farms, the colonists were reliant on a few producers who smuggled in some South American soil and Arabica plants. They produced as much as possible, but given the fact that they had such a small area to work with, only a limited quantity was available for the colonists.

Anastacia managed to beat the morning rush at the café before arriving at the Science Center. It was a three-story building located next to the local school. Kids were pouring into their building, chatting amongst themselves without a care in the world. Every so often while approaching the front doors, Anastacia would hear some of them express their eagerness to grow up and start their career. Every time she bit her tongue to keep herself from interjecting.

No, kid. Enjoy the bliss and ignorance of childhood. Adulthood sucks.

She entered the Science Center and took the elevator to the third floor. The coffee was mostly gone by the time she entered the geology lab.

Her small staff was doing their usual routine, most of which comprised of collating data on numerous finds in the area. Rocks were studied, seismic waves were monitored, and new scans were conducted to determine new drilling sites. So far, most of the areas were in the cursed Blackout Hills.

At the moment, Anastacia was concerned with the wreckage from that shrine she inadvertently blew up.

A chunk of it was secured in a glass table. Being a portion with the most intact inscriptions, they decided to keep it for analysis.

One of the lab assistants, Victor Cho, was already at work. A twenty-eight-year-old geology major who wore large-rimmed glasses, he was one of the few people who volunteered to work in the outer rim. His special interest was seismic anomalies and volcanoes. Out here, he had both.

"Good morning, Doctor."

"Good morning, Vic."

Knowing she had grown tired of the well-meaning but nonetheless nonstop 'how's Patrick?' and 'how are you doing?' questions, he went straight to business.

"Should we plan to take a rover out to the southeast fields?" he asked. "Considering what's been happening in the Blackout Hills, I suppose we can't rely on that methane site."

Anastacia rubbed her forehead. Efforts to solve the mysterious disappearances only resulted in another person having gone missing.

Victor read the look on her face. "Or… are we still planning to drill up there?"

"According to Hope Central, we will," Anastacia said.

"Yeah? According to Maya Napier, something's out there picking off our crews. I've spoken with some of the guys. They're not very keen on working in that area."

"We've delayed the project, but they'll only tolerate delays for so long. It's a rich site." Anastacia wasn't sure what else to say. She didn't like the idea of going back to the Blackout Hills as much as anyone else. The area around Mt. Vahara wasn't much better. It seemed wherever they went, World Two either had vicious wildlife or dangerous landscape to hinder progress.

Victor, being a decent judge of character, knew it was best to stray from the subject.

"Oh!" he exclaimed as though a thought had just come to mind. "We've gotten some results from our consultants over in Aswan Colony. They believe, as we do, that the inscription is Martian in nature."

Anastacia stood over the glass table which contained the shrine fragment, admiring the strange language.

"It's related, but not the same. I can't make out any of this. If you ask me, it's an entirely different language."

"Their history goes back many thousands of years," Victor said. "Language changes over time. Maybe it's something long forgotten."

Anastacia eyed the broken edges of the slab.

"That makes it even worse that we blew it up." She gave a longing sigh, simultaneously straining to make sense of this thing while forcing her personal woes from her mind. "Maybe I should take a crew back there."

"Shouldn't we wait until our new crewmembers get situated?" Victor asked.

She shook her head. "I'm not sure we'll be getting new crewmembers. This year's transport is mostly focused on flooding World Two with blood-jackets."

"Maybe the Martians could help explain it to us," Victor said with childlike enthusiasm.

Anastacia chuckled. Victor Cho was always the optimist. While the pessimistic side of her wanted to poke fun at him for it, the rational side believed the planet could use more people like him. Enthusiasm was something hard for her to muster these days. In the coming weeks, it would only get worse. Her world felt like a ticking time bomb, and she was watching the clock count down with nothing to stop it.

Focus.

"I wish," she said. "It would help if they did, but they generally prefer to keep their distance. God knows we've caused enough problems already. It's a miracle they've adapted to the changes we've made to this planet."

"What about Dr. Douglas Warren?" Victor said. "Just a thought. If we managed to get in contact with him... I mean, he's in good standing with the Martians."

"You know the situation, Cho. Dr. Warren is an outlaw." Victor stepped around the corner and helped himself to a cup of water. "You don't sound very convinced."

Anastacia sank into one of the desk chairs. She turned her eyes to the numbers scrolling vertically on the right side of the screen, pretending to ignore the statement.

Instead, she chose to respond. Free speech was still accepted in this colony—something that would probably change in the next hour. Her eyes went to the clock in the corner of the screen.

"That's because I prefer to make my own conclusions," she said.

An intercom on the wall buzzed.

"Dr. Drucus, are you in the lab?" It was Bill Cook's voice.

"Yep, I'm here."

"Please have your lab ready for inspection. Our military supervision is about to arrive. Possibly in fifteen minutes. Lieutenant Caparzo will want reports on all progress, including research."

Anastacia's face tensed with anger.

"Copy." She looked at Victor just in time to see him shrug. "What?"

He grinned nervously. "Nothing important."

"You have something you want me to say to Cook?" she said.

"No. Not at all. It's just..." He shrugged again. "Listen, I'm not head-over-heels about these guys coming either. But who knows? Maybe this lieutenant won't be so bad." He watched her expression sour further. "Oh, come on. Are they all that bad?"

Anastacia stood up, her pessimistic side in full force.

"They're tridents. What do you think?"

CHAPTER 17

Flight Three-Thirteen.

The flight was long and dull. With the cover of night, there was little for the passengers to see through the windows. Only after the Merci Colony stop did things get exciting momentarily. The ship gunner had yelled out 'flyers' and armed his turret. A quick burst of plasma fire deterred a small swarm of winged creatures who had gotten a little too curious about the Whirlybird. "Good thing it was only three," the gunner had said, "or else it would've been a real party!"

Two more stops were made after that, unloading passengers, and refueling. That process was aggravating for the Centauri platoon, whose sleep was interrupted so they could place their rebreathers on before the doors opened up. Only through the perimeter lights was Vince able to see the layout of the colony domes. There were some interior lights on as well, like streetlights in the World One cities. It was his first and only glimpse of Ortega Colony and Asagi Colony, two of the other settlements on the outskirts.

But with the coming of dawn came what seemed like a whole new world. The landscape here was different than that on the west. It brought to mind the term peaks and valleys, for every few miles, the landscape appeared to alternate between the two.

To the southeast was a large mountain. As they continued farther east, Vince realized it wasn't just any simple mountain. It was a volcano.

Lovely.

"Wow!" Lucy said.

Vince did not share her glee. Both had read about the increased volcanic activity. For all he knew, that big piece of rock would burst at any moment. His daughter was suffering from what he called 'it'll never happen to me' syndrome.

Her next "wow" came from the sight of a herd of ollubs feeding on the red plains. Like a herd of buffalo, they traveled in unison. Like their extinct World One counterparts, they had curved horns behind their eyes. Far more dangerous was the third horn, located on their nose. Like that of a rhinoceros, it was intended for uprooting sustenance, or gorging enemies.

Demonstrating that fact were two creatures on the right side. Two big bulls, angry at each other for some reason Vince and Lucy would never know, they touched horns. Like medieval swordsmen, they clashed with enough force to kick up dust. As the Whirlybird put the herd behind them, one of the creatures yielded, limping away while the other stood victorious.

As the flight continued, Vince watched the northeast. He could finally see the Blackout Hills. As many others had pointed out, it was more of a mountain range than a series of hills. Whichever it was, it resembled something drawn up from some artist's demented imagination. Every towering rock had its own unique shape. Between his studies and the pure sight of it all, Vince knew it was a place where predators could easily hide.

The talkative Corporal Tarseas was awake by this point and watching the world go by. His interest was sparked by an erupting methane geyser which spat flames on the southwest. An unlucky flying creature had flown too close, its body smoldering a dozen yards away.

"Home sweet home," the Corporal said.

"That it is," the crewmember said. He looked at the Lieutenant. "Sir, we're about two miles out. Hope the flight was satisfactory."

"Arrival in one piece is satisfactory enough," Vince said. "Have the pilots made an announcement to the colony?"

"Yes, sir."

Vince looked to his thirty-six tridents. "Alright. Wake up anyone who's still asleep. Duty is about to begin. We'll be setting down in three minutes."

***

When Anastacia Drucus exited the exterior airlock, she found Bill Cook and his counsel already awaiting the new arrivals. He was rocking on his heels and twiddling his thumbs. In the coming minutes, he was going to be usurped as the head authority in this area. His title and pay grade would remain, but every decision was subject to Lieutenant Caparzo's approval.

The Whirlybird was only a speck in the horizon, but the winds of change were already gusting. Nobody, especially the outspoken colonists such as Ed Burger, the animal handler, was happy with this change. Many of them looked to Bill Cook to challenge it, but he was powerless.

He tucked his hands behind his back, striking a stance that projected confidence when he saw Anastacia approach.

"Ready to be told how to run your colony by people who've only been here for half a day?" she said.

Bill scoffed. "What's the difference? If it's not them, it's you."

"Oh, you're funny," she said. "Face it. I make this place radiant."

"Oh, right. You're a real ray of sunshine," he said. "That 'smile' on your face lights up the whole colony." He followed the statement with a half-repressed grin. It was as though he feared his joke wouldn't go over well. The reason Anastacia wasn't smiling was not a laughing matter. It was a talk-think moment, which tended to happen during times of anxiety.

She took no offense. To show this, she laughed with him. As the flight neared, their fake laughs slowed to obscurity.

"This is the way of things," Bill said.

Anastacia shook her head. "It doesn't have to be."

"Yes, it does," he slowly said. "Do me a favor: don't stir up too much trouble."

There was a shrug and a smirk. "You're the boss." She looked to the Whirlybird. "For about two more minutes."

***

After twelve hours, Vince Caparzo and his crew laid eyes on their new home and post. The colony was a little over a mile wide. The sun glinted off of its huge dome, shining over the city within. Like the domes in Hope Colony, Centauri was a large metropolitan area, with most of the buildings comprising the northern half of the dome. The south end of the settlement had surprisingly a lot of green. Trees stood high. A little stream coursed in a long, circular pathway. It was a park. In its center was a gushing fountain, jetting water back into the pond where it stood.

"Oh, wow," Lucy said. "Can we look at that when we go in?"

"We'll have plenty of time, kiddo," Vince said.

He watched the rest of the colony. To the north were five huge storage tankers, one of which was currently being filled by a fuel transport. His mind snapped into its role of the officer in charge. One of the first things he would do was get readings on those tankers. By now, all five should be filled and ready for shipment. Large haulers would deliver the tanks to the pipeline west of Omega Colony, where they would flow to the Grey Harbor to be stored for the next delivery.

The other structures outside of the dome were standard. There were garages, work sheds, watch towers, radio towers, the main generators and backup generators. The only thing he didn't recognize was a rusty building on the northeast side, about two-hundred yards left of the generators. The building covered about two-thousand square feet and had several yards of fencing behind it. There was no mistaking the appearance. It was a corral. What it contained, Vince wasn't sure thanks to the dust being stirred by the Whirlybird's rotors.

The aircraft set down. Its engines eased to their resting state, the rotors slowing to a stop. The fuselage door opened.

Lucy was the first to step out. Hopping on the ground, she stretched her arms and exercised her legs.

"Lucy, don't go too far," Vince said. He stepped outside then waited for his tridents to file out. "Tridents, grab your gear, find your quarters. Housing is located in Sectors forty-through-sixty, located on the northwest side of the colony. Ground transports should be waiting near the atrium. Unload your personals then report to Security Headquarters."

"Aye, aye, sir," the Sergeant said. "Move it, tridents."

They hustled to the airlock with the same urgency as day one of basic training, leaving Caparzo alone to greet the colony staff. The colony administrator approached and extended his hand. Behind him was a woman in her early thirties, who was visibly much less pleased to see him.

"Lieutenant Vince Caparzo, I presume," the man said.

"Correct." Vince looked at his outstretched hand with no intent to shake it. Lucy quickly stepped in and shook Bill's hand instead.

"Lucy Caparzo, sir. Pleasure to be here."

"Bill Cook, colony administrator. It's a pleasure having you here, ma'am," he said. Lucy stepped aside to let her father resume business. Bill, taking the hint that Vince was in no mood for pleasantries, got straight to the point. "As you've probably figured out, we have quarters prepped for you and your men. Despite being one of the farthest reaching colonies, I believe you'll find living here to be relatively comfortable. I'm aware you've had a long trip, so I've requested my staff to prepare sustenance for you…"

"Later," Vince said, walking past Bill to look at the dome. "My work starts now. I'm gonna start by taking a look at this pile of glass I've been assigned to."

Bill turned around to follow him. "Yes, of course. Right this way."

Vince took a left, walking along the dome toward the north side. As he did, he reached out and touched the glass. From the distance, it looked smooth and perfect. Up close, he saw every bit of abuse the shield had endured. The exterior felt like sandpaper, though it was every bit as solid as he hoped it would be. The drones were hard at work like bees crawling over their hive.

His first judgement was toward the storage tankers. He stopped near the leftmost one, his face wrinkling as he looked over the dented metal.

"This is where we store the methane," Bill Cook said. "It's a relatively simple process. It's the most conventional one we were able to construct all the way out here. We have extractors in various parts of the region. Workers draw the methane out, transport it in haulers, which deliver it here to be stored. You probably already know of the pipeline…"

Vince nodded. "I want a map of the sites. From now on, there will be a guard assigned to each one."

"To do what?"

Vince turned around. The stern-faced woman had followed them over here. Right away, he knew she wasn't as eager to please as Administrator Cook was.

He looked to Bill. "Who is this?"

"Pardon me, Lieutenant," Bill said. "This is Dr. Anastacia Drucus. She's head of research. Very good at her job, too. She's found our most valuable methane deposits."

Vince didn't listen to anything beyond the name and title.

"Well, Dr. Drucus…"

"Just call me Anastacia," she said.

Vince exhaled slowly, already annoyed. "*Doctor Drucus*, my tridents will be there to ensure compliance from all workers and properly catalogue their progress."

She crossed her arms. "Why not come out and say you don't trust us?"

"I don't. Satisfied?"

"Why's that? Because of what happened at Espinosa? We're all guilty by association?" she said.

Vince looked to the distant hills in the north. "Supposedly, nobody has heard from Doctor Warren in the last three weeks. I find it a little difficult to believe that nobody has offered to assist him. If not offered, at least felt the temptation."

"That's ludicrous," Anastacia said. "We're miles from Espinosa Colony, Lieutenant."

"Your point?"

She scoffed, believing her point to be obvious. It was, but Vince had no intention of giving weight to any of her arguments. Debate was not going to be allowed. It was his way or the highway. And his way was the way of the Alliance.

"He would have to travel on foot to get anywhere near here," she said. "Even if he took the Martian tunnels, it would take a significant amount   of   time."

"Ah, so you do believe he's in league with the Martians," Vince said.

She started to speak, only to stand slack-jawed with bewilderment. Saying anything on the matter, even speculation, would give him cause for further investigation.

Vince began walking with Bill Cook, quickly, and happily, forgetting the geologist's existence.

"My team will monitor all check-ins and outs, fuel extractions and the amounts taken. They will listen in on all communications, interior and exterior, private and duty-related. All research functions will be cleared through   me."

"Cleared through you?" Anastacia said.

He turned around, annoyed that she was still tagging along.

"Correct."

"You don't need to look over our shoulders," she said.

"Dr. Drucus, please stop," Bill said.

"No, *Bill*," she said, noting his sudden emphasis on titles. "Lieutenant, my team is trustworthy. This whole colony is trustworthy."

"If colonists were trustworthy, I would not be here," Vince said.

"Oh, is that right?" she said. "I took a moment to look at your files. I think we all know why you're here."

Vince noticed the sound of laughter which followed that statement. A few workers standing near the tankers quickly cleared their throats and looked away, realizing they were louder than they intended.

Even Bill Cook was nodding slightly. Some of the staff behind him chuckled at the statement.

At this point, Vince knew his reputation had followed him here.

The amusement came to an abrupt stop when he stepped forward, effectively squaring up with Anastacia. Her amusement faded. Anxiety triggered a few minor twitches. She was on alert. The consequences of playing with fire were plain and simple, even without having been voiced.

"I see we're off to a great start," he said.

"The *start* was when blood-jackets stripped colonies of their own fuel supplies, then followed it up by the arresting and jailing of colonists."

"Does rule of law need to be taught to you, Dr. Drucus?" Vince said. "You think you people own the fuel supply and all of this equipment?" He pointed at the dome, the tankers, and all of the technology around them. "Everything you have was supplied by the Alliance. Without World One, you would not be able to enjoy the luxuries of this assignment."

A sharp, brisk wind struck his uniform. Like tidal waves in the ocean came mountains of dust and sand. Vince held still, confident that his mask would keep its integrity despite the onslaught of particles. For a moment, he could only see the silhouettes of Bill Cook and Anastacia Drucus, watching him. Though he couldn't see their faces, he knew exactly what they were thinking.

Luxuries, huh?

When the wind died down and the dust settled, Vince's black uniform was covered in shades of red. He dusted himself off, then found himself in another staring contest with the irritable geologist.

His eyes went to her hip. She carried a plasma pistol. Probably a Beretta V50. One of the better handheld models. How such weaponry got in the hands of civilians was something General Pyre would certainly investigate in the coming days and weeks.

It was a matter Vince fully supported. He had only been on site for a few minutes, and already the tension was at a razor's edge. Many of the colonists outside the dome carried some kind of weapon. Vince and his tridents were far outnumbered. How could he expect to police an armed society like this?

The answer was simple. Remind them who is in charge. The slightest hint of an uprising here would result in gunships descending on the colony. With that knowledge in the back of his mind, Vince secured the confidence he badly needed.

Before he could state these facts to Anastacia, the silence was broken by his daughter's animated voice.

"Hey, Dad! Over here! Come look at this!"

She was standing by the big corral, close to a canopy that towered over a trough. From what Vince could see, it was an old-fashioned barn and pasture. Nothing special. He was aware that the colonists raised certain livestock for food.

Though disinterested, he decided to walk over. Anything beat a back-and-forth repartee with Anastacia.

Lucy eagerly glanced in his direction. "Look. Over here."

"It's a fence," Vince said. He stood beside her, slapping his hand on the top rail. "And what did I tell you about wandering off too far…"

From the canopy's shade came a flurry of black insectoid legs. Their tips marked the ground as they carried the creature out of the shadows. A screeching sound pierced the air as large mandibles frolicked below the arachnid creature's enormous eyes. It was practically a combination between a beetle and a spider, with slight emphasis on the latter. Whatever it was, Vince's defensive instincts kicked in.

He jumped back and armed his gauntlet. The trigger mechanism extended over his palm, ready to be activated.

To his surprise, nobody else was alarmed by this thing's presence. Not even Lucy. Instead, she watched him with the same amused look that everyone else had. Several workers broke out with laughter. Vince could see a few in his peripheral vision, pointing and laughing at their 'fearless leader'.

Even Lucy couldn't help but giggle a bit.

"Whoa! Whoa! Whoa!" From behind the shelter came a man wearing battered clothes and boots that were completely red from soil exposure. He was balding, a little over fifty-years in age, and had an Aussie accent.

The man entered the pasture and put his hands on the creature's head. He gently rubbed it, calming it down.

"It's alright, girl. Did he scare you?" He turned to look at Vince, smirking when he saw the glowing end of the gauntlet, still pointed at the bug. "What's the matter, blood-jacket? Scared of a little bug?"

Vince powered his gauntlet down, his heart rate slowly easing back into a normal rhythm. "You call *that* a little bug?!"

The animal handler smiled. "Around here, it is."

Bill Cook quickly approached. "Excuse me, Lieutenant. We're all getting used to Ed Burger. He's our wildlife expert and animal handler. He's quite fond of them, despite his name. He's very helpful if we have an issue with predatory wildlife or if we require use of the scarabs."

"Scarabs?" Vince said. "That what you call those... 'little' bug things?"

"Correct," Bill said.

At the fence, Ed Burger filled a small plastic bucket with something that resembled tan powder. He waved Lucy over to the gate entrance and let her inside. Vince suppressed his urge to intervene. Even Bill Cook did not seem bothered by what the nutty animal handler was doing.

"Would you like to feed them, missy?" Ed said to her.

"Sure!"

She took the bucket from him, then extended the open end to the scarab. Several others quickly emerged from the canopy, sensing food.

"Wait your turn, fellas," Ed said to them.

Lucy smiled ear-to-ear as the first scarab used an extendable proboscis to eat its foot.

"Good. Just like that," Ed said. He helped guide the bucket away from the scarab so the next one could have a turn. "So, you're the Lieutenant's daughter?"

"Yep!"

"Your life must be full of laughs."

Lucy shrugged. "It has its moments."

"Hey, Lucy?" Vince called. He pointed his thumb to the dome's airlock. "Come on, kid. I've got work to do. Can't be leaving you out here."

"Okay." Lucy handed the bucket back to Ed. "Thanks for letting me help."

"My pleasure," Ed said.

Lucy exited the corral and ran to catch up with her father. As they neared the airlock, Vince glimpsed over his shoulder at Anastacia, who was in the middle of a quick chit-chat with Ed. A moment later, she was headed for the airlock.

Great.

Vince and Lucy followed Bill Cook through the first door and through a solid glass tunnel, with pressure doors placed for added security. After an annoyingly long time passing through the atrium, they arrived on the inside of the dome.

Vince took his mask off and beheld the sight of Centauri Colony.

Though he wouldn't admit it, it was like entering a new world, yet one that was strangely familiar. The structures and layout were somewhat similar to World One, but with cleaner air, green grass, and people who looked, of all things, happy. The dome was decently populated—Vince's puck indicated over three-thousand colonists—but it was not crammed.

Leading straight from the atrium was a main road, comprised of pavement. There were subtle cracks in the ground section where the floor segments of the dome were assembled. Vince's puck had explained in specific detail how the floor segment was comprised, and what was built under the cozy lawns. Unknown to the colonists, there were security details that only he and other high-ranking officials knew about.

"Everything alright, Dad?" Lucy said.

"Hmm? Oh, yes. Just, you know, looking." He stopped studying the ground area and walked farther into the colony. To the left were restaurants and shops, with colonists freely moving in and out of the front entrances. Most of the buildings did not surpass two floors. The only exceptions was the colony hospital, which he could see farther back, the Administration Building, the Science Center, and a couple of others.

On the south side of the colony was the park area. Trees stood high, their bright green leaves flourishing. He could hear the little river flowing and the fountain drizzling water.

Then there was the air. It was amazingly clean. Vince had noticed it back in Hope Colony, but here it really stood out.

Something else that stood out was a flag of Circular Peace waving *above* the Alliance flag. These people had the audacity to develop their own flag in accordance with the local species. Not only that, but they had adopted their own pledge.

In bold black letters, it was inscribed on a marble slab which faced the atrium, positioned as though intended to be the first thing a person saw upon entering the dome.

From the slopes of Olympus Mons
To the craters of Chryse
Through fire and ice,
The blackness beyond the stars,
And the Shadow of Death
We found home in each other.

Before Almighty God
I pledge
My life to my world
My heart to its virtue
My word to the voiceless
My strength to the weak
My wrath against evil.

Against the blackest dark
Our Republic shines bright.

Vince was frozen, staring at that word 'republic'. It was written as though this place was separate from the Alliance. Sure, they flew the flag... a tattered, worn version of the flag, *underneath* the inferior Circular Peace flag.

He was so fixated on this absurdity that he didn't realize that Administrator Cook and Lucy were in the middle of a conversation. A kiss-up type, the Administrator was clearly hoping to gain favor by bonding with the overseer's daughter.

"Wow," Lucy said. She took a deep breath of the clean air. "So fresh."

"The vast majority of industrial activities take place outside the dome," Bill said. "Our artificial atmosphere in this dome does not contain the fumes that World One's inhabitants are exposed to on a daily basis."

Lucy ran up to the nature park. On the way, she passed a half-dozen colonists, each who extended their welcome.

"Thank you!" she repeated. At the fountain, she was mesmerized by the flourishing lilies and sunflowers. Gently, she touched the petals, then looked back at the administrator. "Are these real?"

"They are," Bill proudly said. "They're grown from a few samples that we were able to harvest from World One. We use the water from the ice rivers to wet their roots. Over time, it became a beautiful preserve. It's good for the eyes. Good for the soul, if you ask me. Maybe one day, we'll figure out how to make them grow outside the dome. The original intent was to use these plants to help people cope with the harsh environment. Now, it's become part of what drives us."

"Yeah?" Vince said. He had a scanner in hand, pointed at one of the shops across the main road. "Coping, huh? Is that your justification for letting people operate unregistered businesses?" He completed the scan, then nodded at the building in question. "That bar there. It's not in the registry. If it's not in the registry, then it's not on the tax roster. Meaning someone here has been double dipping."

Bill struggled to maintain his smile. "Double dipping…"

"They get paid by the Alliance *and* they make money from their little tax-free enterprise," Vince clarified. "It's a violation."

"A very miniscule violation, sir," Bill said. Vince's intensified stare made him regret pushing back.

"Miniscule. I've put away many thieves who have used the same logic." Vince shut the scanner down. "I scanned one building at random and found a violation. Something tells me this colony is riddled with 'miniscule' issues. It helps explain why you missed your quota the last two cycles. You people spent too much time worrying about grass, trees, and flowers, making this place look like World One."

"Dad," Lucy said. "It's nice. By the way, it looks *nothing* like World One. Maybe how it used to look…"

"Kiddo…" Vince swallowed, narrowly preventing himself from chastising her in front of the colony staff. Instead, he escorted her to a shuttle that was waiting on the side of the road. It had been a long flight between planets, bookended by a twelve-hour flight in a packed Whirlybird. The kid needed a real bed for a change.

"Mr. Cook, there will be regular inspections for every residence and business starting tomorrow. This is the only announcement I will make on the matter. They will be random and thorough. Later on, I expect a full detailed report on current methane procedures."

"Certainly, Lieutenant," Bill Cook said. At this point, he could not keep up the friendly façade any longer.

Vince opened the passenger door for Lucy, then took the seat next to her. "Sector November-Eight-Seven," he told the driver.

The shuttle took them through a series of streets. All the while, Vince observed the living quarters. They were not high-rises like the others. These were larger, individual structures. They were packed close together, many in two-story buildings, but certainly unlike the approved setup provided by the Alliance.

There were some open areas in each neighborhood which contained playgrounds and various workstations. Everyone was right at home, living life as though they had been on this planet since birth. There was an energy on display here that was lacking even in Hope Colony. Though the tech was all familiar, it felt as if Vince had been assigned to a completely different civilization, one that was detached from the ways of the Alliance.

The shuttle arrived in Sector N-87. Vince opened the fuselage door and observed the neighborhood. It resembled old suburban housing from times past. Most of the buildings over here were single-story. Though crammed together to accommodate the dome's population, they were plenty specious and were even equipped with a front lawn.

Lucy hurried to their property and felt the grass. "It's real."

"Could be synthetic," Vince said.

"Don't think so," she said. "Either way, I like it."

Vince looked at their quarters. "This is it?"

"Yes, sir," the shuttle driver said.

"It's too big," Vince said. He looked at the row of units lining the street. Families moved in and out of their front doors, enjoying family life. Some were even cooking on outdoor grill units. Not only did it feel as though he was in a different civilization, but it was also as though he had gone back in time.

Lucy, youthful and optimistic, ran for the front door. Resigned, Vince dismissed the shuttle driver and followed her inside.

They entered a spacious living room area. It alone matched the size of the living quarters they were used to on World One. There was a sofa and a chair, the fabric a bit used but still in good condition. To the back was the kitchen and utility area, cleaned and shined. Between the kitchen and living room were two small hallways, one on each side of the unit, which led to the bedrooms.

"Wow!" Lucy said. "This was supposed to be your punishment?! If I had known our living situation would be like this, I would've begged you to get reassigned out here."

Vince was not sure what to make of it. Since birth, he had been taught that homes this size and larger were reserved for the powerful and super wealthy. Humans did not need such space. That was the conditioning. You can eat, you can sleep. Grand space was not required for either.

"I've seen worse," he said, feigning disinterest.

"Is it part of your job to be such a killjoy?" Lucy said.

"I'm not here to make friends with these colonists," he replied.

"That's just it. They're colonists, not aliens. They're not our enemies, Dad. They're just trying to make a life for themselves. May I say, they're doing a darn good job of it."

Vince stepped into the kitchen area. "I see you're already making friends."

"That Ed Burger guy? Yeah, I guess. He seems friendly." She covered her mouth and started laughing. "You should've seen your face when that scarab arrived."

The pain of a bruised ego began to throb in Vince's temples. His first impression on the colonists was incompetence and unease. It was no wonder Anastacia was so eager to confront him.

He managed to smirk at Lucy's remark. "You were just as frightened."

"Nice try!" she said. "Scarabs don't eat flesh. Apparently, you didn't study the files on wildlife."

"Sure I did."

"Riiiight." Lucy picked up her bag and took the bedroom on the right. No longer did she sleep in a tiny, enclosed compartment. Now, she had her very own room. She plopped on the bed, which was also larger than what she was accustomed to. "Mmm. This is great. They really live freely here."

"That's the problem," Vince said from his room.

"If you say so."

"They're just trying to make a good first impression," Vince said.

"Yeah, a first impression. That explains why every unit is just like this one."

Vince stepped into the kitchen area. "Everyone has a motivation for what they do, and it's usually self-serving. You saw how everyone was looking at us. Trust me, they are *not* our friends."

"It doesn't make them our enemies," Lucy replied. "We'll be sharing this planet with them. I don't want to feel like we're at war. Isn't it the responsibility of Tridents to protect civilians?"

"Yes. Loyal ones."

"I read somewhere that it's better to inspire loyalty rather than demand it."

"'Read somewhere'? *Where'd* you read that?" Vince said.

Lucy didn't respond, nor did she need to. Vince knew where that nonsense was coming from. It appeared it would take more than a hundred-and-sixty-million miles of distance to rid her of the propaganda of that book.

"I'm just saying it's better to think outside the box," Lucy said.

Vince snorted. "You're a smart girl, Lucy. But don't forget you're only nine. You have lots to learn."

"Ten."

Vince's throat tightened. *Wait a second...* He thought back on the months and dates. Last month was August... her birthday being on the third. It was the end of September now. New humiliation took hold. Vince had been so consumed in his duties, to his loyalty to the Alliance, he had given no thought to his daughter's birthday.

"Ten. Right. I knew that." He returned to his room and began unpacking. "You're a little old for celebrations, I suppose. Now, go get your stuff sorted. You have school at oh-seven-hundred."

"Right." The disappointment in Lucy's voice was distinct.

Vince found himself staring at his bag. Self-loathing compressed his stomach. He hated that he liked this new living unit. What he really hated was the fact that Lucy liked it. He hated his assignment, the failure that led up to it, the policing he would have to do. Vince was a soldier, not a babysitter. His dreams of following his father's footsteps involved commanding battalions, not enforcing rules on measly colonists and reporting methane numbers to somebody else.

Hate. It was the key word, driven into the mind of every trident. Hate your enemy. Hate those who would do you harm. Hate those who go against the Alliance. It certainly made killing easier.

What was one to do when they hated themselves? Killing wasn't the answer. Vince wasn't suicidal, but even if he was, it would only cause more problems. Tridents, especially officers, were forbidden in taking their own lives. The justification was that the Alliance had invested too much time and resources into each soldier for them to be wasted in a moment of self-pity. The punishment would go into the family members, including fines, lashes, and imprisonment.

Thus lay the answer. Endure the pain, for it was only a thing of the mind. Endure it for the sake of the Alliance.

Vince closed his eyes and exhaled. He rid himself of the weight of his burden. It was all in the name of something greater.

The only guilt that remained was the failure of parenthood.

Duty first. She'll just have to understand that. One day, the time will come when she'll serve the Alliance. Maybe then, she'll truly understand. The time for kiddie stuff has come to an end.

CHAPTER 18

Blackout Hills – Several miles northwest of Centauri Colony.

It was night when Godon opened the exterior passageway. The tunnel entrance spiraled, revealing a fairly clear night full of glistening stars. Had the occasion been different, Dr. Douglas Warren would have happily taken the opportunity to admire the rare, cloudless sky. It had been gradually improving over the years. A decrease in the frequency of volcanic eruptions played a role in that. In another few years, the clouds would settle and the universe would gaze upon the colonies. Assuming the Alliance didn't screw it up beforehand.

Preston Gosly stepped out into the open with Warren. The area was black as space. Even with the sparkling skies and the silvery reflection of Phobos, visibility was still low. The surrounding rocks were still barely visible.

Warren turned to the north, only to be quickly grabbed by Preston. Nothing needed to be said. The pointing of a finger directed his attention to the cliff edge that was ten feet in that direction.

"Thank you." Warren backed away. He had not been out of the tunnel for thirty seconds and already he was nearly killed.

"I don't know, Doctor," Preston said, shaking his head. "If we were in the Valley, that would be one thing. But we're in the Blackout. Crossing though this terrain would be suicide."

"Damn," Warren said. "Davy can't wait much longer."

"I'm fine, Douglas."

They looked down the tunnel at their friend. All things considered, he was looking okay. His veins were discolored and he was severely lethargic, but his heart rate and respiration were still okay. It was something that would not last, however.

"If only I had a credit for every time I heard a patient say that to me," Warren said.

He looked at the landscape once more, fighting against his desperation to trek through the hills. A screeching cry echoed from somewhere behind that sea of rocks.

Preston shuddered as something scurried nearby. He could not see it, but the sound of razor-sharp nails scraping against rocks could not be mistaken.

"It is dangerous," Godon said. "We are in an area of death and decay."

"Yeah… it's called the Blackout," Preston said.

"This area is rife with demons," Godon continued. "Soulless beasts that live to kill. Human. *Vactullan.* Animal. There is no peace in this region."

Preston looked to Warren. "Is he implying this part of the Blackout is worse than the other ten-plus-thousand miles?" Warren nodded. Preston lowered his head. "Terrific. We've wandered into an area so deadly, even the Martians are afraid of it. If we make it to the colony, I'm gonna need a fifth of Scotch… if they have any."

"You'll probably have to settle for Red Ale," Davy Austin said.

"Ugh. Generic crap," Preston muttered.

"Godon, are you suggesting we make camp and wait until morning?" Warren said.

"I am," Godon replied.

"What about other tunnels?" Warren asked. "There's got to be a passageway that leads into the valley. Somewhere safer."

Godon shook his head, then panned his long finger at the surrounding area. "All passages are gone. Crumbled to dust."

"Oh, no," Warren muttered.

"What does he mean?" Preston asked.

"There *were* underground tunnels which would've been more convenient, but the earthquakes caused by the gravity alteration caused them to collapse. Previous efforts by the Martians to make new tunnels resulted in many deaths, first from sickness from the changes to the planet, and by… awakenings."

"In other words, demons. *Monsters,*" Preston said. "We brought the whole subterranean ecosystem to the damn surface."

Davy leaned up, still saddled on his scarab. "Relax, Douglas. I'm sick, but I'm pretty sure I've got a few days left in me. We can wait through the night."

Another screech echoed through the hills. Davy swallowed hard. "Yeah, as the sick guy, I'm pulling rank. I'm not going out there."

"Alright." Warren and Preston returned into the tunnel. "We'll make a go for it at dawn."

"Suits me," Preston said. The orange glow of the tunnel orbs felt more welcoming than ever. He found a spot near the tunnel wall and began unpacking their camp equipment, generously provided by the

Martian colony. He made sure to devote a few minutes to tend to his rifle. The last thing he wanted was to travel through the region with a dysfunctional weapon.

Warren helped Davy off of his scarab, then eased him to the ground. Davy leaned against the wall opposite Preston.

"Nice and comfy."

"Just rest," Warren said. "Tomorrow, you'll be in a hospital bed."

"Assuming there's no military presence there," Preston said.

"We'll figure something out," Warren said. "We must."

CHAPTER 19

Centauri Colony.

Zero-five-thirty came bright and early. When Vince awoke, he stared idly at the window. The last grip of night was gradually slipping away. The streetlights were still on, the automation set to switch them off at zero-six-hundred.

There wasn't much of a view outside that window aside from a closeup view of the next housing unit. The space between the units was a measly four feet. Vince could not grasp why the colonists did not simply attach them. During yesterday's afternoon meetings, Bill Cook explained they were meant to instill a feeling of individual ownership, something Vince balked at.

"Individual ownership. You forget, Mr. Cook, that we are part of one alliance?" he had replied.

It was a busy first day. First, he had to arrange shifts and assignments for his personnel. He had to oversee the stocking of the armaments in the armory section of Security Headquarters. Afterwards, he took a ride through the colony to give himself a good idea of the colony's layout. While he had digital maps which would undoubtedly prove useful, he preferred to know the place by heart.

The colonists all kept their distance. Some offered friendly waves, but none dared to speak to him or the other tridents. He wasn't sure if it was due to intimidation, resentment, or both, nor did he care. As he told Lucy, he was not here to make friends.

In the course of the next hour, he cleaned up and got into his uniform. At oh-six-hundred, he heard Lucy's alarm go off. He reminded her that the school shuttle was due to arrive at oh-six-forty.

As the clock neared oh-six-thirty, he placed his gauntlet on his right forearm.

"Lucy, hurry it up."

"I'm coming."

Vince finished drinking his nutritional smoothie. He was used to the bland tastes of these items. For him, it was no different than the field-issue MREs, beans, and nutritional pastes he consumed in previous years.

Lucy did not have the same attitude.

She stepped into the kitchen, wincing while she finished off her own smoothie. Groaning, she tossed the empty bottle into the recycling bin.

"I can't wait to eat real food."

"I'd be lying if I said I didn't feel the same," Vince said. He disposed of his own bottle, then froze after seeing his daughter dressed in blue slacks and a civilian t-shirt. "Wait… where's your school uniform? Don't tell me you spilled your breakfast on it…"

"No, Dad," she said. "I had a virtual meeting with my teacher after you went back out to work yesterday. They don't wear school uniforms here."

"They don't?"

"No. The policy is to dress business-casual. As long as it meets the criteria, we can wear whatever we want."

Vince had many opinions about that, but it would be of no use to express them. Lucy had no power over the school policy. In his mind, it was symptomatic of a larger issue. These colonies were really taking this individualism nonsense to heart. So much so, that they were implementing it into their school system.

They're indoctrinating the kids. This will certainly be in my report.

When the thought concluded, he saw Lucy staring at him inquisitively.

"You're going to say something critical, aren't you?" she said.

"Hmm? Me?"

"Yeah, you! Who else is in the house?"

Vince smiled at that. She was definitely his kid.

"I wasn't gonna say anything," he said.

"You were thinking it. You just have nothing but critiques for this place, don't you?" She picked up her tablet and study bag. "I took a walk around town yesterday. The people are very nice and welcoming. One even offered me a housekeeping present." She pointed at a small package on the kitchen counter.

Vince leaned in to look at it. "Powdered eggs."

"Yeah. They said that when we start to adjust to food grown and processed on this planet, it'll be good to mix it with familiar stuff. Our bodies won't be quite used to the enzymes and protein strands from the food made here. Hence we have to drink the smoothies."

"Yes, Professor. I know why we're stuck with this stuff." He elbowed the stack of smoothies on the end of the counter. Next to them was the clock, which now read zero-six-thirty. "Oh, hell. Let's get out the door."

Vince ushered his daughter outside, just in time to see the shuttle turn the corner at the end of the block. A few houses down was a line of students ready to board the vehicle. Like her, they were dressed in civies.

"Get in line, kid. The thing's coming."

"Yep. See you later."

Vince watched from the front yard as Lucy hustled toward the back of the line. While waiting to see her board the shuttle, he observed the other parents, many of whom were accompanying their children at the line.

Every child had two parents, a mother and a father. From what Vince could see, each couple was *happy*. Some held hands or had an arm around their partner's back. Many of them were dressed for their duties, while others were in simple civies. He had heard of arrangements where one partner remained home and tended to the household: another option provided on this planet that was frowned upon by the Alliance. What good was having these people here if they did not perform the labor necessary for a functioning society?

That critical opinion was overshadowed by a strange sense of guilt. Every kid in that line, like their parents, looked *happy*. There were smiles on their faces. Their bodies radiated a positive energy. Some of them said hi to Lucy when she approached the line.

She had a smile on her face, but Vince could tell it was hollow. Merely a mask to put on for the others. He tried to convince himself that she was just anxious. It was a new school on a new planet. How could she not be anxious? Despite this attempt to dismiss her feelings, that sense of guilt prevailed. Attention to detail was a large part of his job, and he caught the subtle glances Lucy gave when a kid interacted with his or her parents.

The shuttle arrived and opened its side doors. The kids started boarding, many of them waving to their folks.

It was that moment when self-consciousness overcame Vince's strict nature. He raised his hand to wave goodbye to Lucy.

"Have a good day, kid." He wasn't sure if she heard him or not. Once all of the kids were aboard, the doors shut and the shuttle went on its way. Everyone else on the block went about their day, while Vince stood on his front porch, lost in his thoughts.

Pondering did nobody any good. He approached his own personal transport, which had been issued to him the previous evening, and set out for Security Headquarters. Shift change was in twenty-five minutes. There was much to be done today.

***

Centauri Hospital.

"Paging Dr. Drucus. Please come in, Dr. Drucus."

It was the fourth time Anastacia heard the call through her comm device. The volume was turned low. If there was a way she could switch it off, she would have. Sadly, they were designed to be on all of the time to avoid people deliberately avoiding calls. The only way to shut the blasted thing off was to let its battery die.

She was on her knees, leaning against Patrick's hospital bed. Her hands gripped his. He was still unconscious, which was probably for the best. The nurse had just stepped out after giving him the last application of DZ-5. Once this dosage ran its course, the minerals in his lungs would proceed to rot the organs from the inside out.

"Paging Dr. Drucus…"

She snatched her comm and lifted it to her mouth. "What?!"

A long pause followed, the lab assistant unclear whether to pursue the topic at hand.

"We, uh… Hi. Sorry to bother you. We've got new seismic readings coming from the south ridge."

"And?"

"Just wanted to update you. Also, the new Lieutenant is demanding new surveys of the east plains in search of more drill sites."

"I'll get to it when I get to it. Drucus out."

She leaned her head against Patrick's hand. It was too much. The pressure, the strain, the sleepless nights. She wanted nothing other than to resign right now, but that was not an option. Hope Central would not stand for it, nor would Lieutenant Caparzo, and by extension, Bill Cook. She was the only geologist capable of managing the operations out here. The new staff brought in by the Alliance were sent out to the western regions, which were considerably less hazardous.

Three of the five stages of grief were hitting her all at once. She had breezed through denial and had gone straight to anger, bargaining, and depression. At this point, she was unsure if she would ever reach acceptance. Depression was hitting her especially hard this morning. She could hardly focus on her tasks. How could one focus while the love of their life was facing a slow, torturous death? She wouldn't even be able to wake him up to say goodbye. Doing so would only subject Patrick to the physical tortures of Regolith Lung Rot.

Anastacia kissed Patrick's cheek. "Oh, sweetie, I don't know what else to do. Carlos tried to make a call to Hope Central, but they won't send any more meds. What am I supposed to do? I can't lose you."

At this point, the first tears broke free of their confinement and streamed down her face.

She rested her head on his chest and listened to his heartbeat. It was always soothing to hear. A sense of calmness lifted her depression enough for her mind to revert to the bargaining stage.

A thought entered her mind.

Anastacia lifted her head, simultaneously uplifted and nervous. There was one person in this colony that Hope Central might listen to. Unfortunately, it was someone she had already put herself at odds with.

She reread the reports regarding the refinery explosion. Lieutenant Caparzo had led a fireteam into the Alaska station, despite high-ranking officials demanding a chem-strike. There was no other reason to go into the lion's den except to rescue the hostages. A career trident, he had a sliver of compassion, even if he tried to hide it behind a gruff demeanor. Despite his indoctrination, he saw value in human life beyond its capacity for labor.

Perhaps, he would be able to convince Centauri to deliver a shipment of medical supplies. Unlikely, but worth a try.

Anastacia gave Patrick one more kiss, then hurried for the exit.

***

"By now, you all should have received your shift assignments. These colonists may have made the inside of this dome look like paradise, but make no mistake, we are out in the middle of nowhere."

Vince Caparzo walked in a straight line, watching all thirty-six of his tridents standing before him in position of attention. Half of them had just completed their shift on nights and the others had just arrived. Each face was blurred out by a black mask. Only a number on the left shoulder provided identification. Names did not matter in this instance, for they were one unit. They were soldiers, ready to serve and die at the will of the Alliance.

"This may seem like a simple babysitting job," Vince continued. "But make no mistake, we will treat this operation as though we are at war. As far as I'm concerned, we are. The colonists have proven they cannot be trusted. Furthermore, there's the Martians to worry about. They are not on friendly terms with humans, so watch your backs, especially when outside the dome.

"We will set up a check-station at the atrium. Everyone will sign in and out. No more of this free-roam nonsense. We will document which vehicles are being used and by whom. Everyone signs their name. If they don't like it—tough. I want regular patrols in a fifteen-mile perimeter around the colony. I especially want the edge of the Blackout Hills to be monitored. If anyone's hanging around out there, I want to know about it."

The squad responded with a unanimous "Aye-aye, sir!"

Vince looked to the Sergeant. "Have Corporal Tarseas check out the local businesses on Seventy-two and Seventy-eight. See if they're registered."

"Copy that. It will be done, Lieutenant," Tarseas responded from the crowd.

While appreciated, his tenacity failed to impress.

"That is all," Vince said. As his tridents dispersed, he turned to face the front entrance to Security Headquarters.

It was a single story building covering three-thousand square feet of space. It was in view of the Administration Building, where Bill Cook lived and worked. The Alliance flag hung proudly over the west side. The interior featured an office, galley, infirmary, and armory, of which Vince had personally supervised the stocking of during the previous afternoon. If General Pyre had been generous about anything, it was with weapons and medical supplies. Though tridents were seen as units rather than people, they were looked upon with higher regard than the measly colonists. After all, they directly served the powers that be.

Vince stepped into his office. It was a large, spacious area with a horseshoe-shaped desk near the back. The front of the room was a large planning area, complete with both physical and digital maps and graphics. On the east wall was a projection device for virtual conferences. The building was directly linked to the radio tower, allowing him to make calls in even the worst of atmospheric conditions.

He sat at his desk and immediately went to work looking over some digital files on his computer. There were security aspects built into the foundation of this colony that only he and high-ranking officers knew about. Should certain plans go into enforcement in the near future, those security measures would be necessary in preventing an uprising.

A knock on his door caused him to shut the file down.

"Come in," he said in his usual disinterested tone. He looked at the front door, surprised to see Anastacia Drucus step inside. Already, she lacked the aggressive attitude she so eagerly put on display yesterday. Oddly enough, she looked exhausted and even a bit timid. "Oh, you. *Doctor* Drucus." He turned his eyes to some miniature maps on his desk. "To what do I owe the displeasure?"

She snickered at that. "Is this how it's going to be between us, Lieutenant?"

"Yep," he said, without skipping a beat.

Anastacia held her breath. For a second, that feisty attitude looked as though it was about to make a grand appearance. Instead, she restrained herself. With her hands clasped in front of her, she stepped forward, stopping midway across the planning area.

"Listen, I'm here to apologize for coming off a little rough yesterday."

Still looking over his map, Vince simply shrugged and shook his head slightly.

"Your apology is wasted, Doctor. I'm here on assignment. Attitudes are to be expected."

"That doesn't mean we can't get along," she said.

Vince finally looked up, his stern expression triggering a look of worry from the geologist. Blunt and straightforward, he successfully conveyed the look of a man who felt his time was being wasted.

"What is it you want?"

"I'm just here to make peace," Anastacia said.

"I'm sure you are…" Vince stood up, "…because you *want* something." Anastacia's breaking of eye contact confirmed his suspicion. "What is it?"

Anastacia looked him in the eyes. She kept her posture straight and professional. Though desperate, she seemed to be trying not to come off as such.

"My husband is in the hospital with Regolith Lung Rot, which he contracted while out on an expedition," she said.

It was not what Vince expected to hear. He suspected she was going to lay out some excuses as to why she had not located fresh drill sites. In a sense, this would serve as an excuse, but she was clearly more concerned with her personal hazards than her professional ones.

Her words induced culture shock. Only around thirty percent of World One's populations were unified in a nuclear family. The vast majority of the citizenry were focused on their labor, something highly endorsed by the Alliance. Here on World Two, however, people took value in their families rather than their work.

"My condolences," he said. "Unfortunately, I'm not a doctor. I wish there was something I could do, but there's not."

"Actually, there is," Anastacia said. "You have more pull than Administrator Cook. You could get a decent shipment of DZ-5 delivered out here. It's used to stall the effects of Regolith Lung Rot."

"That's an expensive treatment, Dr. Drucus," Vince said. "I can't just make a call to Hope Central and say 'hey, you mind making an eleven-thousand-kilometer trip with one delivery item?'"

"I would greatly appreciate it if you tried," Anastacia said.

Vince sat back down, torturing the geologist with his silence. His education, as the Alliance called it, was serving him well here. Tridents were supposed to look down on non-military personnel and hold no empathy for their personal grievances. If any of his former commanders were in his shoes right now, they would tell Anastacia that there would be more chances to marry in the future, and to be grateful the Alliance still granted that right. In their eyes, it served her right for being disloyal and openly hostile to a military officer.

Loyalty…

Like a virus, Lucy's voice penetrated his mind.

"I read somewhere that it's better to inspire loyalty rather than demand it."

He grimaced. *That damned book.*

His thoughts shifted when his eyes went to her neckline. It was not a crude desire that led his eyes to her skin, but the edge of a blackened mark which revealed itself from the neck of her shirt.

"Plasma scoring. I see it." He pointed at his collar, then at hers to indicate what he meant. "I'd say that's from an energy blast. Either you were a victim of some violent militia movement, or you were in a firefight. I think I already know which. How long were you in the service?"

Anastacia broke eye contact again. It was common for veterans who did not look fondly upon their time as a trident.

"Four years," she said. "Mainly operated in search-and-rescue. Went on a tour in West Africa. Warlords were trying to destroy the embassies over there. We went to extract out team who went to eradicate the problem. We took a barrage of incoming fire in the process."

"I've had my share of those," Vince said. "Did you manage to get the target out?"

Anastacia exhaled solemnly, then shook her head.

"About my request?"

Vince looked at his computer and brought up a file of the South Ridge, suddenly disinterested in her presence. "I'll let you know."

Silence filled the gap between them. In the minute that followed, Anastacia did not budge. She stood, defeated, yet unsure of how to proceed.

Vince looked at her again. "Will that be all?"

Reluctantly, she nodded, then turned around. Vince watched her exit the front door, contemplating her request.

The answer he had given her was the truth. The supply delivery was sent with the personnel. They would have to wait another month at best for another delivery.

He stood up and turned to the back of the room. Scanning his badge against the card reader, he opened the door which led to the armory. He crossed through a room full of carefully placed munitions, weapons, and gadgets, all of which were locked inside steel cases.

At the back of the room was another door, which led into a small hall. On the other end of that hall was the galley and infirmary. The latter was mainly a storage unit for medical supplies intended specifically for military personnel. Any actual treatment would be administered in the colony hospital.

Cases of medicine were stocked atop one another. Painkillers, antibiotics, antivirals, and much more were all stored as securely as the weapons. Each had a label on the lefthand corner, stating the name and purpose of the contents inside.

Midway across the room was a locked, steel case. It was green in color except for the white rectangular label on the corner. *DZ-5 – 35 units.*

Vince's mind went into limbo as he stared endlessly at the label. It was a good thing Anastacia Drucus was unaware that this medicine was already in stock, or else she would be hounding him endlessly. Unfortunately, these supplies were intended specifically for military personnel, not colonial. If he used up his supply on one civilian and had none for his own tridents should the need arise, he would face dire consequences.

Those facts failed to keep him from thinking about the fact that there was an unfortunate individual lying in a hospital bed, about to suffer a slow and cruel death.

It's an unfortunate reality of living here. Dr. Drucus will just have to accept it and move on.

Vince locked the infirmary door and returned to his office.

CHAPTER 20

Blackout Hills, several miles northwest of Centauri Colony.

When Dr. Warren emerged from the Martian tunnel, he saw a world of oddly shaped rocks illuminated in the morning sunlight. The chorus of carnivorous lifeforms had quieted down during the daylight hours. It was a devious silence which would fool a less experienced man into believing that the danger was over. The reality was that the Blackout Hills were only *safer* during the day in comparison to night.

Preston Gosly led the scarabs out of the tunnel, handing Warren the reigns to his ride. "Can we finally get out of here, please?"

"Absolutely," Warren said. The two of them helped Davy Austin out of the tunnel and onto his scarab. "Hang in there, Davy. I know Dr. LaFonte. He has the stuff that'll fix you up."

"I'm fine," Davy said. "Don't I look fine?"

Warren bit his lip as he looked at the sickly colonist's face. "Oh, sure. Absolutely. The ladies will be all over you."

"Yippee," Davy said, before coughing heavily.

As Warren stepped to his scarab, he saw Godon standing idly near the tunnel entrance. He was as still as a statue, watching the cliff edge with both hands clasping his staff.

"You going to wait here?" Warren asked.

Godon nodded. "My Empress does not wish for our clan to travel near your human settlements. I will await your return here for three days. Should you not come back, I will believe you have been embraced by your colony... or are dead."

"Fair enough," Warren said. "Thank you, Godon."

Preston turned his scarab toward the Martian. "Yeah, man... Martian... whatever. Thank you for helping us."

He waved his finger in a semicircular line in a pathetic attempt to perform the Circle of Peace. Dr. Warren, shaking his head, stepped in front of him and did the correct hand gesture. Godon performed his half of the gesture, then bowed his head.

"To Davy Austin, I offer you a phrase once spoken to me by Dr. Warren—'Best of luck to you.'"

Davy held up an 'ok' symbol. "Thanks, man."

Warren took the lead line to Davy's ride, then boarded his own scarab. All three steeds turned to the southeast. Currently, at least four miles of rough terrain separated them from flat ground.

"Okay. Let's go," he said.

The trio began their trek. Immediately, they held their rifles at the ready. There were many obstacles ahead, and many dangers hiding behind them.

CHAPTER 21

Centauri Colony – Business District.

The name of the restaurant was the Red Flower. According to local documents provided by the administration, it was a privately owned business run by a retired driller named Hayden Stevenson. The first red flag was the fact that these documents were not available on the solar-net.

Corporal Tarseas stood alongside Private Nellen Yasutake, watching the front of the building. It was a small little diner, with only a dozen tables inside. Throughout the morning, they had been going door-to-door, scanning businesses, small and large. Already, they had identified three that were unregistered, thus not paying Alliance taxes.

On the outside of the building were large pots, attached to a network of pipes. Each one contained boiling water. Reaching from the edges of each pot were insectoid legs, twitching as their insides were cooked.

Tarseas gulped. He usually had a strong stomach, but looking at that horrible sight quickly killed any appetite he had.

"This place deserves a scan just for serving that crap." He took a step forward, only to stop and look back at his partner. Nellen, despite her helmet and gear, was easily identifiable. Not only was she the smallest and most slender of Caparzo's tridents, but she was clearly very timid. It was no wonder why she was assigned to this place. In all likelihood, she proved to be useless wherever she was originally assigned and dumped here. If she got infected with Regolith Lung Rot or eaten by some large Martian predator, the Alliance would not miss out on much.

"What's the matter, Private?" he said.

"Nothing," Nellen said, her helmet pointing down.

"Doesn't look like nothing." He waved a finger in an upward motion. "Eyes up, Private. You look like a schoolgirl." Nellen leveled her gaze. Her arms were still at her sides, her stance completely nonaggressive. "What's the matter?"

"Is this really necessary?" she asked. She gestured to the Red Flower and the other buildings in this small block. "All of this, I mean. What are we achieving by harassing these people?"

"These are the Lieutenant's orders," Tarseas said. "It's as simple as that. He gives the orders and we follow them. It is all in service to our world. Part of that is ensuring everyone pays their dues. Do you have a problem with this fact, Trident?"

Nellen knew there was only one acceptable answer to that question. Anything other than 'no' would get her reported to the Sergeant, who would then suggest to Caparzo to have her shipped back to Hope Colony. The costs of such a flight, in addition to the circumstance, would result in her having to undergo a cognitive inspection. The best-case scenario would be that they would reassign her into a support position, working at a desk somewhere. The problem, however, was that she failed her aptitude tests, although only by a narrow margin. Typing and mathematical speeds were her downside.

Ultimately, she was looking at a possible discharge. Though not dishonorable, it still essentially meant getting fired from the military. That would reflect on future aptitude tests, making it harder to obtain any career she had any interest in.

"No, Corporal."

Tarseas turned toward the building and scanned the building code. He punched in his own serial number, then waited for the results.

Red lights flashed on his code-reader.

"Just as I thought," he said. "Unregistered."

He glanced over his shoulder to make sure Nellen was approaching. Together, they marched into the diner.

There were seven customers inside, some off duty, others stopping in before starting their shift. All eyes turned to the two blood-jackets in the doorway.

"Attention, everyone," Tarseas announced. "Vacate the building. This shop is closed."

Nobody moved. The looks on their faces said it all. Most of them were visibly irritated, and a couple others amused. One patron, seated at a table nearby, sipped on hot coffee as though the tridents were not even there.

"I'll say it once more," Tarseas continued. "This business is unregistered with the Bureau of Private Business and Tax Services. It will, in turn, be shut down until all fees are paid by the owner. As of now, this building is property of the Alliance."

A door opened behind the counter. From the kitchen area marched a man in his mid-sixties. He was clean-shaven, neatly dressed, and clearly displeased to see the two tridents.

"Is there a problem?"

"Hayden Stevenson, I presume?" Tarseas said. "Former owner of the Red Flower?"

"Current owner."

"Not anymore," Tarseas said. "You see, you started this little establishment after the foundation of the colony. This is unregistered in the World One databases. If it's not in the databases, it means you're not paying your dues."

"I sent the files a year ago," Hayden Stevenson replied.

"Not according to my records," Tarseas said.

"Well, your records are wrong," Hayden said.

"That, or you're simply a tax evader who's been caught," Tarseas said. The Corporal unclipped his stun-baton from his belt. Its end glowed with a radiant blue color, ready to spark at the slightest touch. "Last time I tell you all... *out!*"

Finally, the customers stood up and began to depart. A few tapped Hayden reassuringly on the shoulder on their way out, some wishing him good luck and well wishes.

His eyes remained fixed on the Corporal's black-tinted mask.

"And here I was thinking we humans were gradually moving away from this kind of authoritarian state."

Tarseas said nothing. He deactivated his stun baton and tapped it against his palm, pleased with himself.

"Let's get started, Mr. Stevenson. I want to see your financial records." He waved Hayden toward his office area. "Come on. Don't waste anymore of my time. You owe a lot of credits. If you hold me up, that will result in a fine. Last thing you need to do is elevate your debt."

"This is outrageous," Hayden said. "You blood-sucking leeches already tax us beyond the breaking point, including our so-called pensions. We're all aware of your schemes."

Tarseas pointed the baton at his chest. "The records, Mr. Stevenson. Now."

Hayden shook his head. "I wish to speak with Administrator Cook. He'll set this straight."

"Administrator Cook answers to Lieutenant Caparzo, my commanding officer." He reactivated the baton, the blue tint reflecting off Hayden's eyes. "Last chance, Mr. Stevenson."

Hayden looked at the weapon, breathing shakily. He tensed, his muscles straining. In the blink of an eye, he learned that his business would be stripped away from him and that he would be forced to pay an impossible fee. The punishment for failure to pay would be hard labor, possibly for the rest of his life.

Though nervous, he was a proud man with no intention to back down. He shook his head and sneered.

"No."

Tarseas thrust the weapon into his chest, zapping him. Hayden Stevenson reeled backward as ten-thousand volts surged through his body. The trident stood over the fallen colonist, making sure he was still conscious enough to experience some more punishment. As soon as Hayden lifted his head, Tarseas thrust the baton again, zapping him.

Hayden cried out with each hit. After the fourth time, he reached his breaking point. "Okay! Stop!"

"Oh, *now* you're willing to cooperate, huh?" Tarseas said. He hit the restaurant owner again, relishing in the high-pitched squeal.

"Corporal, that's enough," Nellen said.

"Shut up, Private."

"Corporal…" This time, she was cut off by the arrival of several patrons who stormed into the diner. Tarseas turned around, seeing the four customers who supposedly left a few minutes ago. By the looks of it, they hung around in case their pal Hayden Stevenson needed help.

"Get off of him!" one of them shouted.

"Stop right there," Nellen warned. "Please don't interfere…" She was quickly shoved aside.

Tarseas wasted no time zapping the colonist. The intense shock put the man on his back. The other three charged at once. Right away, Tarseas thrust the baton out. One attempted to grab it, but accidentally touched the electrified end. The surge knocked him backward, right against one of his companions. Both fell to the floor, leaving Tarseas to engage with the fourth.

He effectively dodged a haymaker and countered with a strike to the nose. Next, he struck the colonist with the handle of his baton, cracking a tooth.

As the fight carried on, Nellen stepped away, nearly hyperventilating. It took three attempts for her to activate her wrist communicator.

"This is Unit Two. We have a situation at Red Flower Café. Please send backup."

***

When Vince Caparzo arrived at the Red Flower, Corporal Tarseas had the restaurant owner and four other colonists apprehended in front of the building. Several colonists had assembled around the block, many of whom were protesting the actions of the tridents.

After parking his shuttle, Vince took a moment to observe his two tridents who had apprehended the offenders. Corporal Tarseas, despite the full-body gear, was easy to read emotionally. He was speaking to Sergeant Elias, and seemed awfully pleased with himself as he explained what happened. What Vince found really interesting was Private Yasutake's body language. She seemed withdrawn. Ashamed, even.

He had read her file during yesterday's flight. Nellen Yasutake was trained in the Okinawa Region and was assigned to an infantry unit in Australia. Two months into her tour of duty, her unit was instructed to investigate a residential building in Sydney following reports of contraband. The investigation revealed that some residents had been smuggling Australian shepherd puppies from the farming lands in the Lockyer Valley. In recent years, dogs from that area had been carrying a new breed of flea, which also infected humans. It was not simply a matter of hygiene. Those fleas were suspected of being carriers of a new infectious disease which was currently spreading in that region.

Nellen was ordered to execute the animals in that building. It was an order she failed to obey. According to the report, she admittedly was unable to bring herself to do it, claiming compassion. Thirty days later, she was scheduled on the next flight to World Two.

Reports from her superiors indicated an unwillingness to use force, a conclusion Vince would have believed had he not read her psychological report and training stats. In fact, she was more than willing to use deadly force—against armed combatants. All evidence indicated that she would absolutely defend her life and that of her comrades. Her scores were moderate at best, but the willingness was evident. It was occasions where she struggled morally that she failed to take action.

Looking at her now, he had no doubt she was morally conflicted. Maybe she was too soft. Or maybe Corporal Tarseas jumped the gun.

His eyes went to the diner owner. He was on his knees, bleeding from the mouth. His face was swollen, his shirt marred with electrical burns from a stun-baton. He was hunched over, indicating abdominal pain. The way his shoulders rose and fell with each breath indicated cracked or broken ribs.

It was looking more and more like Tarseas was a little too enthusiastic in his arrest of the diner owner. The only way to find out was to look into it personally.

Vince stepped out of the shuttle and marched toward the building. His presence was immediately noticed by the Sergeant and Corporal, who turned to salute.

"Sir," Sergeant Elias said. "The situation is under control."

"What happened?" Vince said. The question was directed specifically at Tarseas.

"Unregistered business, sir," he said, pointing his thumb at the building. "Mr. Hayden Stevenson, the owner, refused to show us the financial records. I stunned him, then some colonists decided to stick their noses into the situation. So, I handled them accordingly."

Vince looked at the four colonists kneeled beside Hayden. They had similar burns and bruising, though not nearly as severe as Hayden. They resembled political prisoners awaiting a firing squad. All five of them watched the Lieutenant as if expecting some kind of cruel judgement. Each face exhibited disdain and a hint of fear.

He stepped in front of Mr. Stevenson. "Is this true?"

A confused Corporal Tarseas approached the Lieutenant before the colonist had a chance to respond. "Pardon me, sir, but my understanding is that any and all resistance to our authority must be dealt with accordingly. That is why we're here, is it not?"

Vince remained silent, watching the crowd of onlookers across the street. Many of them conversed amongst themselves. While their words went unheard, it was still apparent what was being said. The apprehension surrounding this new military occupation was already reaching a boiling point, and the tridents had only been stationed here twenty-four hours.

In actuality, what Tarseas explained was technically correct. However, there was a factor that the eager trident was not taking into account. There were less than forty tridents in this unit, and over three thousand colonists—and they were armed. He was picking a fight with an enemy he could not win against. The only ace in the hole Vince had was the fact that any revolution would result in gunships converging on this dome. Ultimately, that fact only proved useful as a deterrent. It would take half a day for reinforcements to arrive. By then, Vince's force would have easily been overpowered, unless he activated the secret security system.

The thought made his stomach churn. Vince was no stranger to killing. He had performed many combat drops and had engaged in nearly a hundred firefights during the course of his career. But there was a staunch difference between fighting extremist groups and terminating an entire colony.

Twenty-four hours into this assignment, and already Vince was contemplating violent conflict.

Once again, Lucy's voice infiltrated his mind.

Isn't it the responsibility of tridents to protect citizens?

Vince looked to Nellen, who remained in position of attention near the building entrance. She was visibly uncomfortable, not just with the events that just occurred, but because of anticipation. Vince had seen how compassionate types responded when others were awaiting punishment that was disproportionate to the crime. As far as the books were concerned, failure to register business, and therefore not pay taxes, was considered a heinous offense. If the offender did not pay, the burden was shifted to the next of kin, or other family members. Assault on security and military personnel was another serious offense. With that in mind, Vince could not eliminate the human factor.

Tarseas used extreme measures and the colonists rushed to the defense of one of their own. Separated by decades of self-regulation and millions of miles of distance, they did not view the Alliance in the same light as the rest of the universe.

"Sir?"

Corporal Tarsea's voice broke his train of thought.

"Corporal Tarseas, you and Private Yasutake take one of the rovers from Station Six and patrol the edge of the hills," he said.

"Sir?!" Tarseas was taken aback. There was a hint of betrayal in his voice. Having expected praise for his diligence in handling the scum, he instead was reassigned to a routine, mind-numbing task.

"Is that a problem, Corporal?" Vince said.

Tarseas fixed his posture. "No, sir." He looked to Nellen and tilted his head in the direction of the atrium. "Let's go, Private."

Vince watched the duo walk away, then turned to Sergeant Elias. "Undo the restraints. We've got bigger things to worry about than petty scuffles."

"Yes, Lieutenant." The Sergeant went to work undoing the restraints of the four colonists.

"Word of advice to you all: don't interfere with any of our operations. If you have a grievance, report it to me," Vince explained to them.

One of the colonists chuckled. "Yeah. As if any report against a trident will be taken seriously."

Vince chose not to respond. Instead, he knelt next to Hayden Stevenson. The man was not doing well. He was in considerable pain and appeared to be lightheaded.

"You need medical attention." He lifted him up by his shoulders. "Come on, old timer."

"Need me to call a medical crew?" Sergeant Elias said.

"Negative. I'll take him myself."

**

Centauri Hospital.

Vince stood in the corner of the hospital room while Centauri's lead physician tended to Mr. Stevenson. Dr. Carlos LaFonte was everything his file indicated and more. He was an experienced medical doctor who worked in all kinds of environments, desirable, undesirable, and hellish. He was not intimidated by the Lieutenant's presence. Unlike the vast majority of the other colonists, he seemed entirely unfazed by the change. He worked and communicated as though the tridents had been here for years.

"Looks like Mr. Stevenson has a few contusions, some cracked ribs, scorching along the chest and upper abdominal area. But he'll be fine. I should have him patched up in a day." He turned to face Vince. "You know our EMS team could have brought him in, Lieutenant? You did not have to make the drive."

"It gave me a chance to get a look at the inside of this hospital," Vince replied.

"And your thoughts?"

"It seems like you're constantly busy." It was all Vince could muster. In fact, the hospital appeared extremely well-operated, despite the circumstances. They were dealing with old and out of date equipment, exhausted staff, and three-thousand potential patients. Here on the outskirts, there was no shortage of emergencies and illnesses. Regardless, Vince needed to maintain the image of a stern, commanding officer, even in the presence of a warm and gentle soul like Carlos LaFonte.

"Constantly busy, but nothing I can't handle," Carlos said. "Believe me, I've had far worse."

"Worse than the outskirts of World Two?" Vince said, his interest slipping through the cracks of his emotionless shell.

Carlos nodded. "L.A. 2142."

"The Fusion Wars," Vince said. He thought about the date and location, then realized what the doctor was implying. "L.A. 2142… you were part of the beach assault?"

"Under General Caparzo," Carlos said. "When I heard your name, I had to look you up. Yep, I served under your father. I was a medic in the Third Army. The EMP field set up by the Southern States forced us to storm the beaches armed with old-fashioned lead projectile weapons. We couldn't use aircraft, for they were all computer-based in their operations. Like with the weapons, we had to look to the past to figure out what landing craft to use. Lo and behold, we had to use diesel-operated barges. That was fun."

"Bloodiest conflict since the Second World War," Vince said.

Carlos smiled. "Give it time. Something will come along that'll top it. We humans have a way of doing that." He placed his tablet down and walked around the end of Hayden's hospital bed. "Lieutenant, to say your father was a great general is a vast understatement. I heard he passed away a few years back. My sincere condolences."

"He lived well," Vince said.

"Did he?" Carlos asked. Vince's eyes narrowed in a stern manner. He did not expect the question, nor the bluntness in the way it was asked. Carlos was unfazed by the mild aggression. He crossed his arms and leaned against the side of the bed as though chatting with a friend of many years. "I remember having the honor of speaking with him. He openly stated how he despised conflict. *But* he knew what needed to be done."

"That sounds like him," Vince said.

"What about you?" Carlos asked. He received another questionable look from the Lieutenant. "I read your files… those that are declassified, that is. You volunteered for many risky missions. You did pretty well for yourself… until the most recent operation, that is."

"Are you a psychologist in addition to a medical doctor?" Vince said.

"If I was, I'd say you've been experiencing a tussle with destiny," Carlos said. "For whatever reason, you feel like you need to live up to your father's name, which ultimately landed you here. I'm simply curious as to why, but I suppose I'll never know."

It was a true statement in Vince's view. He hated psycho-babble, even from licensed professionals, let alone someone who had known him for only a few minutes. What made Carlos' opinion even more frustrating was the truth behind it. In the back of his mind, Vince did seek to live up to his father's name. For him personally, that failure was worse than the disaster in Alaska.

"Dr. LaFonte, thank you for your help." He turned on his heel and went for the door.

Carlos remained in the room, watching him leave.

"That's my job, Lieutenant."

CHAPTER 22

Blackout Hills – five miles northwest of Centauri Colony.

Throughout the trip in the tunnels, all three men yearned for the gift of sunshine. The bright orbs underground did little to quell the feelings of claustrophobia and restlessness within the three humans.

It only took ten minutes of trekking through the Blackout to make them yearn for the safety of the tunnels.

Their scarabs stood at a halt while the three men gazed at the small crevice they had come across. It was a crack in the ground, only four feet across at its widest point, and twelve feet long. The depths were pitch black, lacking the luminance of the Martian colonies.

It was not the breach that alarmed the men, but the rotting corpses that were scattered all around it. Numerous species were laid to rest unceremoniously, covered in a silk-like substance, their bodies reduced to skeletons.

"Doc?" Preston muttered. He was in a heightened state of alert, his eyes scouring the surrounding rocks for the slightest hint of movement. His gaze, like metal drawn to a magnet, returned to the horrible sight in front of him. "What is this?"

Warren shook his head.

Preston gently bumped his scarab with his heel, moving it forward. He steered it to the left, avoiding the edge of the pile of death. In spite of his efforts, Preston could not take his eyes off of the mass grave. There were so many different creatures littered about. Some were insectoid, their many legs coiled under their bodies. Some were winged creatures, their flesh completely gone. To the left was the remains of a four-legged animal, resembling a canine in shape and size.

The scarab screeched again, nearly bucking its rider off.

"Whoa, boy. Hang on." Preston pulled on the reins and tapped the insectoid creature on its head. "I promise, we'll get away from this. All we need to do is get around these rocks, and..." He looked to the web-encased mound lying in front of his scarab. He sat up, squinting at the hideous sight. This creature was under six feet in length, narrow in its physical build.

Preston felt his body quiver uncontrollably. This 'creature' was bipedal. A few extra moments into staring at it, he recognized the outline of worker boots, bent arms over the mid-section, and the vacant sockets of a human skull staring back at him.

"Oh!" He backed his scarab up.

Warren remained perfectly still, unable to take his eyes off the human skull. The bone was dark grey in color, the sockets widened. The fabric exposed through gaps in the webbed substance appeared to be thin, discolored, and torn. The bones themselves, even those of the larger species, appeared to be discolored and brittle. There were pockets of severe calcium loss visible in each corpse.

In his medical opinion, these unfortunate victims were exposed to some kind of pre-digestive enzyme.

Preston unslung his rifle and pointed the muzzle at the graveyard.

"Doc? Is there anything in the databanks about animals that... do *this* to their victims?!"

"No," Warren said. "Not on World Two, at least. Whatever it is, I don't want to stick around to find out."

The scarabs screeched, as though agreeing with his statement. They kicked their forelegs, nervously scraping the soil.

"Yeah, let's take a little detour," Preston said. "This isn't just a mass grave—it's a waste pile, and it definitely was not Martians that put it here."

They altered course, traveling a quarter mile eastward.

Every yard of distance was equally unpleasant. The Blackout Hills was a mass graveyard. There was no shortage of skeletal corpses decorating the landscape. These were more natural in appearance than the graveyard back at the crevice. From here on, every corpse they came across was the result of starvation, thirst, or violent struggle. This was the wilderness of World Two, where any breath could be your last.

Traveling these lands was a reminder of the impact mankind had had on this planet. For millions of years, no life dared to touch the surface. It only took mankind a few years to change the course of history. They were now on the surface, evolved to survive the gravitational changes, and adept to the temperature and atmospheric alterations. Their base instincts remained the same. For most of the creatures roaming the hills, their primary instinct was to kill.

After a quarter mile traveling east, they came across a rare open area. The rocks had been broken down and bulldozed into large piles. In the middle of this clearing, the ground was heavily cracked. There was a thin cloud lifting from this strange area.

"It's a geyser," Warren said.

"You sure?" Preston said. "Methane gas is invisible, isn't it?"

"It is. The 'cloud' we're seeing is not the methane itself. It's thin sediment being lifted off the crust," Warren said. "They found a hotspot. They're going to build an extractor over this thing."

Davy Austin lifted his head and looked at the discarded equipment and vehicles.

"If that's the case, then why aren't they out here now?" He stared at the vehicles and their rusted metal exteriors. A tarp flapped against a rock, having been blown away by the wind. The stakes were piled near one of the tires. Whoever was here last did not bother covering the vehicles.

"Looks like they left in a hurry," Warren said.

"But why?" Davy asked.

It was a question they were not sure they wanted to know the answer to. Looking at this work site sparked a sense of alarm. It was against protocol to leave equipment lying around like this. The vehicles had been left unattended and uncovered for a couple of days at least. With low winds and relatively clear, sunny skies, there was no reason for the work crews not to be out here during these morning hours.

There was only one explanation: something was deterring the crews.

Warren and Preston looked at each other, both thinking of the cocoons over by that crevice. Though they could not prove it, they had no doubt it was related to this oddity.

"Let's keep moving," Warren said. "The edge of the hills is two miles south of here. From there, it's another two-and-a-half miles to the colony, but on much better ground."

"No argument here," Preston said.

They took a right and continued on.

The next mile was slow and tedious. There was not a single square yard that was even ground. Every few yards was some kind of jagged obstacle. There were high rising hills, rock towers, deep pits, and steep hills.

The next half-mile was a little better. It was still rough terrain, but there were larger stretches of relatively smooth ground. Visibility was better here and the scarabs were a little less nervous.

They could see the valley up ahead. A sharp contrast from the Blackout Hills, it was a vast smooth landscape with great visibility. Once there, they could easily pick up speed and race to the colony.

"Oh, finally," Davy said.

"I hear ya," Preston replied. "I'll be more than happy to put this ugly place behind me."

They closed within a thousand feet of the end of the hill when Dr. Warren signaled for them to stop.

"What's the matter?" Preston said.

"Wait…" Warren said, keeping his hand raised. Silence overtook the group. After a few moments, Preston could hear it too.

In the distance was the roar of a rover's engine.

Warren lifted his binocs and looked southeast. "Oh, hell. Get down. Now."

His friends quickly followed his instructions. Even the sickly Davy Austin dismounted his scarab with haste. They ducked by a row of rocks, keeping their heads down. Warren peeked once more to get another look at the vehicle.

"Could it just be diggers or construction crew?" Preston asked.

Warren shook his head. "It's military grade."

Preston groaned. "Oh, no. They've got a military unit at the colony."

It was his first drive on this planet, and already Corporal Tarseas was growing impatient. With the rover sealed and supplied with its own oxygen tank, he was able to take his helmet off. The first fifteen minutes of the patrol was spent with him griping about the events at the diner. It was unfathomable that an Alliance officer would show pity on unruly colonists. Law-abiding ones, maybe. But tax avoiders?

In his peripheral vision, he noticed Nellen glancing ever so slightly in his direction. Unlike him, she followed regulation and kept her helmet on. He did not care if she wore it or not. What he did care about was her ability to even do her job.

"Got a problem?" he said.

"No, Corporal." She kept her eyes on the road. It was not long before she glanced at him again. "You sure you don't want to put your helmet back on? It's regulation."

"Gonna tattle?"

"No. But if something happens to this rover…"

"Like if a window breaks?"

"Yeah."

Tarseas slammed his elbow against the window. Nellen winced, expecting to hear a loud shatter. To her surprise, all she heard was a *thump*, followed by a chuckle.

"These things aren't made of tissue paper, Yasutake. You can relax. It's kind of a good rule of thumb in general." He rested against his door, studying her. She had both hands on the wheel, intensely watching the red landscape ahead. "Thanks for backing me up back there, by the way."

"Oh… it was nothing, I suppose."

"Damn right it was nothing, because you *did* nothing," he said. "You just stood there and let me have all the fun."

"Fun?"

"Yes, fun." He smiled. "Gosh, no wonder they sent you out here. You wouldn't harm a fly. Why the hell did you become a trident if you hate violence so much?" He waited for an answer that never came. "I'd tell you you're in the wrong business, but it's too late now. This isn't a youth center. This is the military, where we use violence to maintain order. Better get used to the idea, otherwise this place will eat you alive. Maybe literally."

Nellen did not have a retort. She simply nodded and followed the gravely terrain, keeping the vehicle steady at forty miles per hour.

Tarseas gave up on the conversation and watched the hills as they drove by. It was an ugly landscape of twisted rock and rutted ground. The files on his study tablet did not do it justice. The moment he laid eyes on the Blackout, he knew it was a place he had no desire to explore.

"Good grief," he said. "I can't begrudge those people for making the inside of that dome look so pretty. I've only been here a day and I feel like I'm in hell. How do those Martians stand living on this planet?"

"They live underground," Nellen said.

She speaks.

"That sounds even worse," Tarseas said. He pressed a button on the dashboard, bringing up a holographic map of the region. "Keep going straight. There's supposed to be an extractor unit a few miles ahead. They could probably use a check-in."

He noticed Nellen look over at him. Not very self-aware, she clearly thought her mask hid the expression on her face. While true, she was unaware that the way she conducted herself made her thoughts obvious. She was worried that Tarseas would start another ruckus with the colonists. He did not hide the fact that he got a kick out of beating up the diner owner and his customers. Tarseas saw no reason to. Tridents were supposed to relish in their victories. After all, they were trained to fight. And he was trained especially well.

"Got a problem?" he said.

"No." She turned her eyes to the horizon. "None at all."

As the vehicle approached from the east, Warren was able to confirm the military markings. "Yep. It's definitely a security rover."

"You mean there are tridents all the way out here?!" Preston said.

"We've got problems," Davy said.

Warren lowered the binocs and put his head against the stone. "Damn it. I didn't think they'd send troops as far out as Centauri. The fact that they did means the planet is under full military occupation."

"Occupation?" Preston said. "You mean they're treating Mars like it's an active warzone?"

"That's what happens when government overreaches," Warren said. "It becomes a corporate entity with control over everything. It owns the means of production, and worst of all, it has a monopoly on violence."

"Lovely," Davy muttered. "We shoot at them, even in self-defense—bad. They shoot at us, even when stealing resources that we need for survival—fine and dandy."

"That's the point, Davy," Warren said. He slowly leaned over the rock for another look through the binocs. The rover continued on its path, traveling eastward with no sign of slowing down. "It doesn't look like they know we're here. I suggest we lay low for a few minutes."

"But if they're patrolling around here, that means they're stationed at Centauri," Preston said.

Warren exhaled sharply. "I know."

A groan from Davy Austin made the doctor look to his right. The sick man was hunched over. At that moment, Warren realized that the reality of the situation was making him feel worse.

He moved over to Davy's side. "We'll figure something out. Just hang on."

Davy took a few breaths, then nodded. "I'm fine. I just need to catch my breath." He began to move away with one hand over his stomach.

"If you feel nauseous and have to remove your mask, make absolute sure you don't inhale," Warren said.

Davy gave a thumbs up as he moved back. He found a small crater where he could kneel. Beads of sweat took form under his mask, fogging the glass. His stomach tightened, his insides feeling as though a hurricane was sweeping through him.

A light breeze passed over him. Something about the mild shift in temperature made Davy feel significantly better. The pain in his stomach subsided enough for him to sit up straight. He regained control over his senses, allowing him not to dwell on the physical discomforts.

He decided to remain in this little spot, while Warren and Preston spoke amongst themselves. Their attempts to keep their voices down failed miserably.

"What do you think we should do?" Preston said. "We can't shoot our way in."

"I know," a frustrated Warren said.

"If we surrender, they'll never let Davy get the care he needs," Preston continued. "So that's not an option."

"I know."

A mild crunching sound to his right took Davy's attention from the conversation. A couple meters away was a small rock mound. From behind it rose a small cloud of dust and sediment. Listening hard, he detected the sound of scraping.

Something was moving on the other side of that rock.

"Guys?"

Warren and Preston continued their debate.

"We need to get Davy into that infirmary," Preston said.

"I know," Warren replied sternly.

Davy looked to the rocks again, seeing another dust cloud. There was the sound of clawed feet marring the ground. *Many* clawed feet.

He inched backward on his hands and knees.

"Guys?!"

"We're in a pickle," Preston said. "If we go there, we're dead. If we don't go in there, Davy's dead."

Warren punched the rock. "I know!"

In the blink of an eye, that scraping noise mutated into a flurry of scurrying legs. A storm of high-pitched screeches followed.

"GUYS!"

This time, Preston and Warren turned to look.

All three men stood up in unanimous alarm at the sight of thrashing legs from two different species. The scarabs attempted to run, but were overtaken in a blur of motion. The sounds of struggle concluded with agonized screeches and sudden stiffness.

All the men could see was a sea of legs and arachnoid bodies moving all over the place, dragging the stiff scarabs beyond the forests of rocks.

These things, familiar, yet totally alien in their appearance, laid eyes on their next victims.

"RUN!" Warren shouted. All three men unleashed a wave of blaster bolts, then retreated down the hill.

"What the... Wait! Wait! Wait! Stop!" Tarseas shouted.

Nellen hit the brakes and leaned to the right to see out through the passenger window. Immediately, she saw the flashes of V-13 Blaster rifles. There was movement on the hill. She adjusted the rover for a better view, pointing the engine at the rocks.

There were three men running down, each dressed in worn out dusters and boots.

"Colonists," she said. "Are they drillers?"

"No. Not the right attire," Tarseas said. He lifted his binocs and zoomed in on the three strangers. A smile took form. "Well, I'll be damned."

"What?"

"I think we found our fugitives."

"What?" Nellen took the binocs and took a look for herself. "Are you sure?"

"Sure I'm sure," Tarseas said. "Centauri has nobody working in the hills as of right now. Plus, it looks like these fellas have been outside the dome for quite a long time."

"Nobody in the hills..." Nellen said, remembering the colony report. The construction forewoman had informed the Administration that something was lurking near the methane geyser. Watching the colonists, it was evident they were fleeing something. "I think something's up there..."

Her concerns went unheard.

Tarseas eagerly put his helmet on and armed his gauntlet. "Ha! First full day of duty on World Two, and already I've located a level two fugitive. Who knows? Maybe they'll give me Caparzo's command."

"Corporal, I think they're running from something..."

"If we see it, we'll shoot it." He looked at his partner. "Floor it, Private. Get us up there."

"In the rover?"

"Yes. We might lose them on foot."

"It's the Blackout Hills," she said. "It's too dangerous to take a rover. We could crash or break down..."

"Do not make me tell you again."

Nellen knew the implication. Tarseas was the type that would gladly throw her under the bus, especially if her inaction stripped him of the glory of apprehending a level two suspect.

With heavy reluctance, she floored the accelerator. She tensed as they neared the edge of the hills. Immediately upon entering, she had to swerve left to wind around some razor sharp rocks.

The two tridents bumped in their seats as the vehicle crossed over the rough ground. Again and again, Nellen had to make sharp turns to avoid crashing. She weaved around a large boulder, found a small stretch of relatively even ground, only to arrive at a blockade of jagged rock towers.

"Keep going," Tarseas said. He pointed thirty degrees to the left. "Right there. There's a way through."

Nellen approached the narrow gap, wincing as the rover passed through. High-pitched scraping of rock on metal made her clench.

These issues did not faze Corporal Tarseas. He had his right fist raised, ready to extend toward his target. They were just a hundred feet up ahead.

"Get a little closer," he said. "Come on, come on, come on." His foot tapped repeatedly on the floor, his only outlet for his pent up energy. Adrenaline and sense of opportunity made him overwhelmingly eager.

Meanwhile, Nellen was trying to keep herself from hyperventilating again. The vehicle bumped over rough sediment. After another twenty yards, she slammed on the brakes.

Tarseas was immediately out the door with his gauntlet aimed at the fugitives.

Warren could hear the creatures behind him. Every time he glanced back, he failed to catch a glimpse, due to the terrain.

Davy Austin summoned every ounce of strength to keep up with his companions. His resilience was most impressive, for he was not only battling the terrain, but horrible fatigue.

Keeping an eye on Davy, Warren slowed down, allowing the frantic Preston Gosly to take the lead. The droid chip repairman was probably the most visibly terrified of the three, his wide eyes and clenched teeth clearly visible through the mask.

"We're in trouble! We're in big trouble..." He hopped over a log-shaped boulder, ready to make a big leap to add some distance between him and the arachnid things behind him. His actions were halted by a new threat standing between him and the relative safety of the valley.

Warren and Davy slowed to a stop, immediately seeing the security rover directly in front of them. A trident with the insignia of a corporal on his uniform was on foot with his gauntlet pointed in their direction.

Preston stepped back. "We are in *serious* trouble!"

"Drop your weapons. Put your hands on your heads," the Corporal said.

Both companions looked to Warren. The doctor had to think fast. He did not want to get arrested, nor did he want to get into a firefight, which would result in reinforcements swarming the hills. Most importantly, he did not want to stay right here. Not with those things closing in.

They were close. Staying here only meant death.

Maybe lying will work. If I convince him we're part of Centauri Colony...

"Listen, sir!" he said, attempting to reason with the Corporal. "Listen, there's a group of..."

The trident fired a warning shot, which exploded at their feet.

"No more talk. You have three seconds to drop your weapons, or I'll kill you where you stand."

"Tarseas?" the driver, a female soldier, said.

"Not now, Private."

The chaos had reached its breaking point. Warren looked behind him, seeing a collection of spindly legs stretching over some rocks.

Preston saw it too. Fear got the better of him. He lifted the muzzle of his rifle with intent to spin on his heel and fire at the oncoming creatures.

The trident saw it differently.

Warren watched the strobe of light streak across the gap between him and the rover, striking Preston between the shoulders. The colonist let out a dramatic yell, his eyes conveying intense pain as he fell from the rock.

"Preston!" Warren shouted. He ran to his friend's side and rolled him to his back. What he got in return was a blank, deathly stare. Preston was gone.

Davy Austin saw it too. His pale face was now beet red.

"NO!"

At the moment, he was no longer fearful of the monsters. Driven by intense hatred, he raised his gun at the trident. His shot went wide, dooming him to the weapon's cooling period.

The trident returned fire. His first shot also missed, allowing Davy to duck behind the log-shaped boulder. The Corporal fired a few more shots in an attempt to coax him out.

Meanwhile, the Private was on the radio, her voice frantic. "Unit Two to Security Headquarters. Lieutenant Caparzo, come in... Shots fired. Blackout Hills. We've encountered the fugitives from Espinosa."

The shooting ceased, the log smoking where the plasma bolts had landed. The trident took a couple of steps forward.

"Come on out."

Warren had his hands on Preston's neck, praying for a pulse. He looked over at Davy, who had his back against the log-shaped rock. The weapon had cooled and was ready to fire.

"No... Davy... don't..."

Davy took a few quick breaths, then emerged from cover.

The trident was ready and waiting, unleashing a barrage of plasma bolts. Two of them struck Davy in the chest, knocking him backward.

"NO!"

Warren threw himself at his friend's side, only to find another deathly stare. Davy and Preston were both dead.

Anger, fear, and guilt flooded his senses. For the first time in decades, Dr. Douglas Warren was utterly defeated. All sense of purpose was lost.

He had led these men all of the way out here, only for them to get killed in a petty firefight with a trident. For weeks, they lived on scraps and crummy-tasting Martian food, hoping to seek refuge in a colony.

It was all for nothing.

If there was any positive in this situation, it was that Preston and Davy would not have to suffer the horrors of the arachnoid swarm. They must have slowed during the chase. Perhaps they got distracted with the scarabs. But he could still hear them.

They were coming in his direction, their motions gradually getting louder.

The Corporal stepped around the rock and closed in, gauntlet pointed. Warren did not bother resisting. That did not stop the trident from knocking him on his back with a kick to the ribs.

"Doctor Douglas Warren, I presume," the Corporal said. "Looks like I've earned myself a promotion." He kicked Warren twice more, then lifted him to his feet by his jacket collar. "Make one wrong move and you'll end up like your buddies." He faced Warren toward the rover and pushed him forward.

Warren, still numb with shock, listened to the sounds of movement. The Corporal did not seem to pick up on it, either through ignorance, or adrenaline from the firefight.

The Private was standing beside the rover. Her gauntlet was deactivated. At first glance, Warren knew she was a nervous rookie who did not even want to be there.

"Look who've I found, Nellen," the Corporal said, pointing at their prisoner. She did not seem to notice. In fact, she appeared to be looking *past* them. The Corporal grew frustrated. "Hey! Radio the boss. Let him know we've got Dr. Warren, the fugitive. His companions are worm food."

The one named Nellen did not appear to pick up on what he said. Her posture grew increasingly nervous, her hands raising partly as she saw something emerge from the collection of rocks.

"Tarseas? Something's coming!"

The Corporal shook his head, groaning. Before he could mock her, he perked up. He could now hear the sounds of movement behind him.

He turned around in time to see the first of the arachnid creatures lift itself over the log-shaped rock.

It was a sight that made his skin crawl. Its body consisted of a head and abdomen, all of which were smaller than the scarabs. The legs, however, were way longer and armed with two curved talons at the end. The head was cone-shaped. Originally a subterranean creature, it did not appear to have any eyes, yet it seemed to see perfectly fine. There were no sign of fangs on its head or a stinger on its abdomen.

Warren was not fooled. He knew from how quickly the scarabs were bested that these beasts were armed with paralyzing venom.

The arachnoid stepped closer, the claw on full display for its victims to see.

Tarseas took aim with his gauntlet, only to retract when over a dozen other arachnoid creatures appeared.

"Get inside!"

He pushed Warren into the rover's back seat, then dove into the passenger seat. Nellen was already in the driver's seat. She engaged the door lock and put the vehicle in reverse.

Already, the arachnoid creatures were all over the rover. The vehicle shook as they scurried over the top, the ceiling threatening to cave in on the occupants as clawed feet pounded down on it.

Warren sat up in his seat, only to immediately duck back down. One of the creatures was directly over his head. Its impacts were heavy and intense, almost as if the thing was slamming its entire body against the rover.

The doctor sat up again and looked to the window. On the other side was a blur of legs, near and far. A clawed foot swung down from the top of the rover, striking the window. Warren scooted to the middle seat, instinctively reaching for his sidearm which was no longer there.

After a few short seconds, the hillside was alive with these spider-things. They came from all directions, seemingly materializing out of thin air. North, south, east, west... every direction Warren looked, there were arachnoids.

"Get us the hell out of here!" Tarseas said.

Nellen slammed on the accelerator and turned right on the wheel. The vehicle shook violently as it moved, both from the terrain and the added weight perched atop of it. After facing the rover south, she put it in forward gear and slammed her foot down on the pedal.

Right away, two of the creatures climbed over the hood, pressing their ugly faces against the windshield.

Their cone-shaped heads parted at the tip and peeled back in four directions. Bending at thin chitin joints, they resembled grotesque flower petals. Unlike the rigid exoskeleton on the outside, the inside was soft and fleshy.

In the center were two enormous black fangs. Dripping saliva, mucus, and venom, they scraped the windshield.

Nellen closed her eyes and screamed. Blinded by fear and physical obstruction, she did not see the rock straight ahead until it was too late.

The rover struck with tremendous force, imploding the engine and cracking the windshield.

Both tridents were flung forward, their faces crashing against the wheel and dashboard.

Nellen sat up. Her hands fumbled with the wheel. Dazed and baffled, she tried to put the rover back in reverse. There was no response from the engine. The arachnoids had been thrown in the crash, giving the tridents a clear view of the engine. It was wrecked.

That clear view was quickly stripped away as more of the arachnoids crawled over the vehicle.

The sound of scraping intensified. The rover rocked side to side, then tilted backward.

"What are they doing?!" Nellen asked.

They felt the front of the rover lift. A series of vibrations shook the floor under their feet.

All of a sudden, the rover *backed away* and *turned*, seemingly on its own.

Tarseas pressed his face to the window, looking down. He could see legs stretching from under the rover.

"You've got to be kidding," he said. "They're taking us somewhere."

He leaned over Nellen to get a look at the other side. Sure enough, several arachnoids had jampacked themselves under the rover and were carrying it on their backs.

His breathing intensified, fogging the inside of his mask. The Corporal, who had been gleefully overconfident minutes prior, was quickly losing his composure. With his gauntlet armed, he grabbed the door handle, ready to unleash a bombardment of plasma bolts.

"NO!" Warren shouted. "As soon as that door opens, they'll flood this rover."

Tarseas looked back at him, ready to shut him up. His eyes went back and forth between the window and the prisoner. Though he would not admit it out loud, he knew Warren was right.

The Corporal eased into his seat, watching the landscape seemingly move past them. Despite the weight of the vehicle, they were able to move at an impressive speed.

Nellen grabbed the radio mic. "Unit Two to Caparzo. We're under attack by hostile wildlife. We're trapped in the Blackout Hills. We've activated our emergency beacon…"

CHAPTER 23

Centauri Colony – General Hospital.

Anastacia Drucus stood up from Patrick's bedside, hearing a rare tense voice coming from Carlos LaFonte. He was in the hall, near the room, speaking through a comm unit on the wall.

"Yep. Absolutely. I'll go. I'll head over to Security Headquarters right away."

"We're not sure if he'll accept our help." It was Bill Cook's voice.

"He'll need to. If anything happens to him or his men on the first day, you can be sure Hope Central will send a hundred more troops. Considering what happened at the diner this morning, I don't think this colony will take well to additional tridents."

"That's a good point. I'll head over to see Caparzo. I'll see you there."

"On my way."

Anastacia stepped out into the hall, spotting Carlos as he began walking toward his office.

"Carlos? What's going on?"

He stopped and turned to look at her. There was a hint of anxiety in his expression, something she rarely saw from him.

"Bill Cook managed to overhear some transmissions from the tridents stationed at the Admin building. One of Caparzo's patrol teams are in trouble in the Blackout Hills."

"So?" she said.

"So, Bill Cook and I are heading over to see the Lieutenant and offer our assistance."

The very thought of helping that jerk made Anastacia want to spit on the floor.

"You're kidding, right? *You're* going out there?!"

"Yes," Carlos said.

"Carlos, it's the Blackout Hills. You could be killed," she said.

"I'm aware, Anastacia."

"You have EMS teams. That's what they're here for."

"As you said, it's extremely dangerous," Carlos said. "Any emergency in the valley, I'll happily send the EMS teams. But in the Blackout? I'm not going to subject any of my staff to go in my place."

"So save *them*?!" she said, her veins bulging through her reddening face. "Those tridents? The same kind of people who shot up Espinosa? The same people who assaulted our people at the diner? You want to save *them*?! Why? Let the Lieutenant go out there. Serves him right. Not you, Carlos. There's people *here* who need you more. Who deserve you more."

Carlos shook his head. Anastacia stood quiet, the hard look he gave her hitting with psychological impact. It was a look, not of judgement, but of grave disappointment. There was no need to address the reason, for Anastacia already knew. He had known her since she had arrived at this colony, and had always known her to be a woman of good character. She was rightfully outraged at the death of her mentor, fellow staffers, and the injuries her husband obtained in the explosion. However, her grief had turned to vengeance, a motivation that Carlos openly despised.

While he understood that violence and even death was unfortunately necessary at times, he had vowed to avoid it whenever possible. Even if the person in question was someone of poor character. He had seen death up close and in vast numbers. It was not pretty, it was not glorious. Anastacia knew this, and yet, she found herself near the point of relishing in the deaths of others.

"Nobody deserves anything," he said, "except for the right to life. Maybe the tridents don't have those principles, but I do, and I will not go back on them because I have fundamental differences with someone." He turned and resumed walking to his office.

Anastacia leaned against the wall and shut her eyes. It was true that Lieutenant Caparzo would be walking into a giant hornets' nest. The Blackout Hills were dangerous under normal circumstances, but this area was especially bad. There was something out there that they had not seen before. Whatever it was, it was cunning, fast, and knew how to blend in. It did not matter how battle-hardened Vince Caparzo was. He was unfamiliar with the territory and the risks therein. Going there without guidance meant certain death.

She looked to her husband. He was in a peaceful state, hands crossed over his stomach, breathing comfortably for the moment.

What would Patrick think if I let such a thing happen?

She knew the answer. Patrick would have sided with Carlos. He was good like that, always putting others ahead of himself.

The office door opened. Out came Carlos, dressed in field clothing.

"Carlos, wait. I'm coming with you."

***

Centauri Colony - Security Headquarters.

"I repeat... ... ... in Blackout Hills... ... ... under attack by... ..."

When Vince Caparzo arrived on World Two, he had heard the phrase 'they don't call it the Blackout Hills for nothing'. That sentiment was made clear by Private Yasutake's transmission. The static fractured the message so badly that only a few scattered words made it through.

"Say again, Unit Two? You're breaking up." He stepped outside and adjusted the frequency. Private Yasutake attempted to repeat herself, but her transmission was garbled. Vince could not make out a single word. Regardless, he heard enough to know this was a hostile situation. "Unit Three and Four, did you copy that?"

"Unit Three here, Lieutenant. Could not make out most of it. Something about wildlife."

"Yeah, I caught that part too. Report to headquarters immediately."

"Copy."

Vince stepped back inside and marched straight for the armory. There, he put an armored vest over his uniform. Blaster tested, it was designed to take over a dozen plasma strikes from M3-grade gauntlets. He was not sure what he was dealing with in the Hills, but he was certain this vest would come in handy. On its center was the trident symbol, displayed in red lines. While shaped like a trident, the lines did resemble rivers of blood.

He turned around, hearing the sound of movement in his office. Stepping out of the armory, he saw Bill Cook, Dr. Carlos LaFonte, and Dr. Anastacia Drucus standing in the planning area.

"Lieutenant," Bill Cook said, "I encountered some of your men and overheard the radio transmission. I understand there's a situation developing in the Blackout Hills."

Vince considered ignoring him entirely and demanding that they leave. The words never came out though. He had enough problems on his plate. Engaging in verbal sparring would not help matters.

"No rest for the weary." He grabbed a mask and secured the armory. "One of my patrols encountered hostile activity. They located and apprehended the fugitive Dr. Warren."

"They found him?!" Anastacia asked.

"How is he?" Carlos asked.

"Not sure. I'm more focused on the 'hostile activity' part of the situation. The emergency beacon on their rover has been activated, but radio contact has been lost."

"They don't call them the Blackout Hills for nothing," Anastacia said.

Vince stepped past them out into the outside. As he approached his rover, he could hear them following him. Stopping at the driver's side door, he turned to glare at them.

"Is there something you people need? In case you haven't noticed, I have serious business to attend to."

"Lieutenant, if you plan to go out there and find your people, you're going to need my help," Anastacia said.

"Mine too," Carlos added. "There's a good chance they might need medical care."

"No," Vince said, decisively.

Anastacia stepped forward, appearing on the verge of squaring up with him just as she had done yesterday morning.

"You don't realize what you are walking into up there," she said. "The Blackout Hills are the most dangerous terrain on World Two."

"I'm aware of that," Vince said. "Hence, I need tridents. Not science majors."

"Oh, really?" she retorted. "Unless I'm mistaken, it's your *tridents* who are trapped in the Hills calling for help."

"Lieutenant?" Bill Cook raised his hand, taking a far less assertive approach in addressing his concerns. "I must urge you to take Anastacia with you. She knows this region of the Blackout Hills better than anybody. You're going to need guidance once you get there. Speeders and rovers are generally unsuitable for the Hills."

"As your people have learned," Anastacia added.

"It's their only chance," Carlos said.

"Listen, I've said my piece on the matter," Vince said. "I've got the situation under control. The last thing I need is to worry about babysitting colonists while in hostile terrain."

"Oh, is that so?" Anastacia said with a smirk. "So, you're doing this out of concern. I'm so moved. Okay, have it your way. Just one question: What should we tell the General when you don't come back?"

LaFonte put a hand on her shoulder and gently eased her away from the Lieutenant. He stepped in her place, his hands clasped unthreateningly over his waist.

"I understand, Vince," he said.

The gentleness of his voice and use of his first name was like a cool breeze on a hot summer day. Only the most coldblooded of people were able to withstand its effect. It was moments like this where Vince questioned how cynical he truly was.

"Understand what?"

"As I stated during our last encounter, I read your file," Carlos said. "I know what happened. You pretend you don't care about people. And maybe you think you don't... but you went into that Alaska facility for a reason, even when everyone else wanted to perform a chemical drop on it. I understand you don't want any civilian casualties on your watch. Believe it or not, we don't want any trident casualties either. None of us here want bloodshed."

"Not even from a blood-jacket," Bill Cook said. "You may be in charge of this place, but believe me, that won't last long if you don't accept our help. Let Dr. Drucus and LaFonte go along."

Vince almost wanted to laugh. The administrator had been so passive since Vince arrived, it was a shock to see him show the slightest bit of assertiveness.

"The agenda is to get Dr. Warren and your tridents back safely," Anastacia said. "The last thing we want is an increased military presence here. If tridents start dying off in the first days stationed at Centauri, we'll have dozens more flying out here by next week."

She paused, letting her statements sink in. She could practically hear Bill Cook's racing heart. Even Carlos seemed a tad unnerved by her brutal honesty.

"What? I admit it," she said. "We don't want you here, *but*... I recognize you're here to stay. Might as well work together. So, what are we waiting for?"

Vince kept one arm on the shuttle door. Part of him was tempted to get inside and drive off. This went against his training. He was a trident, who had been to unimaginable hells back on his home planet. Each time, he came out alive and ready for the next fight.

But this isn't World One.

Though every fiber of his being wanted to handle the situation without their help, there was a voice in the back of his mind shouting the truth. That truth, which he so badly wanted to ignore, was that he needed the colonists more than they needed him. It was one of many realities he would never say out loud. At best, he would only imply it.

He looked to the sky, accepting that this debate was lost, then looked to Anastacia.

"You're a real pain, you know that?"

She chuckled. "That's been said of me."

He groaned, resigned to accepting their help.

"What do we use for transport?"

CHAPTER 24

Centauri Colony – Scarab barn.

"Oh, look at this. Mr. Hotshot Lieutenant thinks he can march out here and requisition my scarabs."

The meeting with Ed Burger was going as well as Vince anticipated. Ed kept his back to the Lieutenant while walking the length of the south fence. He placed buckets of minerals through the gap for the scarabs to enjoy.

Vince's patience was quickly running out, and he was only a minute into the conversation. Stress and mental fatigue tested his self-control. It was no easy thing to maintain the appearance of authority while also pleading for the help of others. Usually, he would take what he wanted by force—something he was trying to avoid for the sake of peace.

On the other hand, time was of the essence, and wasting time in a back-and-forth with Ed Burger was not helping things.

"Well, actually, I do," Vince said.

Ed stood straight and turned to face him. Vince could sense the gears turning in the animal expert's head. He had a whole lineup of one-liner responses, just waiting to be unleashed on the trident.

"Yeah?" he said, grinning. "You mean to say that if I say no, you'd apprehend me and take these scarabs by force?"

"If I have to," Vince said.

Ed broke out in laughter. His reaction had little effect on Vince, who would have assumed it was an act of psychological warfare. The reactions of Anastacia, Bill Cook, and Carlos, however, made it clear he was on the losing side of this discussion. While not as obnoxiously as Ed, they also chuckled.

"Oh, boy. That'd be a sight to behold," Carlos muttered.

Ed's mask was fogging up from the rapid breathing caused by his laughter. "Oh, Lieutenant. You're so cute. Part of me actually wants to see this unfold. So badly, that I think I will say no."

"Is that right?" Vince said. His attempt to save face was a grave failure, for Ed was only amused further.

"Absolutely," Ed said. "You see, I've bonded with every scarab in the herd. I've been there for each of their births. I raised them, fed them, cared for their ailments. They've got the emotional intelligence of dogs, Lieutenant. Your rank means nothing to them. If you cause me any harm whatsoever, then try to take the scarabs... let's just say you'd be lucky if you only end up with a few spurs from their forelegs embedded in you. Even if you managed to mount them, they'd buck you off." Ed crossed his arms triumphantly, maintaining that grin on his face. "What can I say? They're my friends. And they're the most loyal ones you can ever have. So, go ahead. Requisition them by force."

Vince looked past him at the insectoid creatures. "You're their friends, huh?" He looked Ed in the eye. "Makes enough sense that they'd pick the ugliest fella around here. Probably mistook you for one of their kind."

Ed tilted his head, that grin vanishing. His eyebrows slanted and his brow furrowed, putting the Lieutenant on alert. Vince stood ready to fend off a possible outburst from someone whose ego had just been bruised.

Ed glared at him, then looked at the others with a look that read *can you believe this guy?* The others were quietly exchanging glances.

Then at once, they all laughed together.

As usual, Vince was the odd man out. He stood with his arms down, exhaling slowly to keep himself from groaning loudly.

"At least you've got a sense of humor, Lieutenant," Ed said. "I might actually feel sorry if you get eaten by a flying Crossnaught."

"You ought to," Vince said, "because I'll send a message to Hope Central. 'In the event of my death, blame Ed Burger. Won't be hard to find. Look for an ugly guy who hangs out with bugs.' Ever see an F-41 Phoenix? They're the *real* flying beasts."

"I've raised flying lug mantises," Ed said. "They can take your phoenixes any day of the week."

"Alright, alright, alright," Anastacia said, stepping between them. "Let's settle this right now. You guys don't like each other. Ed, you're a grubby rancher who spends more time with animals than humans, and hates government more than scarabs like water. Lieutenant Caparzo, you're an indoctrinated blood-jacket who's used to getting in people's business in service of the almighty Alliance. You're so opposed, we could put your faces on a chess board."

"Make him the dark side," Ed said, pointing at Vince. "And make sure his pieces have big black masks to hide their cowardice."

"You're just jealous, because a face like yours could use a mask," Vince retorted. "The fact that I can smell you through my rebreather speaks volumes."

Ed opened his mouth for another retort, only to get interrupted by Anastacia.

"Exactly the point I was trying to convey!" she exclaimed. "Now, can we get past this. We've got a real situation here. There's no time to measure each other's... blaster muzzles."

Ed raised a finger. "Mine's bigger!"

Anastacia ignored that remark. "This is a rescue mission, Ed. You've been on dozens."

"Not quite like this," he said. "Not rescuing incompetent fools who've gotten themselves in trouble in less than twenty-four hours. It's a bloody record! Ha! These tridents come here, acting all high and mighty, and before you know it, they're calling for help." He looked at Vince. "Did they not undergo briefings of the area? Or are they just plain stupid?"

Vince could not take it anymore. "Anastacia, are you sure we can't just take the damn rovers?"

She shook her head. "Impossible."

"She's smart," Ed said. He gave an exasperated sigh, then waved them to the barn entrance. "Come on. If I don't help you, Anastacia will go on some moral tangent. There's not enough painkillers in the world to rid me of the headache that causes."

Anastacia cracked a smile. "Works every time."

Vince nodded. "I can imagine." He stood at the back of the group while Ed Burger opened the doors.

The inside of the barn was extremely simple. The only section that was equipped with any technology was the office area. Aside from that, the barn could have passed for something built in the 1800s.

For a moment, Vince thought about Lucy and her fascination with frontier life. This barn was the closest to the real thing. There were two aisles lined with stalls. To his surprise, many of those stalls were occupied. Until now, Vince had assumed the colony had maybe a dozen scarabs. As it turned out, there were at least three dozen.

Scarabs weren't the only creatures inhabiting this barn. In the far stalls were snake-like creatures. They were biting down on some dome-shaped droid units, bobbing slightly.

Vince pointed at the oddity. "Mr. Burger, I think your lizards are about to have your droids for lunch."

"Hmm?" Ed looked to the end of the aisle. "Oh, that? No, they're having their glands drained."

Vince sniggered. "Well, that seems a little pointless, doesn't it? I mean, if one of those things bites somebody, their fangs are gonna run through their body. Venom would be the last thing on their minds."

Ed and the others exchanged glances and smiles.

"No, Caparzo. That's not exactly why we're harvesting the venom. We process it as part of our food program."

The hairs on the back of Vince's neck stood on end. Feeling the blood draining from his face, he pointed at the snake-things literally being milked like cows.

"You guys... eat that?"

Ed walked toward a stall on Vince's right, stopping briefly to pat him on the shoulder.

"How do you think those nutrition smoothies are made?" He licked his lips and made an 'mm-mmm' sound before moving on.

Vince gulped, then turned his head so the others couldn't see him grow pale.

No wonder that crap tasted so vile.

Ed opened the stall door and petted the scarab inside. It tucked its head down to receive his offer of scratching its neck.

"Aw, hi there. I'm happy to see you too." He scratched the creature, then led it out of the stall. "Ever ride one of these babies, Lieutenant?"

"No."

"You have no riding experience whatsoever?"

"No."

Ed turned to Anastacia. "Is this for real?! This guy's as good as dead if he goes. It's better if he stays here."

"I'll keep an eye on him," Anastacia replied, her voice motherly.

"Well, if you insist..." Ed shrugged, then handed the reins to Vince, leaning in for another verbal jab. "My gun muzzle *is* bigger, by the way."

"Mine's not rusty," Vince retorted.

Anastacia threw her arms out. "Can we please?!"

While Ed went to collect saddles for the scarabs, she and Vince stepped toward the office quarters.

"After Ed gets them saddled, we'll load the scarabs into the hauler," she explained. "Once we arrive at the hills, we'll mount them and begin the search from there."

"How many are we taking?" Vince asked.

"Six," she said.

"Six? Only six? There's forty of them at least. I can take a whole fireteam," Vince said.

"They're not the easiest creature to tame. Ed's practically the scarab whisperer. They all respond to him. They're all docile, so long as you're feeding them or just in their presence. But only a select few will let anyone but Ed ride them. It's a work in progress. But once tamed, they are loyal, which is good, considering where we're going."

"How many different species of wildlife is out there?" Vince asked.

"Many," Anastacia said. "We've catalogued over two hundred species since this colony was founded. Some are harmless, others are extremely dangerous. Everything living on this planet including the Martians, have been forced to adapt to the new conditions. This caused many subterranean creatures to the planet's surface. From a scientific point of view, it's fascinating. We're witnessing evolution on a planetary scale."

Vince shook his head, failing to see the fascination she was referring to. "Fascinating until one of those things give you a yum-yum face."

"Yeah, there is that," Anastacia said. "We've had over ten people go missing in the Blackout Hills in the past few months. Two of them just a few days ago."

Vince looked away. That statement added weight to an already tense situation. Anastacia was no stranger to hostile wildlife. If she was nervous about the Blackout Hills, then it was for good reason. At this point, he truly understood that he would soon be entering an area where experienced people had disappeared. For the first time since his earliest deployments, Vince was not confident he would come out of this mission alive.

He looked to Ed Burger's office. He thought of Lucy. It was not a passing thought or a feeling of obligation. For the first real time in years, he was thinking of his daughter. Like a machine, he was programmed to raise her—to turn her into a functioning member of the Alliance. Emotions had nothing to do with it, at least, that was what he believed.

He had told himself that was the reason he chose to bring her here. If she survived in this place, it would toughen her as a great adult. Tough experiences built character. She would do great things for the Alliance.

Now, he confronted reality. Bringing her here had nothing to do with serving the Alliance. The truth was that being separated by millions of miles, not even being able to see her grow up, was too painful to bear.

All of his life, he focused on his devotion to his career, as he was raised to do. Today, he learned there was one bond more powerful than his devotion to his duties—the bond between father and daughter. It was something he desperately did not want to fail.

If he died in the Hills, Lucy would have nobody. He would not see her grow up. She would be without him forever.

That, in his mind, would be true failure.

"I'll be back in a minute." He stepped away from Anastacia. Using his security badge, which allowed him access to all facilities and offices across the colony, he let himself into Ed Burger's office. Like the atrium of the dome, the office entrance had a small airlock between two airtight doors. Once inside the office, he was able to remove his mask.

The room was equipped with a desk, a small dining area, and a cot for sleeping. Ed Burger was literally a guy who lived on the job. There wasn't much personalization of the area, aside from a framed photograph on the desk and, oddly enough, a few potted plants. They were on the floor next to the cot with a violet-blue lamp positioned over them for chlorophyll absorption.

Ed Burger was an interesting guy indeed.

On the lefthand side was a wall-mounted comm unit. Vince punched in the dial code.

"Centauri Middle School," a female voice answered.

"This is Lieutenant Vince Caparzo, code Two-Seven-Alpha-Mike-Nine-TACK-Four. Put Lucy Caparzo on the line, please."

"One moment, sir."

***

Centauri Middle School.

It was the middle of economics class. The first day jitters had not yet worn off. Every pair of eyes that turned in her direction carried a sense of judgement. Everyone knew she was the daughter of the colony overseer. Even the teacher, who was nice and polite—really an excellent instructor who kept the class engaged—seemed hesitant to address her. Mrs. Kelleck was her name and she smiled every time she spoke to Lucy. In fact, it was the smile that unintentionally made her nervousness obvious. Lucy could practically read her mind. Mrs. Kelleck's mind was filled with the anxieties of such a high-profile student. She probably wondered whether it would garner negative response from the Lieutenant if Lucy were to receive any bad grades or discipline.

Nobody wanted to talk to her. They certainly did not seem eager to make friends. Lucy tried to brush it off as the newness of her first day.

Eventually, they'll warm up to me. Right?

The normally optimistic Lucy was not so sure. She thought coming to this planet would be a chance for true adventure. For the first time, she was doubting that prospect. Now, it was looking like a lifetime of loneliness.

She kept her eyes on her electronic desk pad, following the instructions Mrs. Kelleck had laid out for her assignment. The classroom door opened and an office assistant stepped in. She spoke with Mrs. Kelleck, who then walked over to Lucy's desk.

"Ms. Caparzo?"

Lucy looked up. "Yes?"

"Can you go with this lady. You have a comm call to take in the main office."

"Oh…" *What's this about?* Rather than ask out loud, Lucy stood up and followed the assistant into the hallway. They walked down the hall and took a right at the nearest juncture, which led them to the front of the building. The assistant directed Lucy to one of the desks. The comm was blinking red with a caller on hold.

After instructing Lucy how to take the device off hold, she stepped out to allow some privacy.

Lucy pressed the button. The red light flashed green.

"Hello?"

"Hey, Lucy. It's your dad."

"Oh!" There was no hiding the surprise she felt. She felt somewhat foolish. Who else would be calling her at school? Then again, her father was not the type to check in. Often, he was gone days or even weeks at a time without ever calling, satisfied that the assigned caretaker was capable of supervising her.

The other thing that caught her off guard was the tenderness in his voice. That was something she was not used to at all, in her personal life nor on World One in general, with a few exceptions. Only here on World Two did she see such affection in full display. Maybe it was rubbing off on him.

"How are you doing? Things going well on your first day?"

"Y-yeah, I guess. Nothing bad to report. Just different, is all. Give it a week and I'll be used to things."

"Good. Glad to hear."

Definitely not the normal dad she was used to hearing from.

"Is everything okay?" she said.

"Yeah. I thought I'd check in and see how you're doing."

"It's not like you to interrupt a class just to check in. You sure everything's fine?"

"Absolutely. I just have to run outside the dome to do an important task. But uh… I was thinking, maybe when I get back and you're done with school, we could go out for drinks. You know, celebrate that tenth birthday."

A warm feeling gently swept away her sense of loneliness.

"I thought I was too old for celebrations," she said.

"No. Not for me, kiddo."

A bright smile came over her face. It was so bright, so genuine, she wished he was here to see it. She would have to gift him with a smile of equal proportions when they met after school.

"Okay. I look forward to it." Immediately, an idea came to mind. "Oh! There's this nice little place called the Red Flower Café! Maybe we could try that!"

To her surprise, her dad gave a long pause before answering.

"Yeeeaaahhhh... You know? How 'bout we try a different one?"

His tone said it all. Lucy shook her head. Somehow, she suspected that he, or at least some of his tridents, had already begun 'making friends' with the colonists.

She leaned in toward the comm. "Dad. Did you do something dumb?"

"Nooo. Of course not."

"Dad?"

He cleared his throat. *"Well, duty calls. I gotta go. See ya later, kiddo."*

She smiled. "Bye."

***

Vince ended the call and exited the office. Back in the barn, he found Ed Burger leading the scarabs one by one into the hauler. It was attached to a large Land Rover to be towed to the edge of the Hills.

He heard the engine of a security rover pulling up to the barn. Stepping outside, he found Sergeant Elias and four other tridents disembarking.

"What are your orders, sir?" the Sergeant asked.

"Sergeant, I need you to oversee things at the colony while I'm gone," Vince said. "You four tridents will follow us in that rover."

"Understood, sir," Sergeant Elias said. "Are you sure you don't want me to go in your stead? It can be dangerous, and we don't want to risk losing our commanding officer."

"I appreciate that, Sergeant, but this is something I need to do," Vince replied.

"Yes sir. Do you wish for the inspections to continue?" Sergeant Elias said.

Vince turned his head slightly, noticing Anastacia and Carlos standing by the hauling rover. They did not appear to be listening, though Anastacia did glance briefly in his direction.

"Yes, but just focus on the scans. Don't confront any illegitimate business operators. We'll handle that later. Just focus on making a record."

"Understood," Sergeant Elias said. He looked to the tridents. "You heard him. Take this rover and follow them to the hills."

"Yes sir," the four tridents exclaimed before boarding their rover. Elias saluted Vince, then returned on foot to the colony atrium.

Vince turned around and joined the others by the hauling rover. Carlos was now seated in the back, Anastacia was standing by the door waiting for him. Ed Burger had all six scarabs loaded in the hauler and was making his way to the driver's seat.

"All set. Ready to go when you all are," he said.

Vince noticed that the three of them had V-13 rifles, supplied by Burger. It was not something that pleased him too much, but now was not the time to argue about civilian access to arms.

He took the front passenger seat. "Ready to roll."

"Aw," Ed muttered. He took his seat and buckled in. "I assumed the lovely Dr. Drucus would be seated next to me. Turns out I'm stuck with you instead."

"Funny. She seemed pretty determined to sit in the back. *Away* from you. If you ask me, I did her a favor."

"Oh, here we go again," Anastacia said. Her head sank onto one of her palms. She looked to Carlos. "They're a match made in Heaven."

Ed hit the accelerator and began the two-mile journey to the Blackout Hills.

CHAPTER 25

Blackout Hills – Cliff edge.

Godon remained poised, watching over the sealed tunnel entrance. He had heard the faint sounds of blaster fire way in the distance. The shooting was fairly brief and was followed by silence. Either the humans had survived their encounter with their threat or had been killed. He hoped in his heart that Dr. Warren and his friends were okay, but understood that it was out of his hands. For now, he could only focus on the *Gojya.*

Guarded, he studied the nearby area for movement. His efforts were fueled by both caution and opportunity. This was his time. Every one of his species had their own special hunt. It was the one instance where competition was encouraged in his clan. Those who killed the largest, most dangerous beasts garnered the most respect. If the kill was impressive enough, the Martian was rewarded with status.

His nostrils picked up many scents, some familiar, others completely new. Both hands gripped his staff.

He had picked up on a very specific scent. This one was both familiar and alien. It was rank with deep soil and rotting flesh from some other surface dweller. Whatever it was, it was coming from the east.

Dr. Warren and his companions were far off now. Even if they turned back, it would take them an hour at minimum to return. That granted Godon plenty of time to investigate.

He broke from his statue-like pose and turned east. Traveling near the cliff edge, he readied himself for combat. After several yards, he could hear the sounds of clawed feet moving around him. They were out of the line of sight, but Godon already knew what he was listening to. *Leshries,* four-legged reptiles with venomous stinger-tipped tails.

As a youngster, Godon witnessed one of those creatures kill a scarab with a heart-stopping sting. The unfortunate steed lurched violently, triggered by an intense pain in its leg. He remembered witnessing the creature attempt to retaliate by slashing its forelegs, but the *leshrie* was an agile creature. Two-thirds the size of an average human, it darted out of range. Had its victim been a wild animal, the creature would have waited for its venom to take effect. On this occasion, however, there were three Martians in the area. Energy blasts from their staffs drove the creature off. For the scarab, it was too little, too late. The venom had shut down its internal organs inside of a few minutes.

A loyal creature, it was given a proper sendoff, wrapped in *Tarweia* silk and cast into the Great Lake. The crystalline, energy-rich liquid bonded with the silk, forming a diamond coffin that would preserve the scarab alongside many fallen Martians from eons past.

Godon had attended many a funeral, and was honored. In many years, as long as he served the clan with honor, he would eventually have his turn. His soul would ascend to the heavens, while his vessel was carefully preserved by his brothers and sisters.

To achieve that honor, he must serve the clan.

To serve the clan, he must deem himself worthy.

The first step was to prove his worth here in the hostile grounds of the eastern Blackout.

With caution, he pressed on.

The sounds, clearly those of a *leshrie*, grew increasingly distant. It moved southeast with a sudden urgency. Either it had found easier prey, or it was fleeing something. Both theories made sense. As dangerous as they were, they were a delicacy, as were most things on this planet.

The strange familiar-but-also-unfamiliar smell strengthened.

Godon stopped.

He remembered the lessons from his youth. The elders had warned the clan of the Watchers. For centuries, they had not been seen. Some of the younger generation doubted their existence, despite the physical evidence preserved in the colony catacombs.

He remembered the scent. It was spoiled with age, but memorable all the same. It was unique, resembling a hot spice mixed with the odor emitted by the worms living underneath the human-named Olympus Mons.

This current odor was stronger and more potent, but undoubtedly similar. Curiosity and anticipation clashed in the young Martian's mind. He gave thought about turning back to warn his clan. By doing so, he ran the risk of betraying Dr. Warren.

Godon decided it was necessary. He could not go back to the colony without confirming if the threat was real.

If it was, and he managed to destroy it, that would mark the completion of his *Gojya*. Furthermore, the uniqueness of this victory would ensure a high status in the clan. He would find himself not only as a warrior, but a future leader, for his actions could potentially save the future of not only the clan, but the species.

Encouraged by these prospects, he pushed on.

On and on he went, far from the tunnel entrance. As he neared the entity, a new awareness filled his mind. The area had gone silent. Very silent.

Silence in these hills only meant death. All life around here was avoiding this area like the plague.

Still, he kept going.

After nearly three-fourths of a mile, he found the oddity—and lived just long enough to regret it.

CHAPTER 26

The drive to the Blackout Hills was considered the calm before the storm. It was two miles of open red landscape. Today, visibility was particularly good. It was only partly cloudy, allowing for the natural sunlight to stream down in its full glory. Looking at the sky, it almost appeared as though there were three suns, thanks to the reflector panels that were actively working on warming the planet's surface.

It was a smooth drive for the most part. The ground was a little bumpy, but nothing that the rovers could not handle. It was an easy route to follow, for the ground was lined with the tracks from numerous back and forth trips over the course of months.

"I hear they're finally starting to build roads near Hope Colony," Carlos said. It was an attempt to make conversation and fill the silence.

"Not when I went there for the conference," Anastacia said. "At least, I didn't see anything. Lieutenant, was there road work going on when you first arrived?"

He shook his head. "Negative. Maybe in the future. Right now, they've got more important things to worry about."

"More important than infrastructure?" Anastacia said.

"Of course," Ed said in his usual snarky tone. "You know the *real* priority is 'security'."

Vince was not sure which he found more bizarre, the abundance of literal alien life or the audacity of these colonists to openly criticize the government. Back on World One, such blasphemy would, at minimum, result in the offender be put on a watchlist.

He chose not to engage in debate. It was likely that special security measures were coming. In a sense, the colonists were already facing punishment for their disloyalty. Those times would come later, and Vince would have to carry it out.

Part of him hoped it would not go that far. This was a different place, in culture and environment, than World One. Enforcing Code Forty-two would not go over well.

Vince forced the thought from his head in favor of focusing on the task at hand. Up ahead were the Blackout Hills.

He lifted a pair of binocs and scanned the ground. "I think I see the trail they made when they were patrolling." He panned the binocs to the left and zoomed in on the rocks. "There. Thirty-five degrees to the left."

Ed snatched the binocs from his hand and, while still driving, looked at the area in question.

"Hmmm... oh, there it is. Scraping on the boulders. Definitely done by a security rover. Only an idiot would drive into a forest of rock towers." He tossed the binocs onto Vince's lap and turned left.

The drive quickly grew bumpy as they neared the elevation. A few small boulders dotted the area, forcing Ed to weave back and forth to prevent blowing a tire.

After another two hundred yards, the rover juddered with every meter of ground it passed over. Vince felt like dice in a cup, held in place only due to the safety belt.

"Alright, we're taking the scarabs from here." Ed parked the rover and stepped out.

Vince undid his safety belt and checked his waist, feeling as though the strap had cut into his skin. He stepped outside and followed the others to the hauler. Ed Burger lowered the ramp, then stepped up to grab one of the scarabs by the bridle.

The security escort parked a few meters back. Its four occupants stepped out and assembled near their lieutenant, waiting for orders.

"I need two of you to stay here and guard the vehicles," he said. "The other two are riding into the Hills with us."

"Don't worry, it's just like riding a bike," Ed said, walking down the ramp with one of the scarabs. He had a sense of glee as he led the scarab to Vince. "Time to mount up."

Anastacia placed a wooden stool beside the creature, then stood back and watched.

Vince watched the creature, loathsome at the fact that he had to ride it. Its mandibles frolicked, its forelegs scratching its head. The mid and rear legs bent as it lowered itself to be mounted. The saddle was on its back, with stirrups propped over the middle leg joints.

There was no declining this horrendous task, especially not in front of his subordinates.

I miss World One.

He stepped aboard the wooden stool, then lifted himself onto the scarab's back. He slipped his feet into the stirrups and took the reins.

Slowly, the creature stood up. Immediately, Vince felt at ease. Perhaps this wasn't going to be so bad after all. The creature seemed gentle, cooperative, and even welcoming.

For about five seconds.

It reared back and bucked its legs.

"Whoa!"

The world went upside down as Vince was flipped head over heels off of the scarab's back.

Ed Burger laughed. Anastacia, while grinning, at least showed a hint of concern.

"You okay?" she asked.

Vince rolled onto his hands and knees. "Yeah. Just dandy." He stood up and gave the beast a burning scowl. "I swear, if I had a giant boot…"

"Oh, be nice," Ed said. He took the reins and extended them to Carlos. "Doctor, would you mind showing him how it's done?"

Carlos approached, his V-13 rifle slung over his shoulder. He took the reins and scooted the stool into place. With a gentle hand, he rubbed the creature's head. It leaned to the left, allowing its rider to continue his show of affection.

"Don't worry, Lieutenant. You'll get the hang of it," he said. He boarded the scarab, which immediately started to resist. "Shhh. Shhh. Whoa…" He grabbed the horn on its head with one hand, holding on tight for the next few seconds. The scarab's resistance slowed after a few short moments.

Tapping its sides with his heels, he directed the creature to walk forward. Using the reins, he steered it to the left, taking it in a circle. There was no further resistance by the insectoid creature.

"Just like animals on Earth, they sense fear," he said. "Show you're not afraid and are in control… without using violence, of course."

Vince exhaled sharply, momentarily fixated on the old-timer's use of World One's outdated name. He concentrated on the task at hand. Ed Burger led another scarab down the ramp and positioned it by the stepping stool.

With no time to waste, he tried again. He took the reins, planted his foot on the stool, then lifted himself on its back… only to get immediately bucked off.

"Son of a—"

"Hey!" Ed pointed a finger. "Watch the language. They're sensitive to that."

Vince sat up and glared at him, unsure if the strange man was being serious or sarcastic.

Meanwhile, Anastacia had already climbed aboard her own scarab and was walking it in circles alongside Carlos.

Humiliated, he stood up again. He took the reins and prepared to climb aboard. Before doing so, he leaned in close to its head.

"Tell you what: if you help me out, I'll give you all the delicious mineral you want—or whatever it is you eat." There was no sign of the creature's acceptance. It stayed in place, cleaning its mandibles, dripping saliva. If nothing else, it at least appeared to be at ease.

Vince shook his head and moved to the stepping stool. He counted down from three in his mind, then lifted himself aboard. He was successfully on the saddle, his feet in the stirrups.

The scarab went to work, pushing on its forelegs in an attempt to buck him off. He leaned forward and grabbed its horn, just as Carlos had done.

"Shhh. Come on, boy... or girl, whichever you are. I'm your friend, despite what Ed might've told ya. Shhh. Shhh..."

Slowly but truly, the scarab's resistance slowed to a halt. The shifting of its body ceased, the creature now standing on all six legs. Vince let go of the horn and sat straight.

He tapped his heels to its sides, making the creature move forward. He tested the reins, steering it right and left. To his amazement, the scarab was taking his commands as though it had known him for years.

Vince breathed a sigh of relief. "Piece of cake." He looked at the others. "Just like riding a bike."

"Well done, Lieutenant," Carlos said.

Vince turned his scarab to face the two tridents that would join them on this journey. They both looked to the other pair, who made sure to stand behind the rover, glad they did not have to partake in the taming of these big bugs.

"Alright," Vince said to the unlucky tridents. "Your turn."

***

Somewhere in the Blackout Hills.

The world had gone dark, and the interior of the rover had warmed by the body heat of its anxious occupants.

Corporal Tarseas was on edge, constantly shifting in his seat while trying to look outside. There was nothing to be seen. The sun had disappeared and visibility was at zero.

"Should we turn on the interiors?" Nellen said.

"No, wait," Tarseas said.

"I can't see a thing," Nellen said.

"Hold on," Tarseas said. "Maybe they've left."

"I doubt that," Warren muttered.

Tarseas turned around to face him. "Doc, it might be in your best interest to keep quiet." Before the doctor could respond, he faced forward and put his face to the glass, trying to see outside. There was not a single speck of light. Wherever they were, it was underground.

Unable to take the pitch darkness any longer, he flipped a switch to activate the interior lights. It was a relief to have some kind of visibility, even if it was just the inside of their own, broken down vehicle. There was still nothing to be seen outside except their own panicked reflections in the window.

"Where the hell are we?" Nellen said.

"Where do you think?" Warren said. "They've dragged us into their lair."

"Fabulous," Tarseas said. "First day on the job, and I'm going to be eaten by oversized spider-things."

"You've got it coming," Warren said.

For the second time, Tarseas faced the back seat. "Care to say that again, old man?"

"Alright... You've got it coming," Warren said, not skipping a beat. "Murdering my friends like you did? The only reason this 'old man' doesn't toss you out that door is because I'm not interested in letting those things in this rover."

"Dream on, Doctor," Tarseas said. "The only reason you don't try and toss me out is because you know I'd break all four of your limbs... and a few other bones just for good measure."

"Can we stop this?" Nellen shouted. For a moment, the tension had gotten the better of her. The young private could not keep still.

Warren watched as she tried adjusting the radio frequency. Right away, he knew she was the more sensible member of the team. She was young and not quite seasoned. Moreover, she appeared to have an innocence that most tridents lacked. More specifically, had stolen from them. She did not take part in the firefight, and had it not been for her, the egotistical Tarseas would have never seen the arachnoids coming. Not until it was too late, that is.

"Unit Two to any unit that can hear this. Mayday. We are trapped somewhere in the Blackout Hills. If anyone can hear this transmission, please respond."

"Is the radio dead?" Warren asked.

"No," she replied. "I think there's too much interference. Unless someone comes within, say, a quarter-mile, any transmission I send out won't get picked up." She leaned her head back against the headrest. "Hopefully our emergency beacon didn't get damaged when we crashed."

"Hopefully they'll pick up the signal if it's even working," Tarseas said.

All three of them perked up. From the darkness came a ghostly sound of pain and suffering. Slight vibrations traveled through the rover, as though it was on the end of a fishing line. On the other end of that line, something was moving violently.

That movement quickly intensified, and the groaning sound elevated into agonized screeches.

"The hell's going on out there?" Tarseas said. He tried to look through the windshield, but could not see past his own reflection. "Do our forward beams still work?"

"No, but our overhead spotlight does," Nellen said. "Are we sure we want to turn them on? What if we attract those things?"

"Trust me, Private," Warren said. "They didn't carry us all the way over here just to forget about us."

Silently agreeing, Tarseas stood up and grabbed a lever on the ceiling, which controlled the overhead spotlight. He switched it on, casting a bright, white stream to the portside. He turned the lever, pointing the light toward the direction of the sound.

"Looks like we're in some sort of cave," he said.

Nellen switched off the front interior lights to keep their own reflections from obstructing their view. She almost wished she kept them on.

What they saw was a maze of thick, white webbing, stretching for what appeared to be the entirety of this dark lair. In that, they were tightly cocooned prisoners. Several different species were imprisoned here, paralyzed and bound, awaiting a horrible fate. Within the group of corkscrew-shaped coffins were vacant, empty ones. Their webbing, which appeared to have been hardened by some kind of resin substance, was torn open down the middle.

Warren thought to the horrible graveyard he and his friends had come across. The mystery was solved.

Perhaps the bastard Tarseas did Davy and Preston a favor. Better to die from a plasma bolt than wait for days on end, cocooned in this place, only to have your fluids drained.

By no means did that absolve the Corporal in his view. If there was anyone who deserved to suffer this fate in Warren's view, it was Tarseas.

"Over there," Nellen said, pointing ten degrees left of the engine. Tarseas rotated the light. He stopped, seeing something dart through the light. He followed in the direction of the creature.

The web was rippling like an ocean under stormy winds. Something else darted through the light, pausing briefly before disappearing. Its eight legs were apparent—it was one of the arachnoids.

Tarseas rotated the light another fifteen feet and stopped, finding the source of the movement and sound.

Nellen clasped her hands as though in prayer. "Oh, God."

Eight large arachnoids, each one as large as a cow, were busy encasing the three scarabs into individual cocoons.

One of the poor creatures twitched violently, its forelegs thrashing. The venom had only partially paralyzed it, allowing for limited motion. It shrieked again, completely terrified of the horrible predators that had captured it.

A few feet beside it were its two companions, both of whom were stiff as boards. One of them twitched, its head and mandibles still visible through the top of its cocoon. Beads of saliva, both its own and the arachnoids', dangled from its prison. The mandibles twitched, as though the creature was trying to squeal for the humans to rescue it.

"They're still alive," Warren said.

"What's it matter?" Tarseas said.

"Just giving you a clue of what we're in for," Warren said. "The venom doesn't kill their victims. Just paralyzes them, leaves them dangling in the nest, waiting to be snacked on."

Nellen nearly fell against the driver's side door, on the verge of passing out. After taking a few deep breaths, she regained control and sat up straight.

Three arachnoids converged on the struggling scarab. One of them peeled its snout back, revealing those horrid fangs. They plunged through the scarab's shell, sparking a tremendous cry that traveled deep into the cave.

For the second time in less than a minute, Nellen nearly passed out. She placed her temple against the window and began practicing deep breaths.

A glob of saliva struck the window, making her jump. She looked to her left and saw the two black fangs twitching on the other side of the glass.

In front of the rover were six or seven arachnoid creatures, enticed by the spotlight. In the blink of an eye, they were all over the rover. The vehicle reverberated as clawed feet tapped all over its exoskeleton. Over and over again, they crawled around the rover, a white stringy substance extending from their abdomens.

Looking at the windshield, Warren could see that the creatures had strung a layer of web around the vehicle.

"Oh, this can't be happening. They're cocooning us," Nellen said.

As she spoke, the arachnoids made a second pass, thickening their cocoon. While they worked, two other arachnoids eagerly scratched at the windows and the ceiling, desperate to breach the rover.

Warren watched as the rear window gradually lost its integrity.

"They're going to get in here sooner or later."

CHAPTER 27

"Up here," Ed Burger said. He was at the head of the group, following the trail left by the security rover.

Vince Caparzo made sure to keep directly behind him. He had gotten used to the scarab during the last fifteen minutes. The animal was considerably gentler compared to their first meeting.

The trail was easy even for a novice tracker to detect. The patrollers had raced up here in a hurry. Given the harsh terrain, it was remarkable they did not crash.

Ed Burger trotted ahead, weaving through a grove of granite structures into a clearing. A moment later, he reappeared, now facing the group.

"Carlos? Gonna need you."

The doctor tapped his scarab with his heels, doubling its speed. The others followed suit, the tridents clinging tight to their reins in fear of getting tossed from their rides. Cutting between a space between the structures, they arrived at a small clearing.

Carlos dismounted his scarab and hustled behind a thick, log-shaped rock.

"What is it?" Anastacia said.

"Two bodies. Colonists," Carlos said. "Both deceased."

"Can you identify them?" Vince asked. "Either of them Doctor Douglas Warren?"

"No," Carlos said. "They're not one of ours, either. My guess is that these men were the colonists that went into hiding with him after the Espinosa incident."

"Davy Austin and Preston Gosly," Anastacia said. She whispered a small prayer then performed the symbol of the cross with her fingers.

"What happened? Casualties from wildlife?" Vince asked.

Carlos shook his head. "No. Plasma burns. Military grade, judging by the scoring."

The three colonists gave judging glances in Vince's direction. The Lieutenant did not give any acknowledgement. He was not going to rush to judgement. For all he knew, the fugitives fired on his tridents, forcing them to defend themselves.

He reactivated his tracking device. Now that he was farther into the Hills, he hoped he was able to pick up the emergency beacon. The signal was cutting out frequently, essentially making this search the equivalent of finding a needle in a haystack.

"This is where the beacon was originally broadcasting from," he said. "I'm getting a new reading. It's now half a klick in that direction." He pointed northeast.

"Why the hell did they drive out that way?" Carlos said.

"I don't think they did." Anastacia dismounted and approached one of the rock structures on the west side of the clearing. The side of the rock had been smashed, the textures reduced to pebbles which layered the soil. Mixed with those rock fragments was bits of metal. Slivers of a rover bumper and underside mineral shielding, black and silver in color, resembled salt and pepper sprinkled all over the red ground. "They crashed here."

"If I had to guess, I'd say they tried leaving in a hurry," Carlos said.

"The way they hit this rock, they were definitely flooring the accelerator," Anastacia said. "Considering how hard they hit this boulder, I doubt they were able to drive the rover anywhere."

"If they suffered that much damage, they wouldn't have gone anywhere but down the hill," Vince said. "The only other option would be to hole up inside the vehicle until reinforcements arrived."

Ed dismounted his scarab and walked to the boulder, noting several markings in the soil. "Lieutenant, your people reported hostile wildlife, did they not?"

"Correct, but I lost contact before they could specify what it was exactly," Vince said.

Ed walked back to the log-shaped boulder. He ran his finger along some thin markings on its top. He kept his eyes to the ground, studying every groove, every displacement of soil, and the location of every piece of metal debris.

Most of the scrapes were accumulated in one location—except for a few others, which were scattered a few yards to the northwest. He followed the trail, finding a few more mixed with a long path full of these strange grooves. The markings were packed tight, as opposed to being scattered near the log and the bodies.

He returned to the clearing and took the reins of his scarab.

Vince knew the look of a man who was eager to leave. "What's the matter?"

"You see those markings?" Ed said, tilting his head at the new trail as he lifted himself over his scarab. "The rover was either pushed, dragged, or carried. I'm guessing carried, judging by the lack of tire tracks."

"Carried?" Carlos said. "Carried by what?"

"Whatever it is, it's up by that ridge to the northwest," Vince said.

"Not too far from the new methane geyser," Anastacia said. "Where our people had gone missing."

Vince groaned. "Wonderful."

"I'm putting my money on this being more than just one creature," Ed said. "We're probably dealing with multiple organisms, capable of working in unison. If we continue this search, it might not end well. The fact that ten people have encountered these things and not lived to tell about it—that says a lot right there."

"What about the colonists' bodies," Carlos said. "Why did the thing, or things, not take them too?"

"That actually worries me more," Ed said. "I'm only guessing... and I'm a good guesser... but I think these things require live prey. Possibly for their blood. It's your call, Lieutenant, but it's likely your people are dead already."

Vince looked at the ground, his mind debating itself on whether it was worth the risk to continue. Turning back could be viewed as an act of cowardice by the Alliance. Continuing on could equally be viewed as an act of stupidity and poor judgement. At the end of the day, tridents and workers could be replaced.

There was one other factor to consider.

"Dr. Drucus?"

"Yes?"

"You said there is a methane geyser in that direction?" he asked.

"Correct," she said.

"We keep going," Vince said. "Even if we don't locate my people, we still need to identify the threat in order to resume work at the site. That is, after all, the reason we're on this planet. Mount up. We're moving out."

Ed shut his eyes and cursed under his breath.

"I knew I shouldn't have let myself get talked into coming out here." He looked to the geologist. "Anastacia, I want you to know something."

"Yes?"

"If we go up there, and I die, and you don't... I just hope you feel really *really* bad."

She forced a smile, which quickly disappeared.

Ed led the group northwest, keeping his rifle on his lap, ready to be used at a moment's notice.

Vince and Anastacia were a couple yards behind him, followed by Carlos and the two tridents. As they trekked through the hills, he noticed Anastacia repeatedly glancing at a handheld communicator. The screen was beeping, signifying an incoming transcript message was coming in. A loading symbol appeared on the screen, never to vanish.

She shook the device, as though that would somehow improve the signal.

"Damn it." Giving up, she tucked it away.

"Something the matter?" Vince said.

"No," she replied. It was an obvious lie.

"Message from the hospital?" he asked. She didn't answer, which confirmed his suspicions. "Regolith Lung Rot, huh?"

This time, she looked over at him. "Yes."

"From an explosion, yes?"

"Correct," she said, waiting for him to make his point. "During an expedition. The Alliance had supplied us with satellite images of a ridge, twenty-five miles east of our colony. It was outside of the blackout, but still a large hilly area. We were instructed to clear it out and determine if it was the location of a methane geyser. We planted the charges, moved to what would have been a safe distance had things gone to plan. All of a sudden, the entire landscape seemed to have lifted off the ground. Rock, rubble, and dirt was everywhere. Lost Dr. Platt that day, along with two others. It won't be long before Patrick is number four."

They rode in silence for a few moments following that statement. Vince had heard of the pain of loss, but had never experienced it for himself. The closest thing was the death of his father, but that was a man of senior age who had lived a fulfilled life. There was some mourning, but all in all, General Caparzo's service was a celebration of his legacy. He was something for all in the Alliance Military to aspire to.

The fact was that most civilians were committed to their labor. If there was any loss to be mourned, it was their position and title.

"You're lucky you're not the one in the hospital," he said.

"I would have been, had it not been for Patrick," she said. "As soon as the eruption occurred and the landscape went skyward, he put himself in front of me. Made himself a human shield. Took the brunt of the shockwave and debris. Otherwise, I would be in that hospital. Or dead already."

"So, there was methane there?" Vince said, forcing himself to be unaffected by the account of Patrick Drucus' act of selflessness. "That why the area blew up? Probably should've used less explosives if that was the case. Or just used bulldozing equipment."

"No," she said, annoyed. "In fact, there was no methane there."

"No methane?" Vince said. Anastacia nodded. "Then what the hell did you ignite?!"

"Believe me, I'd like to know," she said. "We're lucky it was far away. Had it been within three or four miles of the colony, there's a good chance some of the debris would have made it all the way to the dome."

Vince nodded. *Whatever they blew up, it might make a hell of a weapon.*

He kept that thought to himself as they rode farther into the Hills.

***

All visibility of the outside was lost, but instead of darkness obscuring their view, it was thick white webbing. Despite the cocooning and abundance of other prey in the cave, some of the arachnoids were not content with leaving the rover alone. They remained perched atop the vehicle, raking their claws against the metal.

What concerned Dr. Warren most was the sound of dripping fluid and a vile smell coming through the hull. He tapped the ceiling then held his fingers under his nose.

"What are you doing?" an unnerved Corporal Tarseas said.

"Figuring out what our friends outside are doing," Warren said. He was tempted to smirk at the Corporal. The blood-jacket was too cowardly to off himself, meaning he was doomed to suffer a horrendous fate, paralyzed in thick darkness until the creatures were ready to slurp on his blood. Warren, on the other hand, would have no problem offing himself. Once the hull was breached, all he would have to do was remove his mask and take a deep breath. Cardiac arrest would spare him the horrors that awaited.

The only one he had any sympathy for was the one named Nellen Yasutake. She was a blood-jacket, but she was different than most of the others. The poor thing was barely keeping it together. Warren's guess was that she was drafted, probably after failing an aptitude test for higher-level employment. She definitely did not seem the type to join the military voluntarily, especially not in an infantry unit.

"What's the matter?" she asked. "You're looking at that ceiling as though it's going to split apart at any moment."

"It just well might," Warren said.

"What do you mean?" Tarseas said. "They've been clawing at it for a while now. They can't break through."

"Go ahead and tell yourself that," Warren said. He touched the same spot on the ceiling again. The warm, moist condensation stripped him of his machismo, for the situation was truly getting worse very fast. "I think they're using digestive fluids to cut through the rover."

"What? Like acid?" Tarseas said.

"Sort of. They break down flesh," Warren said. "I originally thought they sucked blood, but instead, I think they wrap you in a tight casing, splatter fluid thoroughly over you, then when the time is right, slurp your pre-digested flesh right off the bones."

The words had tremendous effect on Tarseas. He armed his gauntlet to maximize the caliber of plasma bolts, then grabbed the door handle.

"That's it. Nobody's coming. I don't see any other option. We need to shoot our way out."

Warren put his mask back on and sat patiently in his seat, accepting his fate.

"Yeah, you do that."

"Don't go, Corporal. If those things don't grab us on our way out, we'll just end up getting caught in the web," Nellen said.

"How are you the lesser rank, Trident?" Warren said.

Tarseas spun in his seat and aimed his gauntlet in the doctor's face. If there was anything worse than a terrifying predicament in a dark, wet place, it was having his ego challenged.

"Listen, Doctor. I'll make sure to take your head off before those things get a chance to touch you. If nothing else, it'll be for my own pleasure."

"Corporal, I welcome it," Warren said. "Believe me, it's better than what awaits you."

A heavy thud on the hood drew their attention to the windshield. The webbing in front of the glass shook, then came down like window shades. In the gap was the snout of an arachnoid. It peeled back into its four pedals, revealing two eighteen-inch fangs protruding on fleshy pedipalps.

Panicked, Nellen grabbed the radio mic for another attempt at calling assistance. Maybe, just maybe, someone might hear this time.

"This is Unit Two. Lieutenant, please tell me you can hear this. Please... Lieutenant Caparzo, we need your help."

She placed the mic down and held her head low, anticipating disappointment.

"This is Lieutenant Caparzo. I read you. State your position."

Nellen raised her head. A new energy, fueled by optimism, flooded her body.

"Yes!" Tarseas exclaimed.

"Exact location unknown," Nellen replied. "We're underground. Probably in some sort of cave."

"Let him know it's a nest," Warren said.

"A nest," she clarified. "We're trapped in the rover. The place is crawling with huge arachnid things. They've cocooned our vehicle in a thick webbing. They're practically Martian spiders."

There was a brief pause on the other end of the line.

"Stand by."

***

Spider creatures, a dark cave; it was enough to make Vince's skin crawl. He lowered the radio and turned his attention to the others.

"You guys hear that?" he asked. They nodded in unison. "Does that sound like anything in your archives?"

Anastacia shook her head, visibly repulsed by the descriptions she heard over his comm. "No."

"As I said before, we might not want to rush into this," Ed Burger said. "She said something about a nest. A nest confirms the presence of multiple organisms. Don't forget, these things were able to carry a two-ton rover across nearly a half mile of this landscape."

"We can't afford to wait," Vince said. "If they're that strong, they'll figure out a way to break through the hull. Come on, let's move." He tilted his head decisively to the northwest, then raised his comm to his lips. "Hang tight, Private. We're on our way."

His posse followed without hesitation, save for Ed Burger. The animal handler hung back, begrudgingly. At this point, he had no choice but to tag along. Riding alone in this area, even towards the relative safety of the valley, was about as dangerous as what they were about to attempt.

"I guess we can all become lunch together." He brought his scarab to a cantering speed to catch up with the others. "What a great way to bond with the new leader."

He took the lead once again. After all, he would put his head into a fire pit before he would ever let a trident take the lead.

The marks on the ground were present, though difficult to see for the majority of the group. Much of the ground here was rigid, with little to no loose soil. Only Ed Burger could detect the signs of recent movement.

As he led them through the winding path, the bleeping on Vince's transmitting receiver intensified. The signal was getting stronger, meaning they were getting closer.

They crossed another six-hundred feet of landscape before Ed Burger halted his scarab with a sudden yank on the reins.

"Ohhhh boy."

Vince caught up to him, ready to ask what the issue was. Before he could speak the words, he saw the gaping hole in the side of an elevation of earth. A deep, dark chasm, it looked as though it had been carved into the hill by a gigantic earthworm. The entrance was over twelve feet in diameter, the tunnel moving fifteen degrees at a downward angle.

The Lieutenant stepped off his scarab and approached the entrance.

"Careful," Anastacia said. No such warning came from Ed Burger, who watched casually with his hands on his reins, ready to retreat south if necessary.

Vince eyed the edges of the cave entrance. They were jagged, carved from rock. Little icicle-shaped structures dangled from the upper edge, resembling teeth from an enormous beast.

"Does that look like rock to you, Doctor Drucus?"

She inched forward for a closer look. "No. I'd almost say those things were formed by some sort of fluid."

Vince dismounted his scarab and took a few steps toward the cave. Twelve feet from its entrance was a black sliver on the ground. He knelt down and picked it up. It was metal from the rover.

"They're in here," he said.

Ed Burger grimaced. "Well, if there's one thing I've learned while tracking wildlife, here and on World One, is that when there's a cave, there's usually something living in it. It's probably best not to go in."

Vince stood up and turned around. "I think we now know who has the bigger muzzle size."

"Ha!" Ed shook his head, entertained by the insult. "Hey, if you want to go in, be my guest. Shows you have the intelligence of an average trident. Me? I'll gladly sit out here and *not* get eaten."

"You make it sound like you're smart, but really, it just sounds like you're being a wuss," Vince said.

"Oh yeah?" Ed said. "Well, from where I'm sitting, it looks like you're waiting for me to lead the way. Who's the wuss now?"

Vince did not dignify the animal handler with a response. It was a waste of energy, which needed to be spent coming up with a gameplan.

He looked to the entrance, studying it and the deep black throat behind it. He aimed a flashlight, the white stream stretching for thirty feet, finding nothing but more darkness.

The word 'risky' did not do this mission justice. If he went in there, he would be going into the lion's den. Or, to be more accurate, the spider's web. In spite of all of this, he could not bring himself to abandon those inside.

This was the price of inspiring loyalty.

"Tridents, wait out here," Vince said. "Provide me with some cover fire in case I need to make a quick exit."

"Do you not wish for us to go in with you, sir?" one of his men asked.

"Negative. I'm going in alone. See to it that the animal handler doesn't soil himself while you're all waiting."

"Oh, ha-ha-ha," Ed said in an exaggerated tone.

"You're going in alone? Are you crazy?" Anastacia said. She began to dismount her scarab.

Vince turned around and held his hand out. "Whoa! Doctor Drucus, you're not coming—Doc? *Doc?!...* Anastacia! Will you listen a second?!"

"No." She planted her feet on the ground and pulled her rifle from a sling in her saddle. She clicked the safety off, then approached.

"You don't get a say," Vince said. "I'm going in alone."

"Oh, how brave of you," she said. "Of course, we'll have no way of knowing if anything happens to you."

"I'm coming too," Carlos said.

Anastacia spun to face him. Now, it was her hand that was raised. "Carlos, wait. I'd feel better if you waited. There's a good chance we're gonna have to move fast. I know you stormed the L.A. beaches, but... no offense, it's been three-and-a-half decades. I'd rather you wait out here with the tridents."

Carlos gave a bitter expression, following it up with a grin. It was hard to accept he was getting up there in years. His mind was sharp, but his body, while fit, was not what it used to be.

"Be careful," he said. He turned his eyes to Ed Burger, who was content with sitting on his scarab outside of the nest.

Though he kept his gaze on the cave, Ed could feel the doctor's judgmental expression, guilting him into action.

Cursing under his breath, the animal handler swung his right foot over the scarab's head, then hopped onto the ground.

"Well, I suppose it's been a while since I've done anything stupid. I guess I'm due. Besides..." He clicked the safety off of his V-13 rifle and ignited the flashlight on the barrel's underside, "...the Lieutenant called me a wuss."

Into the breach they went.

Darkness encompassed the three brave souls, filling their hearts with fear. The reach of their flashlights seemed ten times brighter now.

Vince had his arms crossed, ready to blast anything that dared to emerge from that darkness. With his free hand, he held his own flashlight, which panned left and right.

The air in here was cooler than outside, yet it also felt oddly humid. The air had a wet, sticky quality to it. Though he could not smell the air, Vince's imagination went into overdrive, feeding his mind with a smell of rot and waste.

Sixty seconds of walking put them a hundred-and-twenty feet into the lair. The entrance was getting smaller and smaller, the interior wider and darker. More crystal shapes dangled from the ceiling, and frozen rivers of resin substance lined the walls.

Ed took the initiative to inspect some of the substance. Standing by the cave wall, he unsheathed his knife and pressed it into one of the frozen rivers. The substance broke off of the wall with ease, crumbling away like dried crust. It was not the texture that he found odd, but the scarring on the rock where the substance had been.

He waved Anastacia over. Taking a brief glance at the section of wall, she nodded, confirming his suspicion.

Acidic burns.

They continued on, taking deep slow breaths to keep their heart rates in check.

Nobody said a word. Their concentration was fully devoted to detecting movement. There was a faint sound coming from deep within. It resembled scraping of some sort, like the edge of a knife being scraped against a granite stone. Then there was a sticky, peeling sound. It was familiar and alien at the same time, and though they had no idea what it was, it painted a gut-wrenching image in their minds.

At a hundred-and-fifty feet, they found a stringy substance accompanying the icicles on the ceiling. It was wet and loose—exactly like a spider's web.

The further they went, the more residue they found.

Ed stopped and pointed his light to the right side. The rock wall was obscured by a white mesh. The moisture that lined the curtain reflected his light. The strands that made up this mesh went in multiple different directions, each one serving as a potential trap for unsuspecting lifeforms seeking shelter.

Evidence of such misadventures was front and center. The ground was lined with bones and exoskeleton casings, each a different shape and size, representing the many different species that had fallen victim to this nest.

Vince stopped to stare at the remnants of what appeared to be a reptilian skull lying on the ground. A massive eye socket stared back at him, the jaw agape, baring cone-shaped teeth. It was four feet in length, the spinal column severed directly behind the skull. The rest of the skeleton was nowhere to be seen.

A few meters farther in was the skull of one of those rhino creatures he had seen galloping in the plains. Ollubs, they were called. They were big and fierce creatures, not easily overtaken. Yet, this one fell victim to this horde of arachnoids.

Despite the warning in their guts, the trio continued on. There was not a single intact skeleton. Only fragments remained, some of which were still entangled in the web. Claws, hooves, even rib cage portions, decorated the cave's interior.

A massive ripple shook the web curtain, bringing the group to a halt. Gun muzzles and light streams shook as they anticipated some horrible shape emerging from the dark.

Slowly, they advanced.

After twenty more feet, they stopped again.

The webbing was much thicker down here, stretching across the wall. There was no passage from here on. Everywhere they looked, there was nothing but a mishmash of weaved silk substance, with only a few small tunnels for the inhabitants to travel through.

The entire cave was nothing but one enormous spider web, ornamented with the cocooned bodies of unlucky victims. The cocoons were thick and hardened, the prisoners twitching as their conscious minds desperately tried to overcome the paralyzing toxins flowing through their veins.

Thirty feet ahead on the right was one particularly large cocoon. From its top came a bright light which beamed against the white maze. Its body was metallic, carried by circular appendages made of thick rubber designed to carry two-tons of machinery.

They had found the rover.

Perched atop of it were three spider creatures. They were as horrid as the trio had envisioned. Armed with eight spindly legs, they were clawing at the roof while spewing some sort of fluid. Smoke twirled from the corroding metal. The very acidic fluid they used to carve out this lair was now being used to breach the rover.

All three of them turned toward the new source of light. Without hesitation, their snouts peeled apart, exposing their enormous fangs.

In the briefest of moments, Vince felt his body constricted by an intense fear. He was no stranger to risking his life. On many occasions, he had descended into horrible locations populated with hostile combatants. *Human* combatants. There was a strange sense of normalcy about engaging enemies that could shoot back. He was used to it. It was ingrained into his consciousness through training and experience.

This, however, was not normal in the slightest. Nothing, not even technological advancement that allowed colonization of planets, could prepare him for the sight of giant spiders.

His training kicked in. *Do not freeze. Take action. Shoot first.*

Vince fired a blinding blue strobe of energy at one of the arachnoids. The projectile landed directly in its open head, cutting deep into the interior of its body. The creature reeled backwards, its legs kicking as automatic muscular reactions carried out the last of the signals sent by its dying brain.

He shifted his aim to the left and struck the second arachnoid. Once again, it was a perfect headshot. This one fell forward, its legs twitching before coiling under its abdomen.

The third one hopped off the rover, ready to scurry at its new targets. Before its legs could touch the ground, it was met with Vince's third plasma bolt, which struck the back of its abdomen. It landed on its side and rolled onto its back, thrashing its legs violently while letting out a horrendous shriek. Blood pooled under its body, its abdomen hollowing as its insides poured through the crater in its back.

Vince put the creature out of its misery with a fourth shot.

Anastacia and Ed lowered their gun muzzles, both—even the animal handler—impressed with the Lieutenant's speed and marksmanship. Neither even had a chance to squeeze their trigger and take part in the action.

Ed Burger was not too heartbroken. He immediately pointed his gun to the interior of the nest. Deep within that mesh of webbing came sounds of movement.

"I'd suggest you hurry and get your pals out of there before the rest of the family shows up."

Vince and Anastacia sprinted to the rover.

"You guys all right?"

"We are now," Nellen Yasutake said. "Is that you, Lieutenant?"

"Yep, it's me. Give me a second so I can get this webbing off the door." He reached for the strands that covered the side door, only for his hands to get snagged. It required every ounce of energy for him to pull back and free himself.

"You all right?" Anastacia asked.

"Yeah. Don't touch this stuff," he said. "Private, Corporal, move as far back as you can. I have no choice but to blast the door."

He heard movement within the vehicle as the passengers shifted.

"We're ready," Corporal Tarseas said.

Vince hit the rover with four blasts, burning the webbing and singeing the metal underneath it. There was no concern for the vehicle, for there was no chance of recovering it. All that mattered were the lives inside.

"Try opening the door," Vince said.

They heard the latch pop open, then the groan of the hinges as they pushed the door open from the inside. Dr. Warren was the first to step out, followed by the two tridents.

"Doctor!" Anastacia approached Warren. "Are you all right? Where have you been?!"

"Ah-ah." Vince stepped between them. "He's under arrest. Corporal Tarseas, escort him to the cave entrance immediately."

"Don't have to tell me twice," the Corporal responded.

A bitter smile took form on Warren's face. "I'm not sure which is worse. Letting you take me in, or being lunch for the bugs."

"You can whine all the way back to the colony," Vince said. "Just be grateful I was willing to come all the way out here to keep you from being added to the menu."

"Grateful, huh?" Warren said. "And what about my friends, Davy and Austin? Whom your Corporal murdered. What about them?"

"What happened?" Anastacia said.

"Hey!" Ed shouted. "Can we do this later?! We're lucky we've only seen three of those things."

As though on cue, the entire nest began to vibrate with the motion of a hundred arachnoid legs. The group bunched up and backed away, watching the web shifting back and forth.

The first few emerged from the funnel-shaped passageways and descended to the ground. Others scurried over the rock ceiling, lowering themselves down by a string of web like soldiers fast-roping from a helicopter.

Once again, Vince was the first to open fire. His first shot struck one of the creatures, exploding its abdomen in a visceral display of guts and exoskeleton. Before its remains hit the ground, he aimed high and blasted a second arachnoid as it descended from the cave ceiling. A fraction of its abdomen dangled from its string, while the rest of it fell free. The moment it touched the ground, it was hit by a second and third bolt, reducing its body to several smoldering fragments.

Tarseas, Anastacia, and Ed Burger joined the fray, lighting the dark lair with burning hot flashes of plasma.

Nellen Yasutake hesitated, her body locked up by fear. Only the goading of her prisoner, Dr. Warren, snapped her mind into focus.

"Might wanna join in, kid," he said.

Raising her shaking arm, she joined the firing squad. Her first two shots missed, forming two smoking holes in the web. The arachnoid she aimed for made its way to the ground, ready to spring at the congregation of humans. A blast from Ed Burger brought it to a dead stop.

The two colonists backed away, their weapons requiring their frustrating cooling period. Meanwhile, the three tridents continued hammering the wave of spiders. Green blood splattered with each scalding impact.

Once the painfully long twenty-second cooling session reached its conclusion, Anastacia and Ed rejoined the fight.

SPLAT! SPLAT! SPLAT!

Whether it was skill or divine influence, everyone's shot was on point. Left and right, arachnoid parts twitched on the ground. Fangs, legs, and internal organs smothered the floor, seared by the projectiles that killed them.

Finally, the remainder of the nest departed into the depths of the lair.

Vince lowered his gauntlet and gazed on the heap of charred shell fragments and flesh. Here, he exercised the true meaning of a trident's purpose. Control of the air, sea, and land—including subterranean land. Nobody and nothing could overpower the sheer force of the Alliance military.

Fear turned into pride.

Now grinning, Vince looked to Ed Burger. "Big, huh? I thought you said the scarabs were the smallest bugs on this rock. Those things didn't seem that big to me."

A new tremor rippled through the cave. The smile on Vince's face slowly reverted back to a grimace. These tremors weren't traveling through the web, but through the earth itself. *Under* his feet.

A low-pitched screech erased the tense silence. The web curtains peeled outward, making way for the enormous, eight-legged shape that emerged from the back of the cave.

Her size made clear her role in this nest. She was the one whom the nest served. This cave was the house of an unbreakable family unit, and Vince and his posse was looking at its matriarch.

Her legs, spiked and thick, were crammed against the walls. Her snout was surrounded by appendages with pincer tips. As large as a bulldozer, she was armored with a thick exoskeleton lined with curved spines. Up close, her body resembled the very hills she lived within. Twisted, rigid, and grotesque.

Vince slowly backed away, his mind grasping the reality of what he was looking at.

Pride turned to fear.

"Yeah... *that* one's big."

As if in direct response, the creature shook the cave with a deafening screech.

Do not freeze. Take action. Shoot first.

Vince pointed his gauntlet and fired repeatedly. Plasma bolts erupted against its shell, two on its head, two on its back, and one on its front left leg. The projectiles disappeared in puffs of smoke, leaving behind mild burn marks that the arachnoid hardly noticed.

Anastacia quickly backtracked. "And armored!"

"And *pissed off!* Thank you very much!" Ed Burger turned on his heels and was the first to sprint for the cave entrance.

Vince and the others quickly followed. It was every person for themselves, each one desperate not to end up in the mother's grasp.

Massive and angry, she pursued.

Her rigid shell scraped the ceiling, grinding stone, sediment and resin. Her days, largely spent slumbering behind a thick curtain of web, barely hindered her strength and endurance.

What did hinder it was the narrowing of the cave as she approached the entrance. Her legs raked the walls with each step and her body pressed even tighter against the ceiling. In the early days of digging the tunnel and forming her nest, she was smaller, not comprehending the possibility of chasing out intruders. That was the job of her offspring, in addition to securing food and being the mother, her job was to live in the darkness and birth new arachnoids. Only when the offspring failed did Mother need to step in.

She was successful in driving these intruders from the nest, but that wasn't enough. Only their deaths would satisfy her.

Vince looked back, seeing the gargantuan arachnoid struggling to squeeze herself through the tunnel.

They reached the entrance within seconds, finding a bewildered Carlos LaFonte standing beside the two escorts.

"Doc! Get away from the cave!" Anastacia shouted. "Go! Run!"

"What's going on?! What's the matter?" he said. A deafening screech from the darkness answered that question. He backed from the entrance, his eyes widening when he saw the enormous legs emerge. The mother pried herself free, quickly turning her attention on the scattered humans. "Oh hell!"

The scarabs wailed in fright. Only their loyalty to Ed kept them from turning around and abandoning the humans outright. They backed away, raising their forelegs aggressively, ready to defend themselves—futile as that may be against the arachnoid mother.

The tridents took aim with their gauntlets.

"No! No!" Vince shouted.

He perched himself on a boulder several yards northeast from the entrance. The others raced south, some of them boarding the scarabs. Tarseas reinforced his order to the other tridents, explaining that shooting the thing was useless.

Vince had to think fast. There was no doubt that retreat would only result in everyone's death. This thing was out for blood. It would likely not stop until it slayed all eight members of the group. There was no way it would stop at one.

Unless one enraged it to the point of forgetting about the others.

A hundred thoughts and considerations raced through Vince's mind in the span of an instant. What he was about to do was borderline suicidal. His fear of not seeing Lucy again would be realized. She would be alone, far away from anyone she ever knew, at the mercy of people who despised her father's presence.

This did not deter Vince. He was a trident. It was against his very nature to back down from any challenge or threat.

Images of dead workers at the Alaska refinery flashed in his mind, followed by a fiery flash of his failure. The enemy won that day, even if they didn't live to see it. People loyal to the Alliance had been stripped of their lives, the surrounding region stripped of energy.

All because he failed.

Not again. Not today.

Vince took aim with his gauntlet and committed to his fate. Numerous blue strobes of plasma struck the arachnoid's abdomen. Though failing to penetrate its shell, it was successful in drawing her attention.

The beast turned around, spotting the perpetrator.

A few short yards south, the group looked back, seeing their leader staying behind.

"Caparzo?!" Anastacia shouted.

"Go! GO!!!" Vince shouted back. "Get down the hill! I'll keep it occupied!"

"Won't get any arguments from me!" Ed Burger said. Mounted on his scarab, he led the retreat.

Vince hit the mother with several more blasts, irritating her further. She leaned forward, raking the ground with her forelegs. At that moment, Vince realized just how huge the claws on her feet were. Sickle-shaped and edged like a sword, they cut through the hard soil with ease.

Her head peeled apart, revealing black fangs that matched the length of his body.

Vince swallowed. "Should've thought this through..."

He turned east and leapt off the rock, narrowly dodging a swipe from one of the mother's legs. He landed in a summersault, rolling to his feet and sprinting east.

The mother swiped the boulder once more, breaking it in two. Knocking the two halves out of the way, it continued pursuit.

***

It was no longer behind them, but the sense of danger was still present. The tridents all ran on foot, their scarabs running beside them. Only Anastacia, Ed, and Carlos had managed to board their steeds before fleeing the mother.

Everyone was on edge, their nerves fried, their minds frantic. Only Dr. Warren, as he raced beside Corporal Tarseas, appeared to think beyond the simple objective of escape.

For him, the colony did not offer refuge. Imprisonment, at best, was his future. Mostly likely, he would be sentenced to a forced labor camp. Somehow, some way, the Alliance would make an example of him. It would be a life of pure misery. Warren understood this when he started the rebellion on Espinosa, but that did not mean he was going to willfully subject himself to such a life. He had an avenue. The Martians would accept him. If he could just reach Godon, he could return to the Martian colony and plan from there.

First, he needed to slip away quick. The Corporal was matching his speed and would certainly notice. Even during this retreat, there was no doubt that he would shoot Warren in the back if he tried to escape. That left only one option.

Nellen and the other tridents were moving to the left in an attempt to wrangle their scarabs, their backs facing Warren and Tarseas.

The opportunity presented itself.

He pivoted to the right and threw himself at Tarseas, tackling him on his back. The Corporal's head bounced, the impact against the rock-hard ground putting him in a daze. Just for good measure, Warren drove an elbow into his ribs and put a knee in his groin. The assault felt good. Gratifying. Had it not been for the situation at hand, he would have gladly continued. But time was of the essence.

Warren got to his feet and ran northwest. It would be a long trek on foot, but it was his best shot. In the confusion, the others would probably not follow immediately, if at all.

Into the Blackout he went, disappearing behind a field of rocks and elevation.

"What the..." Carlos pulled the reins on his scarab. He had stopped to see if the tridents needed help getting control of the scarabs. When he realized only three of the four tridents were gathering near the creatures, he glanced about to locate Tarseas, only to find him sprawled out on the ground. "Man down!"

Everyone converged on the fallen trident.

Nellen Yasutake was at his side, checking for a pulse. "Corporal?!"

Tarseas grabbed her hand and angrily threw it from his neck. He sat up, humiliated, glaring at his peers before looking over his shoulder in the direction Warren ran off.

Nellen stood up, put off by his hostilities. "Where's the doctor?"

Ed Burger steered his scarab a few meters behind Tarseas, watching the ground. "Looks like he went this way. Don't know about you guys, but I have no intention of going after..."

Carlos saw the way Ed was squinting.

"What's the matter?"

"Where's Anastacia?" Ed asked.

Carlos looked around. She was nowhere to be seen.

***

For once, Vince was grateful for the irregular topography and its granite obstacles. The arachnoid, while spry for her size, was a creature that relied on the element of surprise to catch her prey rather than pursuit. The Blackout Hills suited her perfectly for stealth, but hindered the efficiency of chasing down this pesky human.

If only she wasn't so persistent.

Vince peeked over his shoulder just in time to witness the mother burst through a rock tower. Huge fragments, some the size of rover tires, came crashing in his direction.

One landed directly in front of him, forcing him to stop. He dropped to his knees, avoiding a bowling ball-sized rock which flew over his head. The delay gave the mother the opportunity she was looking for.

He glanced at her again, seeing one of her forelegs swing high like an axe.

"Oh sh—"

He dove over the rock. The claw came down, plunging two feet into the dirt. Vince was back on his feet, but only for a split-second. The mother, frustrated, raked her claw forward, knocking the large rock fragment against his back. Vince fell face-first, throwing his hands in front of his mask to keep it from cracking against the ground.

The creature knocked the boulder to the side with a swipe of her leg, then closed in on the human. It raised its leg high, ready to finally skewer him.

Vince saw the narrow shadow stretching over the ground. In a last ditch effort for survival, he pushed off the ground and rolled to his left, settling on his back.

The claw plunged beside him, kicking up bits of dirt and stone. The mother did not appear to be fazed. It was a mere delay to his death. She stood over him, her fangs twitching on their pedipalps. Saliva dripped onto Vince's chest as though to taunt him.

It reared back, then shifted downward to drive the fangs home. Suddenly, the creature flinched. Springing off of its victim, it turned to the east, just in time to be struck by a second plasma bolt.

Vince scampered backward, then looked to the direction the shot came from.

"GET UP!" Anastacia shouted. She rode on her scarab, rifle shouldered. Her third blast struck the creature in the soft flesh of its pedipalps. This time, the mother reared back and brushed her forelegs over her mandibles.

Vince sprang to his feet and raced in Anastacia's direction.

"Come on, Trident!" she shouted. "Hurry it up!"

Vince wasn't sure if he wanted to tell her 'shut up' or 'thanks'. The echo of an enraged beast made him decide it wasn't an important dilemma.

They retreated northeast, quickly gaining several yards of distance while the mother was distracted. That grace period quickly ended, the continuation of her pursuit cued by the sound of crashing rocks.

"Up this way!" Anastacia said. "We can hide in one of the construction site vehicles Maya Napier left by the methane geyser. Hopefully it will still be functional."

A thought hit Vince as he ran beside her scarab.

Methane geyser...

His mind flashed to the eruption outside Hope Colony, and the flight crew member having a laugh at the misfortune of the crews involved.

"A methane geyser formed there about a month ago. They've popped up everywhere since the gravity alteration. All it takes is a little flame to make them go boom..."

After traveling a few hundred feet, they came across some fairly level ground. This small area was fairly clear of rocks, due to the prep work done by the colony's construction crews. On the other side of the clearing were two large construction vehicles and scattered equipment. Directly in the middle were a series of thin, but deep cracks.

They had arrived at the construction site.

Vince stepped across the geyser then charged his gauntlet.

"Whoa, whoa!" Anastacia said. "What are you doing?! There's gas coming up through there. You realize it would not take much to set that thing off, right?!"

"Exactly."

Right away, Anastacia understood his plan. She rode the scarab across the geyser, then dismounted. She slapped the creature on its abdomen, forcing it to run off, then stood beside the Lieutenant.

"Get in the vehicle," he said.

"Shut up, Caparzo."

The ground shook under their feet. Heavy legs pounded in the distance, quickly getting nearer.

Finally, the beast emerged. It entered the clearing, its fangs still exposed. The left pedipalp, dark and scabbed, twitched. The thing watched the two humans, as though deciding which to kill first.

Vince and Anastacia knelt slightly, ready to sprint. First, they needed the thing to cross the geyser.

"Come on, you oversized tick," Vince muttered. "What are you waiting for?"

The creature began to approach, but stopped. It clawed at the ground with its front legs, seemingly bothered.

"I think it senses the gas," Anastacia whispered.

"Don't tell me it knows what we're up to," Vince said.

"No, but insects and arachnids breathe through their sides," she said. "It's probably trying to determine whether it'll get poisoned if it continues."

"How long will that take?!"

She scoffed. "Don't know, Lieutenant. Why don't you ask it."

He groaned, then stepped to the edge of the geyser. Fright gave way to frustration. Aiming high, he delivered two blaster bolts straight into the mother's jaws. Flesh and saliva splattered, the beast shrieking furiously. It stumbled back, once again brushing its legs over its jaws.

Rage and self-preservation overrode any concern of breathing toxic fumes. The mother committed to the attack, crossing over the fissure.

Vince aimed his gauntlet and fired repeatedly. The blaster bolts struck the fissures, igniting the methane at the ground level.

A volcanic fountain burst through the ground, consuming the mother with ten-thousand degree flames.

Vince fell backward, the edge of the fire mere inches from his boots. He scooted back, unable to take his eyes off the huge mass flailing in the tower of flame.

The mother slashed her forelegs blindly, unable to fend off this mysterious fiend that had risen from the ground. Driven mad with pain, it darted across the worksite, its body encased in fire. As it made distance, it resembled a burning meteor, trailing a thick tail of smoke. It darted left and right, crashing into every obstacle in sight.

Unbearable heat finally took its toll. The mother arachnoid slowed to a stop, and after one final screech, it toppled on its side. Its legs, still burning, coiled under its body.

The arachnoid was dead.

Anastacia knelt by his side. Vince's uniform had some mild burns on it, but otherwise, he was unharmed.

"You all right?"

"I'm good," he said. He got on his feet and stood side-by-side with Anastacia, watching with astonishment as the carcass burned. "So... they expect you guys to work out here, huh?"

Anastacia tightened her lips and nodded. "Yep."

"Hmm." He shrugged. "You must be thrilled."

She snorted, her current exhaustion keeping her from descending into full laughter.

"Yes. Very ecstatic," she said, matching his sarcasm. "As you can see, we have the time of our lives here on World Two."

CHAPTER 28

The liquid nitrogen sprays left over by the construction crews came in handy. After extinguishing the flames and sealing the breach, Vince and Anastacia made their way south. Their exhaustion was soothed by a powerful sense of reprieve. The mission was accomplished with no casualties, the arachnoid mother had been killed, and the rest of the nest would soon be burnt out and sealed.

It was a sobering experience for Vince. His second day on World Two, and already he found himself at death's door. It was something the colonists here dealt with every day, especially those expected to work here in the Blackout Hills.

Vince patted down his uniform as he walked beside Anastacia. Her scarab, which had circled back to the site after running off, trailed behind them. It was still a little worked up, so she led it by the reins instead of riding it.

For several minutes, they walked in silence, each mentally recovering from the recent endeavor. Both, though they wouldn't say it out loud, had an elevated appreciation for the other. They owed each other their lives.

In Vince Caparzo's mind, that was the hallmark of a dedicated unit. Maybe there was more to these people than he was led to believe. Maybe ruling with an iron fist like the Alliance intended was not the best route to success. Regardless, Vince knew the road ahead would not be easy. The people of Centauri Colony were vigilant and set in their ways. They wanted to fulfill their duties and be left in peace.

At the same time, Vince Caparzo was sent here for a specific mission. For the first time in his life, he questioned if the mission was wrong. Back in Alaska, *he* was wrong.

Am I wrong this time?

It was a question that would be answered in the days to come. For now, perhaps it was better to earn the respect of his colonists, rather than demand it.

"Dr. Drucus?"

Anastacia looked over at him. "Yes?"

"That medicine you came to visit me about?"

"DZ-5?"

"Yeah..."

He took a moment to consider the proposal he was about to put forth. It would not go over well with Hope Central if they found out he was using his limited military medical supplies on colonists. Especially those with Regolith Lung Rot, a condition that was only suppressed by DZ-5, not cured. To them, it would be considered a waste of precious resources.

On the other hand, deliberately letting a human life slip away was an equal, if not greater waste.

"Listen, there's something I didn't tell you," he said. "At headquarters, we have medical supplies in storage, including a couple cases of DZ-5."

Anastacia stopped in her tracks. As though hit with an electric current, she stood stiff as a board, realizing what the Lieutenant was saying. She did not say a word, the look on her face implying she was trying not to get her hopes up in case her suspicions were wrong. They were not.

"I'll talk with Dr. LaFonte when we return to the colony," he continued. "In the meantime, I suggest forming a team to develop a cure. Even my supplies won't last forever."

"I..." A smile broke through her tough exterior. Her thoughts were plain on her face. *Maybe there's more to this trident than meets the eye.* She wasn't going to waste this offer, so she kept her response simple. "Thank you."

***

"My, oh my! I thought you were goners for sure, Lieutenant!" Ed Burger said.

The team was gathered a quarter-mile south of the construction site, having disobeyed Vince's orders to retreat to the colony.

"You sound disappointed," he said.

"Not at all!" Ed pointed at himself. "Can't you tell?! This is my happy face."

Vince grinned. Slowly but truly, he was getting used to the animal handler's witty sarcasm.

Carlos approached and gave him and Anastacia a quick look over. "You guys all right? We saw the smoke."

"Yeah," Ed said. "Where's the big one?"

Vince tilted his head in the direction of the smoke. "Is cooked bug a delicacy around here?" He did not expect Ed Burger to be actually enticed by the mention of such a thing. Vince looked away, grimacing.

Why am I surprised? Instead of asking that question out loud, he looked around to do a headcount. His blood rushed when he realized there were only six people here in addition to Anastacia and himself.

Two colonists, four tridents, and no prisoner.

"Where's Dr. Warren?"

All eyes turned to Corporal Tarseas, who looked away, his humiliation at an all-time high.

Ed Burger groaned, knowing the group would go after the fugitive.

"I've already picked up his trail. He went northwest toward the cliffs," he said.

Vince approached his scarab and mounted it. "Let's not waste time."

***

The trip up the Hills grew rougher and less pleasant as they neared the cliff edge two miles north. Nellen and one of the trident escorts followed on foot, Tarseas having commandeered one of the scarabs—not without resistance from the steed.

Thanks to Ed Burger's skill, they were able to follow Dr. Warren's trail. During their trek, he pointed out that the doctor had run much of the way, but slowed down after the first mile due to fatigue. He was able to point out every instance when Warren stopped and investigated his surroundings. How he could do this, Vince would never know. He understood basic tracking, but the signs were beyond his skill level.

When they arrived at the cliff edge, Vince was silently irritated to see there was no fugitive. His first belief was that Warren had escaped underground again. Before he could declare he would have this area bombed to reveal the tunnel entrance, Ed Burger was already walking east on foot.

"He went this way," he said. "Looks like he stopped and looked around. Maybe he got lost. Whatever the case, he took off in this direction."

"Just my luck," Vince said. "That's not too far away from the construction site. Had I known he escaped, I could've headed north and intercepted him."

"Oh, quit your whining," Ed said. He proceeded to lead the group east along the cliff edge.

Vince watched the world on his left. After a thirty foot drop, the Hills extended as far as the eye could see. Even through the twisting maze of rocks, boulders, and elevated soil, he saw lifeforms darting about. Some were even watching, hoping that one of the humans would take a tumble to their doom, thus making an easy meal.

They proceeded for another half-mile, during which Ed surmised that the doctor was slowing down. At this point, Warren was searching rather than fleeing.

After crossing an additional three-hundred meters, they found their target.

Dr. Douglas Warren was kneeled several meters from the cliff edge. His hands were on his knees, his body hunched forward. He was not only exhausted, but emotionally spent. Defeated. Given up.

Everyone dismounted their scarabs.

Vince and his tridents slowly advanced on the doctor, taking flanking positions.

"Time's up, Doctor," he said. "Come peacefully. The day's been busy enough for my liking."

Anastacia raised her hand calmingly. "Please, let me."

Vince held back, allowing the geologist to diffuse the situation peacefully.

Anastacia closed the distance, then gently put a hand on the doctor's shoulder. "Douglas, it's me, Anastacia Drucus. I don't like this either, believe me, but you can't keep running."

Vince slowly approached with cuffs in hand. All of a sudden, Anastacia stood up in a shock, looking at the object a few yards in front of the doctor.

"Oh!"

Vince stood ready to blast whatever it was into oblivion. When he first arrived, he thought it was just a boulder. It was red in color, almost blending in with the surroundings. Upon closer view, he noticed what appeared to be several vines protruding from its center, almost resembling a thorn bush.

Except it could not possibly be a plant, for they did not grow in Martian soil. But it was not a rock, nor did it appear to be an animal. It was fairly large, roughly the size of a scarab. Thorn-covered vines coiled inwards to resemble a demonic crown.

In the middle of this crown, impaled by the thorns, was a humanoid body. A Martian.

It was dead, its weapon lying a few feet right of the vines. Its final expression was one of agonizing pain and terror. Vince Caparzo did not know about the Martians, but he did know they rarely showed fear.

"What happened here?" Carlos said.

"Is that a Martian?" Tarseas said.

"What's left of one," Vince replied.

"Yeah, but what is that?" Anastacia said, pointing at the plant.

Together, they stared in unified shock. This was a mystery none of them could comprehend.

CHAPTER 29

World One.
Rome. Capital Building – Archives.

It was a typical day for Gregorio's assistant. When she woke up, she reminded herself it was a privilege to work at the capital. Here, she was provided with the cleanest environment, the best food and shelter, though it paled to that of the people in power. She did not care if her quality of life was inferior to the Chancellor or High Counsel members, it was still better than most of World One's laborers.

Today, she was assigned to cleaning services. She had finished going through the offices of Senator Rominski and Counselman Kirk Wilder. Next were the archives.

With two droid units following her, she proceeded down the hall. As she neared the doors, she slowed down. There was a voice coming from within the archives.

"…and the seeds of which they plant shall sprout fire, and cleanse the earth for their arrival. The world will be their garden, the oceans their fountains, the core their domain."

The assistant slowly opened the door.

Scrolls, electronic and physical, were scattered across the marble floor. Kneeling in the middle of the mess was Quintus Julio. His face was white, his eyes glazed over, his teeth clenched, as though fighting back tears. He was either in great pain, or deathly frightened.

He dropped the scroll he read from, then lowered his head.

"I never thought I'd see the day."

"Sir?" the assistant said. "Are you okay?"

Quintus shook his head. "None of us will be okay, young lady. Not after they arrive."

"Arrive? Who?"

Quintus looked up at the projector. The screen was fiery red, with some sort of demonic, crystal shape at its center. An emblem of doom.

"The Vallachians."

The End

CHECK OUT OTHER GREAT SCIENCE FICTION BOOKS

LOST EMPIRE
by Edward P. Cardillo

Building on their victory in the last Intergalactic War, the imperialist United Intergalactic Coalition seeks to expand their influence over the valuable Kronite mines of Golgath. Reeling from their defeat, the warrior Feng are down but not out. The overextended UIC and the vengeful Feng deploy battle groups and scramble fighters as they battle for position in the universe, spinning optics and building coalitions. Captain Reinhardt of the Resilience and the elite Razor's Edge squadron uncover the Feng Emperor Hiron's last ditch attempt to turn the tables with a new and dangerous technology. With resources spread thin, the UIC seeks to exploit Feng's weakened position through a very conditional peace accord. Unwilling to submit, Emperor Hiron must hold them off and quell the growing civil unrest of his starving, warrior people just long enough to execute the mysterious Operation: Catalyst. Commander Massa and his Razor's Edge squadron race against time to stop Hiron's plan, and a new race awakens, led by a powerful prophet set on toppling the established galactic order through violent acts of terrorism.

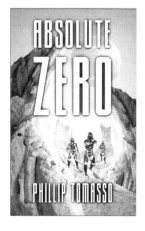

ABSOLUTE ZERO
by Phillip Tomasso

When a recon becomes a rescue . . . nothing is absolute!

Earth, a desolate wasteland is now run by the Corporations from space stations off planet . . . A colony of thirty-three people are part of a compound set up on Neptune. Their objective is mining the planet surface for natural resources. When a distress signal reaches Euphoric Enterprises on the Nebula Way Station, the Eclipse is immediately dispatched to investigate.

The crew of the Eclipse had no idea what they were getting themselves into. When they reach Neptune, and send out a shuttle party, they hope they can find the root cause behind the alarm. Nothing is ever simple. Something sinister lies in wait for them on Neptune. The mission quickly goes from an investigation into a rescue operation.

The young crew from the Eclipse now finds themselves in the fight of their lives!

CHECK OUT OTHER GREAT SCIENCE FICTION BOOKS

WARNING: THIS NOVEL HAS GRATUITOUS VIOLENCE, SEX, FOUL LANGUAGE, AND A LOT OF BAD JOKES! YOU MAY FIND YOURSELF ENJOYING HIGHLY INAPPROPRIATE PROSE! YOU HAVE BEEN WARNED!

MAX RAGE
by Jake Bible

Genetically Engineered. Physically enhanced. Mentally conditioned.

Master Chief Sergeant Major Max Rage was the top dog in an elite fighting force that no one in the galaxy could stop. Until, one day, someone did.

The lone survivor, Rage was blamed for the mission failure and court-martialed.

With a serious chip on his shoulder, Rage finds himself as a bouncer at the top dive bar in Greenville, South Carolina. And, man, is he bored with his job.

At least until he gets a job offer he can't refuse. Now, Rage is headed halfway across the galaxy to the den of corruption known as Horloc Station.

With this job, Max Rage may have a chance to get back to what he was: an unstoppable Intergalactic Badass!

RECON ELITE
by Viktor Zarkov

With Earth no longer inhabitable, Recon Six Elite are sent across space to scout promising new planets for colonization.

The five talented and determined space marines are led by hard-nosed commander Sam Boggs. Earth's last best hope, these men and women are the "tip of the spear". Armed with a wide array of deadly weapons and forensics, Boggs and Recon Elite Six must clear the planet Mawholla of hostile species.

But Recon Elite are about to find out how hostile Mawholla truly is.

Made in United States
Orlando, FL
19 April 2023

32244613R00120